THE DAYS OF ELIORA

Katy Hollway

The Days of Eliora

SozoPrint
SozoPrint.com

ISBN 978-0-9929404-0-9

Contact or follow the author

www.KatyHollway.com
www.facebook.com/KatyHollwayAuthor
www.twitter.com/KatyHollway
www.pinterest.com/katyhollway/

Dedication

To my husband, there is no one else I would rather adventure with.

1

New

Eliora was alone. She thought that this was surely the most beautiful place there ever was. How could she possibly consider working here to be as awful as the pits? True, she did feel a little uncomfortable. It felt dark and oppressive inside the thick walls of the palace despite the early morning sunlight but she put it down to her feeling apprehension about how she would be received.

'Keep up!' her mother had warned. 'We can't be late.'

Eliora scurried after.

She had risen early and had got dressed in her new cotton tunic. Her mother had applied the irritating eye makeup to herself before turning to Eliora. It felt stiff against her young skin but she was happy about the distinction it gave her.

Everything about this morning was new. The time, her appearance and her mother's demeanour. She had seemed agitated and nervous somehow. What there was for her to be nervous about, Eliora had no idea. She was the one who was going to meet the most powerful woman in the known world for the first time.

Eliora's new simple sandals cut into her feet as she sped from the hot little house towards the cool palace.

The heat of the morning was creeping over the sands and into the shallow river valley, but all of that was left behind as they entered through the statued gateway. The smooth stone floor left a chill in the early morning. The silence was punctuated by the lonely, echoing tapping of their sandaled feet. Eliora gazed at the scale of the corridors and the clean crispness of the architecture they passed by. Huge columns in the shape of elegant palms held the roof high above. Guards stood alert at either end of the hall.

They hurried through a series of doors, each one with a guard stationed outside.

The last room was beautiful yet terrible. The walls were decorated with colourful paintings depicting people walking and sitting. The images were mesmerising but made Eliora feel uncomfortable. She felt a shiver go down her spine as she saw half human half beast depictions.

There was very little furniture to be seen. A couple of shining gilded stools sat to the side of a large opening that welcomed in the sound of rustling rushes of the river. The scented breeze wafted the light cotton curtains.

'Wait here!' Eliora's mother cautioned. 'Don't touch anything,' she added before quietly rushing through the ornate door opposite the window.

And so Eliora was alone.

The polished floor gleamed as beams of shimmering morning light bounced from the surface and highlighted a section of the wall painting. It depicted a man kneeling with his arms outstretched and flowing from those arms were green and red feathers, as if he had wings. It was unnerving and exotic. Eliora focused instead on the regular patterns of triangles and circles that bordered the image.

Suddenly three other women rushed into the room through the door Eliora had come from. They wore pristine white tunics, tied at the waist with a gold and green braid. Their faces, although quite different, all bore the same almond emphasised eyes and rouge lips and cheeks. They each raised their chins and glanced down at Eliora as they passed her, entering the same door that her mother had.

Eliora felt, maybe for the first time, small and insignificant.

Gentle and hushed voices could be heard from the neighbouring room. Eliora could now hear her mother's voice singing a slow but elegant tune and the slightly shriller voices of the other women giving instructions.

Eliora waited. She rubbed her sleepy eyes and yawned.

Another voice, more commanding and authoritative spoke, although the wooden door muffled what was said.

Eliora fidgeted a little. She leaned over and peered out of the window. It was already a hot morning and the breeze that drifted in was full of promise that it would get hotter still. She welcomed the clean light in this unfamiliar place. She wandered over to the curtain and drew it back. The rushes nearly came up to the window ledge. A ramp, that appeared to be suspended in the air, gradually led down to the water's edge. This was not part of the river, but a hand dug pool that branched off from the water source in the distance. This pool was secluded and private. This is where it all began.

I stand on the ramp. She remembers as a story told, I recall it perfectly, as I was here.

Eliora jumped as the door behind her opened. She spun around and saw the most elegant looking woman framed in the doorway. The woman was tall, slender and pale skinned. Eliora could not help but look into the beautiful face, even though her mother had warned her not to. She looked as perfect as the images painted around her. There appeared to be no imperfection. There was something about her dark eyes that was frightening. Eliora quickly diverted her gaze to the floor and gave an involuntary shudder of fear.

'Who is this child?' Eliora glanced up. The woman's voice was richly toned and strong. She had a long neck where she wore multiple gold necklaces, and a chiselled face. Her dark eyes were enriched by her carefully painted makeup. Her long, thick, dark hair hung completely straight, and woven into her crown was a bright circlet of jewel encrusted gold.

'She is my daughter your Majesty,' Eliora's mother said, standing behind the queen, her head bowed. 'You commanded me to bring her before you when she reached her age.'

'Will you work hard in my household?'

'Yes,' Eliora stuttered, how could she refuse to do so? 'Your Majesty.' She remembered.

'You shall be called Ebonee.'

Eliora heard the stifled giggles of the three other women and looked up. Her mother looked on Eliora with concern.

Her own mother had been named by the queen when she was Eliora's age but she never used it outside the palace.

'If you are like your mother, you will be good at singing. Is that correct?'

'Yes, your Majesty.' Eliora struggled not to look into the queen's face. It felt rude not to make eye contact, although she had no desire to feel that fear again.

'Then you will be assigned to the care of my cats. Sing to them.'

'Thank you your Majesty,' Eliora said aware of her mother's relieved sigh.

'Simra, show her the way.'

Eliora's mother bowed low and escorted her daughter from the room.

'Simra. What does that mean?' Eliora asked, barely out of the room. 'What does Ebonee mean?'

'Oh Elli!' Her mother sighed. 'Simra means song. That is my name here. And you are to be called Ebonee. That means black.'

'Black?' Eliora looked at her mother confused.

'Yes black.' She pulled a small square of muslin from her braided belt. 'You will need this.' Eliora took the square. 'Look at your reflection in the disk here.' She led her daughter to the mural, and the gilded disk held by the horns of the painted symbol.

'Oh no!' Eliora said mortified.

As she looked into the disk, her reflection stared back, only it was not the pristine and beautifully made up face of this morning, but a kohl smudged, black eyed child who looked back at her. She had rubbed her tired eyes and smeared the makeup right up into her eyebrows and also halfway down her cheeks.

Eliora began to scrub away at her face. 'What is wrong with my own name? It seems unfair that I have to have her choice.'

'Here, let me.' Her mother took the muslin and carefully rubbed away the traces of unconscious sabotage. 'You could have waited until she had named you before you did this!' she laughed. 'Now you are stuck with that name!'

'How come you ended up with a nice name like song?' Eliora pouted.

'It was grandmother's voice that she heard first. She was singing to your uncle. I inherited her name.'

'Do you think she will change my name?'

Simra laughed.

'I'll take that as a no then.'

'It isn't all that bad. At least you are not a number like the others.'

Eliora frowned.

'You have been given a great honour, to take care of her cats. To you that is nothing, but to these people, that is a big deal.' Simra stood back from Eliora and nodded. 'You'll do.' And led the way down the corridor.

Eliora checked her reflection. The result was not as neat as this morning, but she was looking Egyptian again.

'Ebonee!' her mother called. 'Eliora, come on!'

'You never told me she was so frightening.'

'You think so?' Simra hesitated a moment. 'Yes, I suppose I had thought that to begin with.'

'You aren't scared of her now?'

'No. She says she needs me.'

'But her eyes.' Eliora shuddered again.

'I told you not to look into her face.'

'How can you not do that? I mean, haven't you looked into her eyes?'

'Not for a long time,' Simra said quietly.

'I don't know how you go to her every day and not die each time.'

'Elli, don't be so dramatic.'

'Why does she need you? Those other women didn't want you there.'

'No one wants us here.' She sighed. 'The queen says that my singing calms her soul.'

'And her soul definitely needs calming. You should have seen her eyes.'

The two of them strolled through a series of empty rooms before they came to a blue painted door surrounded by carvings of cats. The guard at this door was muscular and severe looking. He took no notice of the newcomers and allowed them entry without question.

Inside was a bright sunlit room with many cushioned seats and the sound of a gentle purr. Many cats lounged on the soft chairs and at the tall windows. The floor was littered with excrement. The stench made Eliora retch.

'Keep this place clean, and for your own sake, keep these cats happy.' Simra marched over to the ornate cupboard in the corner, opened it and pulled out a broom and a pan. 'Waste must be taken to the pile, outside the kitchen, and food can be found with the cooks. You should have no trouble.' She held out the broom to her daughter. 'Ask the guards for directions. They are allowed to speak to you as you wear the royal servant colours in your belt.' Simra pointed to the embroidered stitches that adorned Eliora's belt and kissed her on the cheek. 'Work here until your replacement comes.' She looked anxiously at her daughter.

'I'll be fine. How difficult can this be?'

'Alright. I'll see you at home,' Simra said and she closed the door behind her.

It was difficult work. Eliora had been fooled by the cats' graceful movement and soft purring. The cats had wills of their own. They were quick to pounce on the broom and quite happy to attack with their claws out. She had finally collected all their mess and left the room having sustained two angry looking scratches to her forearm.

The bald headed guard was far too frightening to ask for directions, so, Eliora, left to her own devices, searched for the kitchen herself. Every corridor looked the same, every doorway led to similar rooms, every wall decorated in the typical Egyptian manner. In the end it was the smell of cooking that led the way. But of course, Eliora had not paid attention, and was uncertain of the way back.

I walk with her. I stand guard over her. She is lost and is panicking.

I quickly transform.

Eliora was lost. She took the next turning on the right and nearly bumped into an elderly man, sweeping the floor.

'I'm sorry,' she apologized. The guard standing a short distance away flicked his gaze towards her. He looked confused as to whom she is talking.

'Easily done, my dear.' The old man was kind to her. She was relieved, at last, to find a kind soul.

'Excuse me sir, I am looking for the queen's cat room. I don't suppose you know ...'

The old man gave her directions, telling her to take note of visual aids to guide her. She would not get lost again.

As Eliora walked past the guard, she glanced up into his face. He pulled away as if he considered her crazy.

Eventually, and reluctantly, she returned to the cat room.

It was lonely work. The cats were very poor company and vicious with her. She felt very sorry for herself as she cautiously sat on the cold stone floor. As the day had progressed, it was her own soul that could do with calming. The images painted everywhere disturbed her, the long echoing corridors and unfriendly faces disheartened her and her unappreciated job depressed her. This was the place she was destined to be. Why did her family have to be picked for this? What had her friends been doing today down in the pits? It would have been hot, but at least they would have had someone to talk to.

She feels lonely. Turquoise shimmers and pulses from her. But she will not be alone. I cut through the musky scent of cats with calming aloe.

2

Beginnings

Eliora perched on the rough brick steps in the shadows.

Today had been her first day of proper work. Her family were set apart in many ways. Eliora had now followed in her mother's and grandmother's footsteps and worked for the royal household. There was no brick making for them.

She could see her own people wearily walking the streets, back to their homes, caked in mud and covered in dusty sand, but she didn't feel sorry for them. Her life was so much worse than theirs, and now she would be in trouble with her mother all over again.

What else could go wrong today?

She wiped her nose and tucked the cloth back into her belt. Glancing up she saw a familiar person trudging along towards her. She lowered her head, not wanting to be noticed.

He slowed his walk as he approached her. She didn't look up at him so he sat down next to her.

'What's up Eliora?' laughed Caleb. 'Someone take your doll?'

'I don't play with dolls,' she sobbed.

Caleb smelt of stale sweat and was covered in the crusted mud and grime of his day's work. At least it was finished and he could go home to clean up.

'Are you crying?' he asked, suddenly concerned as he bent down and pushed away her thick dark hair from her face.

'No!'

'Yes you are.'

She was certain he could see the smudged trails of kohl and tears on her cheeks so she quickly rubbed her face with her hands.

'What's the matter?' he asked gently. 'Did they work you hard in the palace?'

'How did you know about that?'

'Everyone knows that is where your family are destined to work.'

Eliora stared at the dusty ground again. At least news of her first day had remained a secret.

'I just went to get Mother some fish,' she finally said quietly.

'Well, that's nothing to cry about.'

'I know,'she replied angrily. 'Let me finish.' She paused, expecting him to interrupt. He didn't so she continued. 'I went down to the market and that idiot Kenaz, pulled my hair so that I dropped my money. I can't find it. Now Mama is going to get mad at me too.'

'Where did you drop it?'

'I've looked and I can't find it.'

'Well show me where, maybe I can find it.'

'You won't find it.'

'Eliora!'

'Okay, I'll show you.'

She took him down towards the market, a place they had been together so many times before. The houses were closer here, and sounds of family life were drifting out to them. Mingled aromas of meals being prepared flowed out into the street. Eliora was slowing her pace as they reached the larger open square of the market.

'It was round here.'

'What was it you dropped?'

'Just a small bronze, but it was all Mother had left.'

They searched the dusty floor as many walked past them. Eliora, after a few moments decided it was a fruitless task. The coin was lost to them, and more than likely found by another.

You have a bronze, Caleb.

Caleb was bent close to the ground when Eliora had her back turned to him.

'I found it!' he announced holding out the coin.

'Oh Caleb! Thank you!' Eliora turned towards him, her face alight. 'Thank you!' And she flung her arms about him.

'That's alright!' he said ruffling her hair. 'Squirt!' Even though he had used *that name*, she could see he was delighted to have found the coin.

'Oi!'

'It isn't the first and I doubt it will be the last time I help you out.'

Caleb was ten when Eliora was born. He had told her she was a loud, scrawny thing, which held very little interest for him. He had been coaxed into holding her for a few moments before she began to squirm and scream when she was a few weeks old. He never did that again.

But as they grew up, living in houses that neighboured each other, they saw each other daily. Caleb played with younger brothers and other friends and Eliora had a habit of tagging along. She was annoying, she knew that. She always turned up when they were up to mischief and had the habit of telling everyone that they were to blame. She would beg to join in with their games, and if they shooed her away she would run to his mother crying, which inevitably meant that they were forced to include her.

By the time Caleb was fifteen, and Eliora was five, everyone seemed to see them as brother and sister. They would fight as siblings would but were close nonetheless. Eliora had celebrated her fourteenth birthday only last week. She was now required to work at the palace.

'Do you need any more help?'

'No! I'm done with you now.' Eliora was already rushing off to the fish stall.

'Come up to my place when you're done. I have some herbs that will go nicely with your fish.'

'Thanks Caleb. See you later!'

Eliora didn't think how strange it was that the coin was warm as if it had been inside someone's pocket.

Caleb was still trudging back up the road but was nearly at home when Eliora caught up and grabbed his arm.

'Nice fish!' Caleb complimented as he nodded towards the basket. 'Come in and I'll get you those herbs.'

The sweet smell of bread and bitter herbs filled the cool room. Caleb's younger brother lay stretched out on the window seat lightly snoring but his mother was nowhere to be seen.

Caleb turned to Eliora. 'Shhh!' he said with a finger to his lips.

He crept up to his brother and firmly grasped the woollen blanket he was laying on and pulled as hard as he could. The young man span off the seat and landed with a loud thud on the earthen floor.

'Oi!'

Eliora began to giggle.

'Kenaz!' Caleb greeted his brother quietly.

'What did you do that for?' Kenaz raged, red in the face.

'No reason.'

Kenaz raised his fist just as their mother came through the open doorway with a bowl of dried dates.

Eliora contained her laughter behind her hand.

'Stop that at once!' their mother ordered.

'He attacked me!' Kenaz protested.

She raised her eyebrows and looked at Caleb. 'Really,'she tutted. 'I would have thought you two had grown out of this by now.'

Caleb restored the blanket to its original place and went outside to wash.

'You have got to do something about him mother,' Kenaz moaned. 'Find him a wife!' And he smiled at Eliora, who stopped laughing immediately

'Kenaz that is not funny.'

'Never said it was,' he mumbled.

Eliora heard Caleb sigh.

'I've got enough on my plate with your wedding,' his mother said. 'When that is over, maybe I will seek another bride for him.'

'No you won't. You like having him around too much,' Kenaz complained.

'Enough. Are you clean for dinner?'

Caleb walked in with a handful of fresh green leaves in his wet hands.

'So Kenaz, how is Martha?'

'How would I know? I thought she had been moved to your team today.'

Caleb shook his head. 'You know, a girl likes to know that you care about them. She was at home, unwell. We had to work her quota today too.'

'Ill?' Kenaz asked. 'What was wrong?'

Caleb shrugged.

Kenaz got up, grabbed his jacket and headed for the door.

'You are not going anywhere until you have eaten.' His mother pointed out.

'But Ma!'

'No buts. She can wait until you are fed. I don't want her parents thinking you are unfed and unable to put food on the table.' She nodded towards Eliora as if she would appreciate such an important thing.

Kenaz sat down grumpily obviously concerned about his bride. Their mother had been very careful in her choice for each of her boys. Only Caleb was unmatched now but that had not always been the case.

'I've got to go,' Eliora said breaking the awkward silence. 'Mother will want this.'

'And these,' Caleb said handing over the herbs.

'Thank you. See you tomorrow?'

Caleb nodded and Eliora left them to their meal.

'You know what Ma, I have an idea for a bride for Caleb ...' Eliora heard Kenaz say loudly from inside the house.

'You two are acting like children!' Their mother shouted. 'Stop that now!'

Eliora couldn't help but laugh as she walked home.

3

Normal

The fish dinner tasted good. Eliora was hungry after her tiring day.

She sat at the table with her mother and grandmother. It had been a few years since her grandmother had worked at the palace, but she too had endured the hardship of being different.

'So tell me, Elli, how did you like the cats?' her grandmother asked.

'Not very much,' she said sulkily, turning to her mother. 'I don't like the work mother. Please don't make me go back.'

'I am sorry, but I have no choice,' Simra replied.

'It was what was destined for you,' Her grandmother said sadly.

Eliora picked a small roll from the plate and began to pick at it.

'How is it fair? Reuben got to work in the pits, why can't I?'

'Eliora!' Her mother frowned. 'How can you want to work there? Have you not seen? Have you not experienced the torture our people go through?'

'You didn't see the cats!' she huffed.

'Cats are nothing compared to the whips.' She tutted. 'Be grateful you have been chosen. Surely even you have heard their complaints.'

'I don't want to be chosen mama.' Eliora crumbled the crust into her plate. 'I want to be like everyone else.'

'Your uncle Aaron will be here soon,' her mother said, seemingly ignoring her plea. 'Wash up so that he will be welcome.'

'Uncle Aaron has a place in his team. Martha is not well. I heard it in the market. He needs someone else to help meet his quota. Please mama, can I join his team?'

'I wouldn't want that kind of work for anyone Elli,' her grandmother said. 'Please, be grateful that you have a few scratches and not a back covered in lashes.'

Eliora knew that her grandmother's words were final and that the queen's words were the law. She would be going back to her own kind of torture in the palace.

Uncle Aaron arrived shortly after. He was old, Eliora's great uncle, but his face was so lined by the years in the baking sun he bore the signs of a greater age. He stooped as he walked as if burdened with the days quota of bricks. He lit the lamp and sat by the fire barely saying a word.

'Ithamar and Beth are expecting again,' he finally said as he sipped from the cup her mother, his niece, had given him.

'Oh Aaron, what wonderful news!'

'No, not really.'

'But all children are a gift from God. And more grandchildren for you!'

'How can they be a gift if they are born into this slavery? Another will be brought into this burdensome life. I didn't want this for my children and definitely not for my children's children. What a life!' He sighed.

There was little to say. Eliora was certain that now was not the time to ask her Uncle about working with him. She kissed him gently on the cheek.

'Congratulations Uncle. Please tell Auntie Beth I will pop in to see her soon.' And she left the darkened atmosphere.

The evening air was cool and crisp. Eliora thought about visiting Martha but then remembered her encounter with Kenaz and decided it wasn't worth the risk of bumping into him again. Instead, she considered meeting up with her friends at the well.

The streets were not busy. The occasional open doorway bathed the dusty pavement with light and homely chatter. The well was situated in the middle of the Levite settlement and would often be the place where groups gathered. Tonight was no different.

Eliora recognised the girlish giggle of Dinah, her best friend. Even in the dim evening, lit by the flickering torches, Eliora could see the brightly dressed, and soft curved form of her friend. She had gathered a group of three around her.

'Elli! How was the fish?'

Eliora turned. Caleb sat with a group of his old cronies also enjoying the still evening.

'Oh! Good thanks.' She laughed as she strolled past him.

As Dinah turned her head to the sound of Eliora's voice, her head scarf fell away and Eliora thought she saw a flicker of annoyance flit across her face.

'Hello. How are you?' Eliora asked.

'Fine.'

The girls had stopped talking.

'What were you talking about?'

'Nothing much,' said Dinah. Eliora felt unsure of her friend. There was something different about her.

'What news?'

'Oh, nothing of importance.'

'My auntie Beth is having another baby,' Eliora offered.

'That's nice.' One of the other girls said smirking then raising her eyebrows at Dinah.

'Is something the matter Dinah?'

'Eliora, we are a bit busy tonight,' Dinah said and turned her back.

'Busy doing what?' she asked, but none of them even acknowledged that she had spoken.

Eliora just stood for a moment, not really understanding what was happening. Then confusion gave way, they were busy doing anything as long as it was without her.

It seemed a harsh reality. She no longer fitted in anywhere. The people in the palace hated her or thought she was crazy, except maybe that old man, and her now her own friends no longer wanted to be with her. Ebonee was a curse in this settlement.

Eliora could feel the prickling of tears pooling in her eyes. She turned from her lost friends and hurried away, head bowed.

The scene has not gone unnoticed. Caleb has seen the anguish in Eliora's eyes as she turned away. He scowls at the girls as they whisper and giggle to one another.

I do not understand. Humankind have a narrow view of life. Eliora longs to be included but she will never quite fit in. The plan for her is quite different. Each lesson she learns builds character, and it is her character that will be tested in the end.

She needs a friend.

I see Caleb. He sits with friends yet is not really part of who they are either. He has known such sorrow already yet he burns with gold at times. I have seen it. I have witnessed his faith even when others deny it.

That is why I have named myself Faithful for this mission.

Caleb will follow her. He will know what to say. He hears things whispered in his heart.

'I'm going to head home now,' he says casually to his friends as he gets up and stretches. 'Busy day and everything. I'm tired.'

They wave him on and continue to chat.

Caleb walks in the direction of his house but as soon as he is out of sight from his friends he doubles back to the path Eliora had escaped on. He thinks he knows where she has gone. He quickens his stride, and sure enough, there she is ahead of him. Her pace is slow and almost aimless. Perhaps her feet were taking her to her quiet place without her even thinking about it.

The tightly packed houses are thinning a little now, and the way is only intermittently lit by household lamps. A large area of darkness patches the horizon. Caleb continues to follow, trying to think of something to say to her. But every formula sounds wrong to him.

Eliora bent low to pick a few flowers from a plant, and crushed them between her palms. The sweet smell of lavender saturated the air. She moved slowly through the carefully planted rows of vegetation and stepped over the irrigation channels, squinting in the starlight, until she reached the boulder that marked another family plot. Dropping the used stalks to the ground, she turned and sat on the rock with a sigh. Hearing someone approach, she wiped her eyes and looked up.

'Oh, what are you doing here?'

Caleb shrugged. 'Not really sure.'

'You didn't need to check on me,' Eliora began, 'I am alright you know.'

'I know.'

Eliora looked down to her feet and started to draw patterns in the dirt. She felt Caleb sit beside her.

'So,' Caleb said after a few moments silence, 'The fish was good then.'

'It was alright.'

'You are chatty tonight!'

Eliora looked up at him and smiled weakly before returning to her patterns.

Caleb laughed quietly.

'So,' he tried again. 'Ithamar and Beth are having another baby.'

'Yes,' Eliora said confused. 'How did you know?'

'Overheard your conversation by the well.'

'Conversation!' Eliora shook her head. 'It wasn't a conversation. To have a conversation you need two people talking.'

'You've not had a good day have you?'

'No!'

'Do you want to tell me about it?'

'Not really.'

'Fine,' Caleb sighed staring up at the myriad of stars above him.

Eliora took a quick sideways glance at him. Caleb had a contented smile.

'Why are you smiling? Are you laughing at me too?'

'No, I was just thinking that it is really peaceful here that's all.'

'I guess.'

'I haven't been here for a while. I forgot what it was like.'

Eliora sighed again. 'She called me Ebonee.'

'Who did?' Caleb asked casually.

'The queen.'

'What did you do to earn that?'

'You knew that they gave out names?'

'Sure. Why would they make do with our names when they have the power to do what they like and call you whatever they like?' Caleb said with a hint of bitterness.

'Do you have a name that they have given you?'

'No. I am just a number.'

'Oh.'

'So what did you do?'

'I smudged my make up over my eyes, so she called me Ebonee, it means black.'

'Oh dear.' Caleb puffed. 'She didn't get that right then did she?' he murmured.

'What do you mean?'

'You are far from black, Elli.'

'Oh, right,' she said confused.

Caleb laughed at his own embarrassment. 'You are more like a star in the night sky. A bright light against the black.'

'Thanks!' Eliora said resting her head on his shoulder. 'That's a really nice thing to say.'

Caleb laughed a little. 'That's alright squirt!'

'And then you have to spoil it!' Eliora laughed with him. The laughing felt good. It chased away the mess of the day.

'What are you going to do about Dinah?' Caleb finally asked.

'You heard that too then.'

Caleb nodded.

'I don't know.'

'Do you know what I think?'

'Not often.'

Caleb smiled, 'I think she will come round eventually.'

'I don't even know what I have done,' Eliora said peering up at him.

'It isn't something you have done.' He looked down at her and sighed. 'I think she would like to work at the palace too.'

'I would happily trade with her!'

'It can't be that bad.'

'I have been given the honour of looking after the cats,' she said sarcastically. 'I hate cats.'

'Well, maybe the job isn't to your liking, but I suspect that Dinah thinks, your job is better than hers.'

'It probably is.'

'I'm glad you see it that way Elli, because I think it is too.'

Eliora returned to drawing patterns in the dirt.

'Doesn't mean I have to like it though,' she said sulkily.

'No.' Caleb puffed.

'But ...?'

'But, you should be grateful for it.'

'I know.'

Eliora looked up at the stars and smiled. She was like a star. That was a warm thought. Tomorrow, when her name was called she would think of that.

'What are you thinking about?' Caleb asked as he saw her genuine smile.

'Oh nothing.' She looked at him. 'So, how is Kenaz?'

'He has a nasty bruise,' Caleb said nodding.

'Really!' Eliora said shaking her head. 'Why's that?'

'He fell off a chair!' Caleb winked.

'Excellent. I would have liked to have seen that happen!'

And they were laughing again.

'Thanks for coming to find me Caleb, that is the second time you have rescued me today.'

'You are welcome,' Caleb said getting to his feet. 'Squirt!' and he ruffled her hair.

'Oi! It took me ages to get it looking like this.'

They stepped over the plants and headed in the direction of the glowing lamps.

'Just be yourself. You don't need to impress anyone.'

'Yeah. I made a great impression on the queen already!'

'What's done is done. Tomorrow is a fresh day.'

'With a whole new set of hazards!'

4

Found

It had taken a full six months for Ebonee to learn the palace layout, and that is who she was when she was at the palace. Now, after a year, she was an expert. Several times, she had found that one of the cats had decided to go missing and had therefore given her the opportunity to explore the palace a little further than the stuffy cat room. She never enjoyed capturing the wild animals. They seemed to know just how to be crafty. She had found that the queen's advice to sing to them did produce a calmer atmosphere, but whether that just worked for her she couldn't tell. She had discovered that she didn't like cats at all.

The guard opened the door. His vast size, dwarfed by the scale that the palace adopted, still intimidated Ebonee even after a full year of working here. She quickly got to her feet. She had been teasing one of the kittens with a bulrush stalk.

'You are missing one of your charges,' he said with a frown.

'Pardon?'

'A cat has been found near the queen's parlour.' He smiled vindictively. 'I'd fetch it if I were you, before you get sent back to where you belong.'

'Thank you.' Ebonee bowed her head. It wasn't the first time that someone had commented on the fact that she didn't fit in. It was considered a great honour for the Egyptians to work in the palace and as she was not of their race she had been shunned. It hardly seemed fair that she was given this treatment in forms of comments, looks or food rations. It was not her fault that the king's mother had singled out her family. Even when she returned to her home she didn't fit in. After all she worked at the palace while they worked as slaves. Theirs was obvious slavery; her slavery was just dressed up differently.

Ebonee slipped her feet into her sandals, lifted the kitten back into the basket and left the room.

She walked casually down the wide corridors checking her reflection in the golden sun disks and bowls. She wore her hair as straight as possible, although by the end of each day it had kinks in it mostly because she spent the day twiddling it around her forefinger in boredom. Since coming to the palace she had spent a lot more time dwelling on her own appearance. Every day she applied her eye makeup with care and had even taken to adding creams and lotions to her skin to keep it pale and tan free. The kohl enhanced her large dark eyes and secretly she thought that it looked better on her than many of the Egyptian women. As she looked down, she tutted at yet another irritation of being with cats. Her crisp white tunic, freshly laundered, was covered in short, dark cat hairs.

The queen's chambers were decorated with her image and the king's. They sat and stood among the numerous gods. There were so many of them, Ebonee hardly knew one from the other, but they all had their place in the palace. Each one was supposed to perform a certain task yet was somehow limited too.

On one wall the king was depicted, sat with his queen and his sons and daughters lined up before him. Ebonee recognised the first few in the line, as they had, on occasion, been to visit their mother and took part in different ceremonies. The king however, had many wives, and therefore many children. But it was this wife that he favoured and had honoured by paintings and statues. He had given her a rank of importance.

Ebonee heard the loud crash of something shattering on the stone floor, from a side room.

'Stupid cat!' she muttered and dashed into the room.

A once elegant, pale blue vase, lay on the floor, broken into pieces, in a pool of water. The lilies had been tossed haphazardly and were now scattered over the table and lay crushed on the floor.

'Where are you, you stupid cat?' Ebonee hissed. 'Now I'll have to clear this mess up too.'

She bent down low to look under the table but the cat was not there. She knelt down and peered under the couches, yet she knew that her cats would never stoop as low as hiding under there.

'Are you looking for this?'

Ebonee spun round to find a young man, maybe a little older than herself, although it was difficult to tell with his shaven head, holding the purring culprit in his arms. He wore the common apparel of a white linen kilt and had a bare chest.

Take care Eliora. He is not as he seems.

I see the creature winding its silken body around the young man before me. It will not see me until the correct time. I am obedient and stand back, but I could easily take on this creature. For now my beautiful bow and true arrows will stay slung at my back.

'Yes I am. Thank you.' She held out her arms to take the animal. 'How did you get in here?'

'Don't you like him?' he said casually rubbing the cat's ears causing the gold armlet, he was wearing, to glisten in the sunlight.

'I don't think that is any of your business.' She walked forwards a little with her arms still raised hoping to take the cat from him. 'Can I have my cat back now?'

'It isn't your cat.'

'And it isn't yours. Give it to me or I'll call a guard, I'm sure he will be interested to see you in here. Anyway, that cat is the queen's property.'

'Then you should look after it better.' He scowled. 'Don't want anything to happen to the precious queen's property do we?' he hissed.

'You shouldn't speak like that.'

'Why not?'

'Because you could get into serious trouble for saying things like that about the queen.'

The creature speaks to the man it binds.

'Look at her,' it hisses, 'She doesn't belong here.'

I see the way it looks at her. I want to destroy it now.

'She is one of them,' it concludes. 'One of the tribe that says they don't follow me, but they do, they all do really. They are lost. They are bound. They are all mine.'

It does not know that at all. That is not the truth. Some are still faithful.

'You should take her. She is pretty in her human way. Don't you want her?' it whispers as the man watches her. 'You should punish her for defending the so called queen. 'Oh, you want her alright. You can have whatever you like. If it means she gets hurt, I don't care.'

The Creator cares. I am here because He cares for you Eliora.

'What difference does that make to you anyway?' He looked at her. 'She isn't your queen.'

'No,' Ebonee said angrily. 'That's right, she isn't. But she is yours.'

There was a moment's silence. The young man shrugged his bare shoulders.

'I'll hold him if you like,' he said smiling a little, 'while you clear up the mess.'

Ebonee was not overly eager to take the cat.

'How did you get in here?' Ebonee asked again, warming a fraction to his smile.

'I followed the cat.'

'So you let it make that mess?' her tone changed a little.

'It was an accident.'

'So you made that mess?' she asked angrily.

'You can't prove that.'

Ebonee huffed as she bent down and set to work in picking up the pieces. She took a cloth from her belt to soak up the water and then marched over to the window.

The Nile was a fair distance from the palace but there had been long channels and a pool dug close to the queen's chambers for her to bathe. The noise of the chirruping frogs was intense. The din calmed a little as Ebonee leaned over to wring the cloth out.

The sound of frogs calling out to one another is continuous. The humans do not think it strange that the usual night time behaviour has crept into the day. It will be a good year for frogs.

Eliora guards herself. She is suspicious of this young man. Silver threads hang in the air around her while ammonia flowing from the creature attacks her defences and slowly eats away at the threads.

She carefully collected the sharp shards and lilies, but now had her hands full.

'I'll carry the cat,' he suggested. 'After all, I don't want it to cause even more trouble.'

Ebonee sighed and stood up straight raising her chin slightly higher than normal. He seemed to be enjoying her annoyance a little too much.

'Very well then.' And she left the chamber without even glancing at him. He followed after her looking a little smug.

She led the way to the pile behind the kitchens where she threw the rubbish. The servants she passed stared even more than usual. Perhaps she would be made to pay for the breakage.

'I can take him from here,' she said as she turned to him and opened her arms once more.

He passed the purring cat over to her, which hissed a little at her touch. He chuckled and she ignored him.

'I don't know your name.' he said as she made to leave.

'Ebonee.'

He looked a little confused. He would of course know what the name meant. He quickly studied her fair complexion and her dark brown hair that was nowhere near as dark as the traditional Egyptian wigs. Ebonee was glad that the name didn't seem to fit her at all.

'Do you know your way from here to your quarters?' she asked.

'I'll find my way.' He smiled. 'Hope to see you again Ebonee.'

'I don't think that is likely. I spend all my time with the cats.' He couldn't help but notice how she spat the last word.

'They're not that bad,' he encouraged.

'You don't have to spend all day with them!'

She turned away, tossing her slightly kinked hair and marched her way back to the cat room with the squirming cat in her arms.

I stand guard. They will not cross this threshold.

'We will be back young Ebonee. There is no doubt about that!' the creature spits as the young man strolls away.

I know that they will and I weep for Eliora.

5

Secrets

Ebonee was aware of the whispers. She had grown used to them in the palace. But things had changed over the last few days. The whispers were louder, as if they wanted her to react to them. She shut them out and set her mind on the task of taking care of the cats.

In her room, she sat cross legged, perched on a cotton cushion on the floor. She had found some papyrus and was busy with charcoal, copying some of the paintings that decorated the walls. The day was hot outside, but here, with the large open windows, a refreshing breeze played with the delicate curtains. Bright patches of sunlight danced on the floor and the cats dozed the day away.

Amon, the creator god, with his big hat and long beard looked almost normal against some of the others. Ebonee captured his likeness, then set about studying a young female cat that was suckling her kittens. She was absorbed.

Oh Eliora! She has taken so much into her life that doesn't belong there. She sees no danger in studying these false gods. They are humorous to her.

Every day, she takes Ebonee back to the settlement, but brings less and less of Eliora here.

I am glad she finds the cats to be a better study.

He creeps through the window, I see them enter. The young man and his possessor. There is malice in the air. I have been given power, yet I have to restrain myself.

'I like it, Ebonee.'

Startled, Ebonee physically left the cushion and drew a dark gash through her drawing of Amon. The young man, she had met with the cat, stood behind her, dressed as before, although in his hands he had a folded piece of cloth.

'Oh, he won't like that!' he laughed.

'How did you get in here?'

'Through the window. You know, if you want to keep an eye on your charges, you should keep it shut.'

'They won't go out this time of day. It's too hot for them.'

He reached over to one of the chairs, grabbed a cushion and sat down next to Ebonee.

'Don't you have anything better to do?' Ebonee asked as she rubbed at the unsightly mark.

'No.'

'Then they should give you something to do, instead of making a nuisance of yourself.'

'I completely, utterly and totally agree! Maybe Ptah will grant me the truly amazing gift of stonemason,' he said sarcastically.

'You should watch yourself. Your gods won't like you mocking them.'

'I think I'll take my chances.'

Ebonee returned to her drawing and tried to ignore him.

'I don't believe I told you my name when we met the other day.'

Ebonee said nothing although she was slightly inquisitive.

'Don't you want to know?'

'Do you want to tell me?'

'I just thought it would be good as I will be visiting you every now and then. I thought you needed a friend that's all.'

'I have friends.'

'Egyptian ones?'

Ebonee was silent again.

'I thought not,' he said proudly.

'What is it to you anyway? You don't want to be seen with me. It will jeopardise your future.'

'I won't be seen with you,' he said casually, 'at least not for a while.'

'And what is that supposed to mean?' Ebonee said looking at him angrily.

'Just that I will be coming in through the window. No-one will know I am here.'

'Well then, I have no escape. If I shutter the windows I'll boil and if I open them I'll get a visitor.'

'Exactly! So do you want to know my name?' he smiled.

'You want to tell me so I guess I will listen.'

'I am Horusisus.'

'Named after a god. That's ironic.'

'Indeed,' he sighed. 'You can call me Si.'

'So, Horusisus, what kind of job do you have that allows you all this time on your hands?'

'Well done young one' it chants in Horusisus's ear. It pollutes the air with its foul deception. 'You must soften her. Let her feel sorry for you.'

It plays a nasty game. And to this creature that is exactly what it is. But this no game. Eliora is not a worthless piece to throw around. She is valuable and is treasured.

'It's Si and that's not important,' Si said almost sadly. Ebonee noted the change in his tone and looked at him closely. 'I bought some food. I thought we could share a meal.'

Taken aback by his sudden genuine manner Ebonee just gaped.

'Of course, I'll go if you don't want me here.'

'No Si, that's fine.' She tentatively smiled. 'I'll fetch my food.'

She got up and flattened out her tunic, although now the linen was creased beyond repair, and gathered up her own meal from the side table.

Si had already opened his cloth and had laid out several unusual looking items. Ebonee unpacked hers. It contained a small loaf and hunk of cheese. She also had a few grapes and figs.

'Do you want to try this?' Si asked holding up something wrapped in a vine leaf.

They exchanged food and chatted together. Si said that the grapes were far better than the ones they grew in the vineyard. This pleased Ebonee as they were picked from her family plot. Perhaps pretending to be an Egyptian and living Ebonee's life wasn't so bad.

She was surprised to find that Si wasn't as he first appeared. He seemed friendly and warm, although he would never say exactly what he did in the palace. Maybe it was an embarrassing job with low rank, thought Ebonee, although the clothes he wore were richly embroidered.

As the afternoon faded and time for Ebonee to finish for the day drew near, Si became downhearted again.

'Can I come to see you another time?'

'I don't think there is a way to stop you!'

'No, there is no way to stop me.' Ebonee saw a flicker of power cross his face, but before it had even registered, it was gone. 'Promise me, you won't turn me away. Promise me on the goddess Hathor.'

All afternoon I have had to watch and guard. Eliora is fascinated by this mysterious man. He has fed her lie after lie. He has pulled her in.

I will not leave her. I will continue to stay with her.

'Steer clear of him' I urge but she will not listen to me, his voice is more dominant.

'There is no way to stop me,' the creature shrieks in evil delight. 'Make her swear on the goddess of death. Make her!'

'No!' I bellow. 'She will not pollute herself.'

'I don't promise on any goddess. But you have my word.' Ebonee smiled at him. 'Just bring back some of those delicious cakes.'

'Excellent. Until next time then Ebonee.' And Si stepped out of the window and into the shade of the garden beyond.

'Mama, I'm home!' Eliora called as she entered the house.

Her mother appeared at the doorway. She wiped her hands on a cloth hanging from her sash. She frowned.

I see worry swirling about Eliora's mother, it is grey and thunderous.

'Is something the matter? Auntie Beth, is she alright?'

'Beth is fine, I spoke to Aaron only an hour ago.' She beckoned to the bench. 'Sit for a minute with me.'

'Mama?'

'I have heard some things at the palace.'

Eliora just looked confused.

'I understand that you have been seen with a young man.'

'You mean Si?' Her mother raised her eyebrows. 'He helped me find a cat the other day. It had smashed a vase, well it could have been the cat.' Eliora bowed her head. 'Am I to be punished for the vase. It wasn't my fault. He said the cat knocked it over.'

'No. That was all resolved. No-one is to be punished. Your friend sorted it all out.'

'Really? He didn't tell me that.'

'You have seen him again?' she asked sternly.

'Oh mama, I'm sorry,' Eliora blushed as she turned to her mother for forgiveness. 'He visited me today in the cat room. We had our meal together, that's all. I didn't think it was a problem.'

'Do you know who he is?'

'Horusisus, although I think he prefers Si.' She laughed. 'I don't blame him, who would want to be named after a bird god?'

Not only a bird god Eliora. There is something much more sinister in his name.

'Maybe a son of the pharaoh.'

Eliora stopped mid chortle. 'What?' Her face paled.

'His mother is a lesser wife, but he is a son nonetheless.'

'Mama, I did not know,' she pleaded.

'What is done, is done.' She put her arm about her. 'Maybe stay away from now on.'

'Mama I can't. I promised he could visit again.'

'Oh Elli. What will we do with you?' She cupped her daughters chin in her hand and looked into her face. 'Well, I guess we will see what happens. I don't think you will be able to go back on your word now.'

'I could tell him to stay away next time I see him.'

'It doesn't work like that my love. He has power here, we are just the play pieces.'

'Oh Mama! What can I do?' Eliora had worry in her eyes.

'Nothing,' her mother said looking away, 'But do you think he was a good man?'

'At first he was a little cruel, but today he was quite kind and generous.'

'Maybe there is hope then. Maybe you have found a friend.' She quickly got up and went back to her kneading. 'Why don't you go and find Dinah?'

She seems to have found hope for her only child. But a hope that is connected to the son of Pharaoh is frail indeed. She still worries, even if I could not see her colours I would know. The dough is going to be kneaded very well.

Talking it through with her mother has given Eliora unguarded ideas. Dreams have begun to form. She dreams of a life free from the cats with a powerful friend at her side. I am sad that she may even see some of that dream. How the Creator longs to redeem her. She is his precious treasure.

Eliora was both fearful and excited. A son of the most powerful man had sought her out. He had given her protection with regards to the breakage but was a normal person too. Si had offered her friendship, maybe he could get her a better job.

She washed off her make up, and headed to the gardens. Dinah was still not really talking to her, but she had not spoken to her mother about that.

The streets were busy. There was always a strong smell of sweat at this time of day. Many were returning home from their hard labour, exhausted and burnt by the sun.

In the gardens it was cool. The fruit trees gave shade and the irrigation channels moistened the air. Caleb was tying up some vine branches that had worked loose from their bindings.

'Hey squirt!' he said as he looked up.

'Hey yourself!' Eliora replied pulling a face at the use of the name.

'Good day?'

'It was fine. You?'

'You know, not too bad. Good breeze today.'

Eliora held the branch in place while Caleb wove the cord through the gaps.

'Caleb, do you know anything about the Egyptian gods and goddesses?'

'A little.'

'Who is Hathor?' Eliora asked remembering the goddess Si had asked her to swear by.

Caleb is caught out by the use of that name. He has purposefully tried not to think of it for many years now.

'Hathor?' Caleb gazed at Eliora. 'Why do you ask?'

'I just heard someone talk about her today.'

'Hathor is a goddess of death. Sometimes the masters call her down upon us as they beat us, but they usually use Osiris, the main god of the dead. Hathor had other roles too.'

'Like what?'

Caleb paused in tying a knot. 'She is the goddess of love and birth.'

'Really.' Eliora smiled. Why would Si want her to promise in her name? 'How do you know?'

'Abigail had one.'

'She had what?'

'A statue of Hathor.' Caleb turned away. 'I smashed it when she died.'

'I'm sorry Caleb.'

'It's not your fault. She bought it into the house when she found out she was pregnant. I shouldn't have let her do it. Now she is gone with our son, and I am without ...'

'How long now?'

'Four years. Do you remember her?'

'She was very beautiful.'

'Yes,' Caleb said catching her glancing at him, 'But she should not have turned her back on God.'

'It is easy to do when he doesn't hear us.'

'He hears.'

'You see the impossible situation yet always have faith. You are amazing Caleb.' Eliora frowned, 'Why have you never married again?'

'Lots of reasons. I guess I never found the right woman to have me,' he said snorting a little.

'Where's your faith now!'

'I smashed the statue of love remember.'

'They are all nonsense Caleb. If they were real I would be squashed by now.'

'What do you mean?'

'I drew a dirty great line across Amon's face today!'

Caleb began to laugh. Eliora followed and before they knew it tears were running down their cheeks. When they had calmed down Eliora said.

'You should marry again. Don't you want all the things your friends have? A place of your own, space away from Kenaz. For that alone, I would get married! Do you want a wife and children?'

Caleb started to tie the cords again. 'I've been there and to be honest I'm not sure I want to go there again. I barely knew Abigail and just look where that ended. But then,' he said trying to lighten the conversation, 'I'm sure I want all the money problems, the nagging, fear of the future ... Yeah, who wouldn't!'

'Stop it Caleb!' Eliora felt cheerless listening to him. Marriage was something she felt sure would never happen to her, but for others it bought happiness. She slumped on the wall with a heavy heart.

'What about you huh?' Caleb said putting down the cord once more and trying to change the conversation. 'When am I going to hear that you are betrothed?'

'That won't happen.'

'Why not? You're beautiful, fun, intelligent ... I must admit you aren't that good at cooking but that comes.'

'No. No-one will have me. I am a Hebrew in an Egyptian world. They look at my Mama and remember what happened to my Papa. The two lives cannot mix. No-one would offer their son to that life.'

'I'm sorry Elli.' Eliora was comforted by the use of her name. Caleb sat down beside her. She rested her head on his shoulder.

'Papa will never know what he has left us with.'

He put his arm around her. 'Just look at the two of us. A couple of bad eggs!'

'At least we are bad eggs that can do what we like.'

'Maybe ... but I think both our mothers are expecting us home for dinner.'

Eliora smiled as she got up. 'See you tomorrow?'

'I'll be here.'

Neither of them know of the destiny set before them.

6

Reunited

I stand on the dry and crisp vegetation lying on the roof of the house. I make no noise. The leaves and fruit are not spoiled by my presence. My softly woven tunic is not long enough to touch the ground and is tied at my waist. At my back there appears to be a loosely gathered bundle of straw. But things are not always what they appear to be. If anyone were able to see me, they would consider me an Israelite although my hair is a little lighter and russet in colour.

I am watching for the signal. My eyes sparkle with excitement.

The cloudless night sky is ablaze with the light of the universes beyond. Swirling masses, some circular others more elongated, alight with amazing colours weaving through the speeding particles. Explosions so distant that before the light reaches this small planet a solar system is created and established.

Stars that were set in place in a time past, swathe the kohl black above me. A band of twinkling lights.

Then I see it.

A flash of the brightest light.

I will answer back. I am transformed. A robe so bright, it would destroy the human eye, and a moment so quick it could easily be missed. My true form. My skin shimmers as I let out a joyous cry. I am dressed for battle with my full silver quiver slung over my shoulder.

I load my glistening bow of light with a perfectly straight and beautifully clear arrow. I set it into the night sky. The silver flights flutter as it rises into the air, Its golden tip piercing the darkness.

Briefly, so briefly, the Israelite sky is alight with arrows.

I know he is here and I rush to greet him.

My comrade in arms and dear friend!

He is dressed ready for battle too. His white robe is tied with a golden belt, but instead of a quiver his belt hangs with a long, jewel encrusted scabbard and in his hand he clasps a long sword with a solid gold handle. He has astounding strength and the muscles on his arms speak of battles won. His dark hair frames his beaming face.

'Friend!'

We embrace.

'It has been too long since we have waged war together!' He announces in his deep rumbling voice.

'Well met!'

'So, introductions first,' he says smiling broadly, teeth shimmering against his dark skin. 'I have chosen Release as my name. And you would be?'

'Faithful.'

'Excellent to be with you again brother!'

Our laughter saturates the air.

It was still dark when Eliora woke to the sound of her grandmother's excited chatter. It was joined by a man's deep voice speaking slowly.

Eliora wrapped a thick woollen blanket about her, as the night's chill had yet to pass, and stumbled sleepily into the main room.

Eliora's mother sat perched on the edge of her chair gazing happily at the strange dark haired man opposite her, while her grandmother sat beside him, her hands in his.

'Elli. I'm sorry. Did we wake you?' but before she could answer. 'You won't believe who has come!'

The man turned to face her. His face was dark and weathered. There was a familiarity about him, yet Eliora was sure she had never seen this man before. He did not wear the light, flowing Hebrew tunic, but a heavier and coarser robe. His salt and pepper beard was cropped short and his wavy hair tied at the nape of his neck.

'Miriam? Who is this?' he asked Eliora's grandmother.

'Oh Brother! There is so much to tell.' She sighed a little. 'This is my grand daughter, Eliora.' She turned to Eliora. 'This is your other uncle. Your great uncle Moses.'

'Moses!' Eliora exclaimed.

'Eliora,' he said slowly, 'It is nice to meet you.'

'I have heard stories about you for years.'

'I hope my sister has been kind!'

He stepped towards her and kissed her cheek.

Suddenly the room was full of noise and people. Aaron had walked through the door followed closely by a tall, slender woman and two young men a little older than Eliora.

Eliora was immediately struck by the similarity of the two uncles. Aaron was greyer and slimmer, but the family likeness between the two brothers was uncanny. Aaron appeared so different to his usual demeanour as he strolled in. He seemed to stand taller and straighter, the lines on his face were shallower so he looked as if he were younger.

'Miriam, this is Zipporah my wife,' Moses said as he took Zipporah's hand. 'And my two boys, Gershom' he indicated to the older boy, 'and Eliezer' He then indicated to Eliora's family and introduced them to his wife

Zipporah. 'Miriam is my sister, Jochebed (named after my mother), is my niece and my great niece, Eliora.'

'How wonderful to meet you! I am so glad you have come at last!' Eliora saw Zipporah's shocked face as her mother rushed over, hugged and kissed her, then tried to do the same with the boys.

'You will excuse them please,' Zipporah said, her voice was heavily accented but quite melodic. 'They are travel weary and a little under the weather.'

The older of the two boys shot an angry look at his mother.

'Let us find a place they can rest.' Miriam looked at Eliora. 'Move your things into my room Elli, the boys can use your room.'

If the room had not been filled with strangers Eliora would have complained. The best she could do was to mirror her cousin's glare at her own mother in protest.

Eliora left the busyness and returned to the seclusion of her own space. Sighing heavily, she piled her main possessions on the bed, gathered the blanket around them and moved them into her mother's smaller room.

The overcrowded living space was buzzing with talk when Eliora returned. Zipporah approached her.

'Thank you for letting us stay. I am so happy I have a beautiful niece. It will be good to be with females again.'

'My room isn't very big. But you may use it now.'

'Thank you,' Zipporah said as she stooped to kiss Eliora's forehead. She beckoned to the boys who gathered up the packs they had bought and willingly followed their mother to Eliora's room.

Eliora scowled as they shuffled past, heavy laden. How long were they planning on staying?

Eliora watched as her uncles laughed together. Her mother turned to her and beamed with happiness.

'Elli, come and sit down. There is so much to hear.'

She pulled the blanket around her, moved closer to the group and slumped to the floor resting her back against the thick wall. She would get no more sleep now. At least, she thought, she could nap when she got to the palace.

After a few moments, Zipporah had rejoined the family group. She sat next to her husband, opposite Eliora, who had the chance to take in the appearance of her aunt. Her features were more angular than the typical Hebrew face, but her olive complexion was clear and her eyes bright. She was younger than her uncle, by perhaps ten years. Her clothes were layered and rich in colour, deep hues of green and blue dyed the fabric.

'So Moses,' Miriam began, 'You are here at last.'

'I am.'

'How? Why? Where have you been these past years? A whole lifetime has passed!'

'Miriam,' said Aaron, 'Our brother finds our tongue a difficult one. Don't set so many questions before him!'

'You did my brother, when you first saw me!' Moses replied.

'He has come to set us free, Miriam,' Aaron announced, then whispered in awe, 'Freedom.'

'Not I,' Moses added slowly. 'But the Mighty One, the God of Abraham, of Isaac and Jacob. He will set his people free.'

'When?' questioned Eliora.

'I go to the palace tomorrow.'

Aaron's laughter was bold and contagious. Happiness filled the little house. Eliora noticed that her other uncle, although he smiled, there was an absence of joy in his eyes.

'How?' she asked. 'How will we be set free? Why now?' Her tone was filled with unbelief.

'Eliora, God has heard the cry of his people.'

'It has taken a long time to hear it!'

'Elli!' her mother scolded.

'Well, it has. Why now? And why use you?'

'I don't know why I should be the one.'

'Tell our faithless niece the story Moses!' Aaron said with disapproval in his voice.

Eliora hid the anger that burned inside. How dare her uncle say she was faithless? Was it not him who had so many times declared that God did not hear the cries of the people? Who would moan and complain that God would never come to save him? How could he, with his hypocritical attitude be so self righteous?

'I fled from this place almost forty years ago. So much has changed,' he said smiling at Eliora and turning to his wife, 'yet so much is the same. I feared for my life but I return because I am told to. I am so glad to find that I have family here. Family that has grown in number and courage.' He sighed. 'Your lives have been harsh. Caught in slavery to an unfair master. But God has heard the cries of his people. He has chosen to act now.'

'We thought you were dead,' Eliora said focusing on her uncle. 'Grandmamma, although she hoped you were alive somewhere, thought you were dead. She put off suitors because of you. My own mother was born in her old age, my grandfather dying before he had the chance of seeing his only daughter grow up. Mother's life is so different to the rest of our people but my father eventually won her over, but he didn't stay for long. Didn't even stay for my birth. Why didn't you come back sooner? I might still have a father.'

'Elli,' her mother said crushed by her daughter's words. 'Your father just couldn't cope with our lifestyle. With being so different.'

'I don't claim to understand all that you have been through. All that any of you have been through,' Moses said turning to both of his siblings and reaching out to touch their hands. He then turned to Eliora. 'I wish I could have done something to prevent the hurt you have gone through. I really do.'

'How do you know the time is now?' Elli asked more softly.

'God spoke to me.'

The room was quiet. Everyone gave Moses their full attention.

Eliora hurts. She wants to believe, but struggles believing that the Creator has not acted fast enough for her. Her needs were not met, her disappointments are heavy and her life seems devoid of a father. She only focuses on the things right before her eyes. One day she will look up and see the bigger picture, the wider horizon.

As Moses talks, Release smiles and nods in agreement.

'Tell me,' I say, 'What was it like in your eyes?'

'The Creator chooses those that are not! Moses was one of those! He had been running scared for years; settled, yes, but still fearful of his past. But even with that past, the Creator chose him.

'You know the bushes out in the dessert that suddenly catch alight?'

'Yes.'

'Moses had seen a fair few. The midday sun, igniting the resin. Well, the Creator came and rested near to such a bush.'

As Release remembers, the images flood my own mind.

I see as Moses leads his flock to the west side of the wilderness. The ochre ground, rocky and dry. There is very little to graze here, no lush pastures or cool flowing streams, but still he led them on. He had purpose, he wanted to see the mountain that he had been told about, the place where he had heard of encounters with the one true God.

He wanders over the uneven ground, taking the route that leads closer to the steep mountain side. I see my friend guiding him. Highlighting the path he should take. The mountain is striking against the cyan blue sky.

He saw the bush burning, but not being burnt. He turned form his path and drew near.

Flames of gold and brilliant white, colours that I see, seem to be apparent to him too. This man sees the presence of the Creator and is drawn in. What blessing to be in His presence and not be destroyed.

The voice of the Creator rings out, true and clear. He calls the man's name and the man does not flee. Is he eager for the Lord? He has come to this place for an encounter and will not run even though I can see the fear pulsing from him, but it is right to be fearful. This is the Creator who is speaking to him. The ground about him shimmers in the holiness. His shoes must be removed.

The Creator is all in all. He tells this human that He is the God of Abraham and Isaac and Jacob. He is not an Egyptian falsehood.

Moses hides his face. Other gods that he grew up with are nothing compared to this God. Moses knows a little of the exploits of this God, and the little he knows increases his awe.

The Creator states that He has seen, He has heard and He is aware. He is not a distant God. He cares for the human race in a way they do not understand and will never fully comprehend. He knows their suffering, He feels their pain and He hates the injustice.

He will deliver them. The Creator promises Moses that. Not only will He deliver, but He will provide. He wants His people to have their own land that flows with all they need. What a gift! What a place! Beautiful, lush, green. Rich, expansive, safe. The Creator promises the very best for His people.

'The cry of the sons of Israel has come to Me.' He has heard them. 'I have seen the oppression.' He has seen. 'I will send you to Pharaoh so that you may bring My people, the sons of Israel, out of Egypt.' He will deliver.

But Moses now fears wrongly. He fears for himself. 'Who am I?' He asks.

The Creator knows his fears. 'Certainly, I will be with you. You will bring them here, to this mountain to worship.'

Moses knows that the people will know of many gods and will be living by their idols. He asks what the Creator's name is so that he may tell them.

'I AM WHO I AM.' The Creator who has always existed and will do so, the creator and sustainer of all things, the perfection of righteousness, the only answer to life and the meaning of life itself. The one true God. What a name!

But now to details. 'Gather the elders, tell of My concern and My promise of deliverance and land. Go to the pharaoh. Tell him of Me. Ask him to let My people sacrifice to Me.'

Moses listens. He is determined to do all his God has said.

'But it is not as simple as that,' Moses said with slow words. 'Pharaoh will not let us go except under compulsion. God will strike Egypt first.'

Eliora was amazed at what she had heard. A voice from a burning bush. Her uncle chosen to save them. The hairs on the back of Eliora's arms rose as he began to explain. They were going to be free! With all thoughts of Ebonee gone, Eliora was, in her mind, already packing her things and leaving Egypt. She paid little attention as Moses continued.

'I was not confident in these plans, I am ashamed to say. How could I prove anything to the pharaoh? God is at that mountain to be sure, but as soon as I left, how would I show the power of this God over the others that have such control here?

'He gave me signs that will enable them to see. Yet I was still unable to do all that I was told. I have never felt the fear I felt there. But this God, the God we must follow, was merciful to me. He sent out Aaron, and now we will work together.'

'I just felt I needed to go,' Aaron said, his eyes glazed at the memory. 'Elisheba was not happy and neither were the boys, they took on my quota, but I couldn't get it out of my mind, so I left and walked out, and there I found him. Him, Zipporah and the boys. I am ready for this. At last we will be free.'

'When do you go to Pharaoh?' Miriam asked, her face streaked with tears.

'We will go today,' Moses said sadly.

'Why are you sad uncle? This is great news,' Eliora said confused.

'Indeed it is good news, but it will not be simple. The Lord said he will harden Pharaoh's heart. Your oppressor will not want to let you go.'

'How long then?' asked Eliora impatiently.

The room was quiet for a moment.

'I don't know. But it will happen,' Moses stated confidently.

Eliora's spirit soared. She would be free.

7

Request

Ebonee yawned widely as she settled herself on the floor.

'Not sleeping at work I hope!' Si's voice startled her and her eyes flashed open. 'Can't have the precious Queen's cats unattended, can we?'

'Si,' Ebonee bowed her head, remembering she was in the presence of a prince. 'Work started very early and I've been really busy.' It was midmorning, the cats were fed and the room cleaned. Ebonee had only just sat down and was enjoying a small round raisin cake with her eyes shut when Si had come in.

When she looked up, she noticed his frown.

'I've come to get you away from these vile creatures,' he said with his eyes suspicious. 'There's something I wanted to show you.'

'I shouldn't really leave my post.'

'I want you to come.'

Ebonee didn't protest but got straight to her feet.

'What? No arguing with me?'

'No, not today Si.'

He grabbed her hand and dragged her out the window and into the gardens.

Ebonee was not used to such familiarity. Si was strong though and wouldn't let her wriggle out of his grasp. She felt ill at ease with his hand so tight around hers, but what could she do? He had authority and she was only a Hebrew slave. But there was something about his power that she craved. He could change things for her and she was sure he would.

In the garden the air was thick with heat. Ebonee felt it pound her lungs. It was only a few moments before she longed to be inside the palace wall again, protected from the sun. Si took her through the gardens outside the cat room and then further into the greenery that surrounded the palace.

The air hummed with insects and was full of moisture, so unlike the rest of the dry landscape. The tall rushes scratched at Ebonee's bare legs and prickled her feet.

Si took her to another window, at the back of the palace, and lifted her to the sill. He quickly followed her inside. The room was cool and empty of people. Ebonee had little time to take in the rich furnishings before she was dragged to a door hidden behind a flowing curtain. Si pushed the door and went inside the dark passage. He took the flickering torch from the holder and pulled her along. This space was cold and had no windows.

They walked in silence for a while.

'Where are we?' she finally asked, her curiosity getting the better of her.

'Servants passage.' Si laughed. 'Neither of us is meant to be here, but I don't care. It will take us to the ... just hurry up or we'll miss it.'

'Take us where?' But Si didn't answer. He kept wrenching her hand painfully, making her trip and stumble after him.

'You're hurting me,' Ebonee complained.

'Get a move on.'

Ebonee thought that they must have walked almost the entire length of the palace when Si diverted off on one of the side passages. He seemed to know his way around very well for someone who wasn't meant to be there.

He stopped suddenly and had pressed his ear up to a door. Slowly he pulled on the rope handle and the door swung open slowly and noiselessly. There were echoing voices coming from a vast room beyond. Si let go of her, pushed Ebonee down to a crouch and crept up to the open lattice of the stone balustrade.

She peered through the gaps. They were high on a balcony, suspended at the end of a very large and light room. She hadn't noticed she had climbed any height as she stumbled after Si. The windows were at ceiling level along both sides of the length of the room. The warm air that she breathed was exchanged for cool draughts that drifted to the floor below. The roof above them was held in place by tall stone intricately carved palms, although, unless you were viewing from this height you would never know how perfect they really were. The ceiling gleamed with gold, reflecting the light.

Ebonee caught her breath and gazed into the hall beneath her.

Eliora is fearful. She thinks should not be here, and I suppose she is right in her own mind. She should be working, but this is a scene she is destined to see.

Si thinks he has led her here, but it is I who lead them.

The floor below teems with spirits. The room seethes with obsidian bodies and sickly yellow vapour. Leathery wings beat the smoke in swirling trails. Occasionally a fight breaks out between creatures.

A few of them have taken the form of the paintings that adorn every wall. Others prefer their scaly forms. Red eyes glare at their human hosts and expressions betray their true contempt for them.

The largest beast sits on the throne. It encircles the head of the man who sits there. It is fire and flame, burning slowly and lazily. The flickering flame takes the form of a bird's head with a sharp curved beak and malicious eyes. It closely resembles the god that is so important to these people. It looks on idly, as if the day to day lives of the human race bore it. This creature has entrapped the humans here, they have been made slaves.

I am not fooled by its appearance. I know this one.

I will wait.

The Creator has set a time and a place for everything.

On a polished raised platform, an ornate throne took centre stage. Either side of the throne, and set into the wall, were large carved plaques covered in scrolling images. Two more massive palms stretched up either side of the throne to the slightly lowered ceiling. The illusion made the throne and the person sitting there look larger. Ebonee heard Si make a slight hiss as the man began to speak. She looked over at him, suddenly aware that they were watching his father.

'I will receive them.' His voice resonated throughout the room.

Ebonee shivered despite the heat. She wished she were with the wretched cats.

The movement of the others caught her attention. The room was so elaborate that she hadn't noticed the people gathered down each side of the room to begin with. They almost blended in with the colourful paintings covering the walls.

Si eagerly moved closer to the edge dragging her with him.

Gradually the crowd hushed. Ebonee looked closely to see what had caused their action. She gasped. Her uncles were walking towards the throne. They were out of place here with everyone else dressed in Egyptian finery. They stopped before the throne and bowed.

'Your servants Moses and Aaron, O great one,' said a thin, wispy man, bowing, before backing away.

Ebonee saw a flicker of surprise on Pharaoh's face that quickly gave way to annoyance.

My friend, Release, accompanies the men with full assurance and confidence into the creature filled hall. They have come fresh from their meeting with the elders of the Remnant.

I am happy to see him here, and delighted that the spirits are so uncomfortable.

Their leader hisses, and the throng about him squirm.

Release is not dressed for battle. He is here to ensure the message is delivered through the man the Creator chose. But I do see his sword sheathed at his waist. A strong message to those who would attack.

The fire creature roars and order is restored in his ranks.

'This is my domain!' it declares.

'Speak!' commanded Pharaoh.

Moses stood still, his head held high. Aaron took a step closer to his brother. Moses spoke in a clear and unhesitant voice. He had not forgotten his old tongue.

'This is what the Lord, the God of Israel says: 'Let my people go, so that they may hold a festival to me in the desert.''

Ebonee felt a pang of longing for freedom. Her uncle had commanded it from the pharaoh. She wished briefly that she could be Eliora and enjoy this moment instead of wearing the uniform of Ebonee.

That seems to have done the trick. We have its full attention now. It blazes about the man in fierce anger.

'How dare you! What do you think you are saying? I am the one who reigns here. This is my palace. This is my throne. I am king. I am the Lord.'

Its hordes look on. Do they doubt its strength?

He flares and burns. It grasps the human. 'He is completely mine, as are all his people ... they are my slaves.' The flames penetrate the man's mind and seem to consume him. This is a power that his horde find difficult to resist. To them, their leader is supreme!

'Stand you fool!' The fire beast grabs the man and drags him to his feet.

Pharaoh stood.

'Who is the lord,' He glanced around at the images painted on the walls. 'that I,' he gestured grandly to himself, 'should obey him and let Israel go? I do not know the lord and will not let Israel go.'

'Do not give up Moses,' I hear the calm voice of my friend whisper. 'You knew he would refuse. But the plans The Creator has for you are great. Greater than you can fully understand. The Judge of all the earth will always do what is right.'

Moses nodded at Aaron and spoke again. 'The God of the Hebrews has met with us. Now let us take a three day journey into the desert to offer sacrifices to the Lord our God, or he may strike us with plagues or with the sword.'

'The god of the Hebrews ... he will not take them from me.' His bitter voice screeches through the room.

'Plagues and sword? Really? That is not likely. If they are his people ... which they are not because they are mine, he would not strike them. They are my slaves. They build my city. They will not leave.'

It eyes the sword at my friend's waist carefully. Is it contemplating a fight here and now? I am ready!

Its eyes, as dark and deadly as I remember glint at some thought. It does not attack but sits back on its haunches in an almost relaxed position. There is nothing to trust with it.

'No, let them go back to their tribes and spread the great news that they are still mine. I will not let them go!'

Pharaoh was already angry. Ebonee could see from the expression on his face that he did not want to let her people go and worship their own God. Si sniggered next to her, his attention fully caught by his father. As she looked over at him, she wondered what she had seen in him; he was so different here, almost hungry for a fight. She felt he would have fallen from their vantage point in his eagerness if it hadn't been for the railings.

'Why do you stop my people from working? Go and join them!' Pharaoh commanded.

Moses slouched as if he had taken on a heavy burden. Ebonee realised that her uncle was now one of them. A slave to the lord of Egypt. There would be no special treatment for an adoptive son of the palace. That life was over.

'I will not let them go!' Pharaoh proclaimed.

'Not much of a fight! I am supreme!' the beast declares as my friend and the men leave. It is greeted with cheers of support in the sulphur thick room.

But I watch the beast. Its flames are hesitant and not triumphant. It does not trust us, and with good reason. Perhaps it expected more. Well, it won't be disappointed!

'That was horrible,' Ebonee breathed. 'Did you know that was going to happen?'

'Oh,' Si said with a cruel smile, 'I thought that was fun!'

Ebonee looked down again at the throne. Si's father had sat down. He had a look of determination etched on his face. He beckoned a man servant forward.

'Speak to the foremen of the Hebrew people.' A cruel smile crossed his lips. 'I want them to produce bricks, the same amount as before, but I will not be merciful to them anymore. They must find their own straw. GO!'

The man hurried away.

Ebonee slumped on the floor. How could he be so heartless? Merciful? The man who sat on that throne was far from merciful. Suddenly she could understand why Si hated his father so much. Although Si seemed enthralled by him in this moment.

8

Life

Si didn't stop talking about it all the way back through the passages to the lavish room.

'It was about time. I mean, they don't have any right to come in the Palace and demand all that. Who do they think they are? I thought that Pharaoh was going to squash them there and then, shame really, but I guess that no straw will be a lesson! Didn't you just love the look on their faces as they left? That will teach them to mess with us. You're not saying much,' he finally said as he sat on the couch.

'I can't get a word in! What do you want me to say?' asked Ebonee.

'I just thought you would enjoy it!'

'You don't know me at all then.'

'Oh, come on Ebonee!'

'You really thought I would enjoy that? They are ...'

Careful Eliora. He does not need to know they are your uncles.

'... my people.'

'But my ... oh never mind.' Si scowled.

'I need to get back to the cats,' Ebonee said.

'Why? Why do you work so hard for the queen. Like you said, she is not your people. She doesn't deserve you. Wouldn't you prefer other work?'

'You know at least a little of me. You know I hate the cats.'

'So, you would work elsewhere?'

'The queen has commanded I work with the cats. I cannot choose where I work.' She thought of her uncle, now subjected to the masters' whips in the pits. A place he was never destined for, yet sent there today. 'The choices for my people were taken away a long time before I was born.'

Si sat quietly, a smile playing on his lips.

Eliora stood. 'I'll go now. I have work to do.'

'Alright,' Si said distracted by his thoughts. 'I might see you later. Use the window.'

She dropped to the spiky leaves below the window. 'Fine!' she spat. The air was even more stifling than before, but somehow not as painful as breathing in the throne room.

Ebonee was confused. Did she really want to be a part of the Egyptian world? Being Ebonee had never looked so unattractive. Meanwhile, Eliora worried for her uncle. For her people and the news of a harsher sentence. Of her once friends who would hate her even more now that her family had bought this upon them. Was she really worried about them, or was it herself that she felt sorry for? Her eyes began to fill with tears as she realised how selfish she was. She lived a comfortable life - miserable yes - but not full of punishment and pain, yet here she was considering her own feelings superior to those who really suffered.

Suddenly she remembered Caleb. His suffering was beyond anything she had known, yet she wondered about the response he would give. She began to look forward to their meeting in the gardens. He was sure to have something worthwhile to say.

Ebonee only had the company of the cats for the rest of the day. She was glad of it. She did not want to see Si or the expression of hunger had worn in the throne room again. She took care to work well, thinking of the pits and the harshness of life for the others. She must not complain.

She noticed the weariness of her people as she walked purposefully home. There was very little lively chatter among her neighbours, but plenty of complaining.

Eliora increased her pace at the well. Dinah spotted her and stepped into her path.

Dinah sneered. 'Hope you are enjoying your life of luxury! You and your family ... why do you have to interfere with everything?'

'Pardon? I don't know what you mean.'

'You know full well what I mean,' she quibbled. 'You parade about in your fancy clothes,' she leaned forward and flicked Eliora's uniform, 'thinking you own the place.'

'No I don't.'

'Oh come on! Your family just hate to leave things alone. Your uncle comes along and promises one thing but just gets us all punished instead. Why couldn't he just leave it alone, hey? He should go back to where he came from. I don't see precious little Eliora covered in mud and exhausted though, no we wouldn't want that now would we?'

'That's not fair, Dinah. You know it's not.' Then she added quietly, 'I thought you were my friend.'

'Another thing you got wrong then.'

Eliora stared in disbelief. Dinah showed no sign of taking back her words. Tears prickled Eliora's eyes as she quickly shuffled by, and fled.

It was late by the time Eliora got home. Steaming broth and bread ladened the table as her family waited for her to join them. There was very little joy at the family gathering. She ate as fast as she could and left the sombre room as soon as was possible.

Wrapping a shawl about her shoulders, she walked through the quiet settlement. The joy bleached out of life from everyone around. For the first time, Eliora felt anxious about going to the gardens. Her steps slowed and her feet dragged. A bubble of fear began to grow. There was no way to dispel the feeling. She would have to face him.

She fears his rebuff. He will not abandon her.

He sees and understands much that others have overlooked. He knows who to be angry at and who to trust.

She is safe with him.

He will lead her.

The night was cool, the heat of the day dispersing. A few torches burned from posts in the garden. A shadow moved slowly about the plants.

Caleb looked up. 'I wondered if you were coming today.'

Eliora could not decipher his mood. 'I was working a little later today.'

'You too?'

'Hmmm.' She nervously continued, 'So, you had a hard day?'

'It wasn't what I expected.'

'No, I doubt that it was.'

'Aren't you coming over to sit down? Or are you going to stand so far away we have to shout at each other?'

'I'll come over if you like.'

'Of course Elli. What's the matter?'

'Don't worry about me.' Eliora slumped to the stone wall. 'Are you alright?' she asked, genuinely interested.

'A little tired. I guess you heard about the new working conditions.'

'Yes, I heard. How bad is it?'

'Well, let's just say, the day certainly began better than it finished.' Caleb sat down next to Eliora, leaned back and stared up at the stars. 'Your uncle was put on my team. He is a hard worker.'

Eliora was a little confused, but then realised that Moses was one of them, one of the Hebrews, so would be set to work.

'The people were elated at the beginning of the day,' Caleb continued, 'I think the meeting with Aaron and Moses lifted them.' She saw how tired Caleb looked, physically tired, but there was an energy that he still possessed. 'They do not listen well though. Moses had said that it wasn't going to be easy. This wasn't going to be their last day here. I think many of them truly believed they would be making their way to the festivities tonight. But by the end of the day our work load had doubled. Same quota but double the work.'

'I'm sorry,' Eliora said doing her best to show how sympathetic she felt.

'As far as I see it, the pharaoh must see the threat as real or he would have just sent them away.'

'What do you mean?'

'Our people, they are numerous, if we go, Pharaoh will have to conscript his own people. That will do little for their belief that he is a god. If our people were strong enough to unite together, to be a true nation, we could rise up and leave. But we have been so crushed, there is little hope of that. I saw a glimpse of it this morning, but Pharaoh is clever. He has extinguished that little spark of life.'

'Is that what he is doing?'

'I think so.'

'I thought he was just punishing my uncle. You know getting the people to deal out the punishment.'

'That may be some of it. Our people are calling for old working conditions as if they were being treated like kings only yesterday. I don't think that is Pharaoh's motivation though, I think he may be scared.'

'He didn't look scared, just surprised and angry.'

'Look? Did you see him?'

'I was in the throne room.'

'How? I thought you were looking after the cats.' Caleb was shocked. 'What were you doing in the throne room of a powerful ruler?'

'Si took me. I had no choice.'

'Who is Si?' Caleb asked sharply.

'I thought he was just another slave like me,' Eliora said quietly.

'But he isn't?' Caleb said frowning.

'No. He is a son of Pharaoh.'

'Elli, Egyptians are not slaves.'

'I know that. I get told one way or another every day.' Eliora sighed.

'I'm sorry. I know you know that ... even more than me.'

'I didn't know who he was,' she started, trying to defend herself. 'But I can't get away. I'm trapped.'

'Is he your friend?' Caleb asked harshly.

'Sort of.'

'What do you mean?'

'I thought he was. But today, I don't know - did he take me there to gloat?' Eliora looked away puzzled.

'So ... did Pharaoh see you?'

'No. We were high up on a balcony. No one saw us.'

'Then maybe he was attempting to impress you,' Caleb said sitting down and letting out a sigh. He scrutinised her expression.

'Ha! Well plan foiled! Laughing at my uncles does not count as impressive.'

'Glad to hear it,' Caleb replied smiling. 'But don't underestimate him.'

'What do you mean?'

'Elli, there are people who want to possess you.'

'I have no idea what you are talking about!'

'Take it seriously. I have heard some of the young men talking about you.'

'As if! My family is cursed. Anyone who wants to get close to us ends up paying for it. No one will want to have anything to do with me now, not even old friends. My family caused all the trouble.'

'I think there are some that are willing to risk your so called curse.' Caleb smiled a little. 'Well, one at least. And besides, does this Si know or even care about that curse?'

'I guess not. But there is nothing I can do about it. He comes to me and I can't throw him out.'

'Can't or won't?' Caleb muttered.

'What?

Caleb quickly continued. 'I think you may be onto something when you say Pharaoh is using your uncle. I mean what better way to quash an uprising than to belittle their leader?'

'Maybe,' Eliora agreed. 'Caleb, can I ask you something?'

'Sure.'

'You don't hate me do you?' She asked bowing her head.

'Of course not,' Caleb said gently taking Eliora's hand.

'No one talks to me anymore. I feel so alone.'

'I talk to you. Other people are missing out.'

'I have tried to be patient but no one wants to know me and I think my uncle has sealed that fate for me now.'

'Fate is something an Egyptian would believe.' He gently squeezed her hand. 'Wait a bit longer. When this is over, and I say *when* not *if*, because it will be over one day, people will forget about it. And if they can't, well, are they worth talking to anyway?'

'I guess not.'

'But you still feel alone.'

'Yes.'

'I don't want you to feel alone. If I could I would visit you while you worked if that would help.' He caught Eliora's unbelieving expression. 'Well, I think of you when I work. I think about the things we do and talk of when we meet up in the evenings. Perhaps it might help you to do the same.'

'I did think of you today.' She smiled. 'I was worried you wouldn't want to be my friend anymore after what happened with the straw.'

'Our friendship is stronger than a bit of straw Squirt!'

'Why do you do that?'

'Do what?'

'We start talking, I mean, personal talking, then you call me Squirt.'

'I don't know,' Caleb said gazing up at the stars again.

Eliora thought she caught a darkening of his skin.

'I guess I don't mind really. At least it is only you that calls me that.'

'It is a term of endearment.' Caleb sighed gently squeezing her hand.

She smiled and returned the squeeze. They sat quietly. The clicking of the night time insects making the only noise. Eliora looked up at the dark sky swathed with stars.

'Our God made all that,' she eventually said. 'Not the pharaoh, not his ancestors, but our God. I believe we will see freedom in our lifetime. I think it is in nearly in our grasp.'

'I couldn't agree with you more ... Squirt.' Caleb's voice was quiet, but Eliora heard the tenderness.

'Thank you Caleb.'

'What for?'

'I never feel lonely when I am in the garden with you.'

Caleb didn't reply. But Eliora's hand was suddenly enclosed in both of his. 'I'm glad you feel better.'

The night had started to get cool but Eliora was not cold. She felt a little uncomfortable. Caleb was sat very close and she was unsure this was what she wanted. Eliora released her hand and pulled her shawl tighter around her shoulders.

'I really ought to get home. And you'll have a long day tomorrow too.' Eliora cringed at her icy tone.

'I suppose.' Caleb looked confused.

'I'll see you tomorrow then,' Eliora said as she stood quickly and began to move away. She quickly glanced at Caleb before turning away. She noticed the pain she had caused him. Guilt saturated her and she had to escape.

'Of course. Sleep well,' Caleb called.

9

Objects

Early the next morning, Eliora and her mother hurried to be ready for work at the palace. Moses was already awake and seemed in much better spirits. Eliora wondered what had caused the change in him.

'Elli. Will you please hurry!'

'Go on ahead Mama,' she urged. 'They won't notice if I am a little late.'

Jochebed turned, waved and hurried on ahead.

'Your mother worries about you,' Moses said.

'I know. She was worrying about you last night.'

'Ah, yes. I was also worrying that maybe I had brought this hardship on you.'

Eliora wanted to say that it wasn't her uncle's fault but deep down she couldn't. He hadn't caused it but it was his visit that had set the punishment in motion.

Moses read her silence correctly. 'I spoke with the Lord. He has this in control. He said the pharaoh will drive us out of this land.' He smiled a sad smile. 'Do you understand what this means Eliora?'

'Not really.'

'Well, at the moment he holds us here, but he will get to a place where he has no choice but to push us out. It will be a compulsion. The Lord will have His people, free from the burdens of the Egyptians, we will be called His. He told me we will be free. It will be the Egyptians that will be judged.'

'How long will that take?'

'You may not see the end, but it is there.'

'I can't see any end. I hope you are right.' She gave her uncle a quick but almost unbelieving smile. 'I'll be late for work.'

The sun was barely creeping over the horizon, but the day promised to be unbearably hot. Eliora stepped out of the house and onto the quiet street. She dragged her feet, not feeling an urgency to rush.

'If you don't hurry you will be late too.'

Eliora turned round and saw him striding down the path behind her.

'Caleb. You don't need to be up for a while yet.'

'I know. I just wanted to catch you before you left.'

'Well, you very nearly hadn't caught me! It's my fault we are late. My hair just won't stay straight today.'

'That's because it is meant to have a curl.'

'Not at the palace it isn't.'

'It looks lovely with a curl.'

There it was again, that slightly uncertain feeling as if Caleb had sat too close again. It wasn't unpleasant, just unexpected. Eliora shrugged it off.

'True, but that means I have to get up earlier to get it to lie straight. Why did you need to catch me?'

'I have something for you.' He reached for her hand and placed it in front of him. He dropped a folded and tied green leaf into her opened palm. 'Wait until later to open it. I'll see you in the garden this evening. I hope the cats behave. Have a good day!' He turned and strolled away but had no way of knowing what would lay in store for her.

'You too!' she called. For the first time in a long while she felt guilty about her form of slavery compared to Caleb's. The cats at the palace were spiteful and smelly, but she couldn't complain when she thought of the quota he would have to fill today.

She was tempted to open the package there and then, but thought it best to get to the privacy of the cat room first; after all Caleb had asked her to wait.

The walk seemed longer, even though she hurried now, probably because of the package that seemed to be burning a hole in her pack. Sand and dust swirled through the air as she made her way through the expanse of land that was not occupied byHebrew settlement, the palace nor Egyptian quarters. She was suddenly thankful for the fact that there was a breeze today and hoped that it extended to the pits.

Ebonee was able to reach the cat room unnoticed. Sometimes she thought the palace workers preferred her to be invisible.

The cats were restless but having fed them, cleared their mess and settled herself down on a stool, she pulled the parcel from her pack. She stole a moment to be Eliora in her world of Ebonee. The twine was tied tightly around the leaf, but she managed to pick open the knot. She unfolded it and found a bracelet snuggled into a wad of soft wool.

It was simple but beautiful. The tan leather thongs were woven together and tied in such a way that it could slip over her hand and then be tightened at her wrist. There was a single polished stone in the centre. The square cut, polished gem had veins with shades of green, layer upon layer, as if the colour had bled into the stone itself. Leather threads held it in place. Eliora smoothed her finger over the gem and found it was indented. Looking closely at the surface she saw that a starburst had been represented by precise cuts. Eliora remembered the time Caleb had said she was a star in the dark sky. He had made this for her. Especially for her. Suddenly she felt as if she was not as alone as usual.

Throughout the morning, her hand kept returning to the bracelet around her wrist. It was a comfort. She thought of him and he thought of her. How was he suffering today? Had he received further beatings?

The time with the cats moved slowly. It seemed so wrong that she should be doing such a menial and pointless task when her people, her Caleb, was out there suffering under the oppression of the masters.

I stand with her. Her compassion for her people grows.

She is unaware of the plans put in place, plans that will give her a future and a hope.

I stay close. I am here to protect. She will see things that she doesn't understand. Things that will confuse and test her faith.

Si disturbed her internal raging.

'Ebonee! You've got to come quickly. They're back for more.'

'What? What do you mean?'

'Those men are waiting to see Pharaoh again.'

She wanted to run from this, but felt such a need to see what would happen from this encounter that she went with Si.

As they crouched on the balcony, Ebonee was aware of the different atmosphere. Pharaoh was angry. His advisors and officials hung back from him.

Si was just as enthralled and mesmerised. Ebonee felt shaken by his thrilled expression.

I see the scene. I am not fearful but saddened.

The king of this land, so consumed by evil.

I see the creature that sits on his back.

It is full of arrogance and pride as it has exulted itself above all others.

My friend approaches guarding Eliora's uncles. His stance is one of stubbornness. He will not be moved today!

After long moments her uncles approached the throne.

'Back again Moses! Do you want me to punish your people further?'

But it was not Moses who spoke. There was a wordless exchange between her uncles. Aaron stood straight and confident. 'The Lord, the God of the Hebrews, came to Moses, and has sent us to you, saying "Let my people go so that they might worship me."'

'You think you are above me, too superior to speak to me personally Moses?' Pharaoh retorted angrily. 'Who are you that you come to me but refuse to speak? Do you consider yourself a god over me? And this ... slave ... your prophet?'

There was silence. Moses smiled a little but said nothing. Aaron waited for Moses' instruction. Nothing came. Then Pharaoh grinned.

'You consider yourself powerful, yet I see the evidence of working in the pits in your mud caked skin.'

Still nothing. Moses stood silently waiting for something. The people observing the scene began to snigger and laugh. Ebonee was close to tears. Her uncles were being made into some snide form of entertainment.

'Fine Moses, you will not speak to me. Perhaps you will demonstrate some of your obviously hidden power. Work a miracle, then perhaps I will listen.'

Aaron turned to Moses who nodded. Aaron threw down his staff before Pharaoh and his servants.

Before Ebonee could blink the staff had transformed into a large serpent, writhing and coiling on the stone floor.

'What is this? You fight with my images, my gods?' the flames burn deep green.

Oh yes! The fire creature has noticed us. We mean business. We know that the serpent was set in their histories by this same beast to bring fear and we use it against them.

I don't think it will take this challenge meekly.

'Apep,' stuttered Pharaoh, but quickly recovered. 'Magicians, sorcerers, wise men. Show them!'

There was a bustling of bodies as half a dozen men came forward. None of them wanted to approach Aaron's serpent. They took wax models, shaped like snakes and laid them on the floor. They began chanting and stamping and calling out to Wadjet, cobra goddess, the protector of the king. The wax models began to move and shimmer. They had come to life.

'This wonder is not hidden from me!' the beast laughs.

His hordes love the spectacle.

'Let them call on me. Let these feeble humans call on my name. Their trust lies with me. How ironic, since I am the father of lies!'

The humans give themselves over to his lies. In each act they please him more. His power is strong here, we don't doubt it and we don't underestimate it. So many lives are caught up by his leading.

He commands the wax models to be possessed. Small demons creep to the models, lifeless and useless. They will be animated. They move easily to position. The atmosphere in the throne room is one of welcome to this force.

I see them approach the models.

'Be cobras,' he shouts, 'Destroy that snake.' They slither and vaporise into the wax forms. 'I am the ruler of Egypt!'

The company of creatures shout and scream in agreement. The air is thick with sulphur and the beating of wings.

The cobras attack.

Ebonee was astounded. What was happening down there? Si glanced over at her; he thought she was impressed. Eliora moved closer to the edge in fear for her uncles. If those snakes went near them, if they attacked, that amount of venom would kill them.

But it was far from over. Aaron's rod serpent was large. Its focus was on the other snakes there. One after the other it struck, sinking its fangs into the bodies of the magicians' creations. It opened its mouth wide and one after the other, swallowed them.

Look at it. See it is shaken!

The Creator is all powerful. You will be shown. You will drive out this people. You have no choice!

I raise my fist in the air and salute my friend. He smiles. A great victory has been won today. A stumbling block has been set in place.

Eliora felt like cheering and dancing, but here she was Ebonee so she remained silent. Her uncles had truly shown Pharaoh a miracle. He would listen now.

Si fell back from the railings, gasping for air. All audacity blown away. Sweat poured over his face and he had turned pale.

'Si, are you alright?'

'Swallowed into the non-existence,' was all he muttered.

'Pardon? I don't understand.'

'Apet has swallowed them into the non- existence. The worst place to be. Wadjet cannot protect us.'

'What are you talking about?'

But Si was silent. He was getting back in control of himself.

'Si, is everything ...'

'Let's get out of here,' he said with his confidence returned.

Ebonee was confused and scared.

Back at the cat room, the events that had unfolded before her eyes seemed distant and unreal. Si was distracted but would not leave her to her own thoughts. He talked endlessly about the power of Egypt. It was only as he was leaving that he mentioned something that jolted Ebonee's thoughts.

'I've got you a new job. You start tomorrow.'

'What?'

'Don't thank me then!'

'Do I need to thank you?'

'Absolutely. It wasn't easy getting you moved.'

'What is it I am supposed to be doing?'

'You will be a handmaiden to one of the princes.'

Ebonee was suddenly faced with what she had wanted for such a long time. It was a strange sensation, but now that it was presented to her, she felt ill at ease. Si had used his power to secure this job, and seeing Si properly now, made Eliora frightened, maybe being Ebonee was not what she wanted after all. She did not want to be a slave to a prince. A prince that he had not named yet, but that may well have been him. She did not want him to have that power over her. She had to stay where she was.

'Si. You have to undo this. I don't want that work. I won't fit in at all.'

'Of course you will.'

'No I won't. Those positions are reserved for the privileged Egyptian families.'

'That doesn't matter.'

'I don't want it. Please Si, change it back.'

Si's expression became hard. Ebonee could see the anger rising and was unsure of what to do. He looked dangerous.

'Careful Eliora!' I whisper, 'He will become treacherous.'

I move between the young prince and my frightened charge.

He is precariously angry.

The creature screams in frustration from the floor in front of me.

'You own her,' it says. 'What right has she got to disobey you? Take her now!'

Si hears so clearly the mocking of the spirit. Having been shaken so much by the events in the throne room, his whole life seems to be swirling about him. Anger could so easily consume him.

I have been given my orders. I will warn him.

'Si,' I say calmly. The creature hisses and splutters at my sudden appearance. 'Si, she is not yours, you know that. She is not one of your people. Let her go.'

'She may not be an Egyptian, but she belongs to you!' the creature shouts.

'She is not an object, to be possessed or owned ... or taken.' As I declare the truth, the creature's voice catches in his throat. I will silence the lies it speaks here. 'Si, you go. Leave her to her work.'

It is done quickly. Si turns to leave. The creature cowers on the floor before scuttling after Si. As they leave I hear the scratchy creature's voice freed from the restriction I had over it. It speaks in an oddly calm voice. 'She is nothing. Not worth it anyway. A complete waste of time!' But I see Si shake his head.

'Continue working here then, if that is what you want,' he calls over his shoulder and is gone.

Eliora is visibly shaken. She staggers to a stool and sits.

I cup my hands before me and breathe into the small space. A glowing sphere of light appears. Slowly I move my hands away and blow it towards Eliora. It moves steadily and rests over her head. Gradually it opens like a water lily, each petal unfurling in turn. A beautiful perfume flows out from the centre and permeates the room. The smell is one of home.

Eliora takes a deep breath and sighs. Her heart rate drops to its normal rhythm and small smile appears. She is safe. She is peaceful.

10

Meaning

The evening was brightly lit by the moon. The heat of the day gone and the cold air swept through the gardens. Insects chirped from the plants but other than that the gardens were quiet and still.

Eliora watched Caleb stretching high to tie a vine to the post he had replaced. Suddenly she was unsure how to approach him. She wanted to go over and hug him but that seemed too familiar even though she had been doing so for years. She fingered the cool stone at her wrist and decided. She wrapped her arms around Caleb's waist making him jump and drop the young shoot.

'Thank you!'

'You're very welcome.' Caleb laughed, 'but for what?'

'The bracelet!' she said letting him go. 'Do you want a hand?'

'No, I've got it.' Caleb swiftly tucked the tendrils of the plant through a twisted branch until they were caught firm.

Eliora wandered over to her favourite spot and sat down.

'It really is beautiful,' she said rearranging the bracelet.

He sat next to her. 'I'm glad you like it.'

'Where did you get the stone from?'

'Sometimes the mud from the Nile contains little gems. I found it a while ago.'

'I love the star,' Eliora said, tracing it with her finger.

'Hmm, me too.' Eliora looked up at him wondering at the meaning. 'It is what you are, you know *a star in the night, a bright light against the black*. So...' Caleb sighed and quickly asked, 'how was work today?'

'I remember you telling me that on the first day,' Eliora recalled. 'The palace was ... interesting.'

'Now, that's got me inquisitive!'

Eliora explained all about the meeting in the throne room and the spectacle with the snakes.

'That would have been fun to watch!'

'Well, it wasn't. I was scared that those snakes were going to kill my uncles.'

'What a great example though! I mean for God to do a miracle using the snake. Do you know about Apet?'

'No.' Eliora remembered Si mentioning that name.

'Apet is a god of the Egyptians, the enemy of the sun god Ra. In theory the enemy of the pharaoh. Our God was challenging Pharaoh's god.'

'The magicians called forth Wadjet.'

'She is the god that protects the king.'

'But they were killed. The staff snake killed them and ate them.'

'Wow! I think that would have shocked Pharaoh. To be eaten by the snake and taken to the void, the place of non-existence!'

'Si said that. What is it?'

'A place where the after-life doesn't exist, where nothing exists. A fear the Egyptians cannot face.' Caleb fidgeted a little as he asked, 'Was Si there?'

'Yes. I didn't want to go but I knew Uncle Aaron and Moses would be there. I wanted to see what would happen to them.' Eliora looked down at her feet. 'Are you angry with me?'

'No Elli. Life in the palace is complicated. You may not be covered in mud, sweat and lashes, but you suffer from slavery too.'

'Si almost forced me to change jobs today. He said he had found me a new place to work as handmaiden to a prince.'

'What? But Elli ...' Caleb grabbed her hand. 'You can't.'

'It is alright Caleb,' she said, smiling up into his panicked face. 'I told him that there was no way I could work there being a Hebrew. He was cross - no more than that - he was angry.' Eliora recalled the almost flames rolling over him. 'I am to stay with the wretched cats.'

'Be careful Elli.' The cool breeze played through the gardens and tossed a lock of hair across Eliora's face. Caleb caught it and tucked it back behind her ear. 'I mean it Elli. Please stay safe.' His tone was urgent.

She placed her hand over his and squeezed it hoping he would understand her motive. 'Thank you.'

He lifted her hand and brushed the surface with his cheek then tenderly kissed it.

She closed her eyes and leaned into him, resting her head on his shoulder.

He had understood her.

'I can't protect you there. Stay safe for me.'

'Of course!' she promised. 'I've got to go.' She sighed. 'Early start in the morning.'

Caleb slowly stood not letting go of her hand. 'Let me walk you home.'

11

Blood

Eliora sat at the window of the stinking cat room gazing out over the dry land and to the river. The window offered her mind some escape from her work. The reeds below were brown and curled up in death. Such a contrast to the budding life she felt.

She was still reeling from the revelation that it wasn't just friendship with Caleb anymore. It had been such a slow and steady thing. But her feelings for him were stronger than they had ever been before.

Caleb had always been a part of her life. He had been there before she even knew of his existence, but now it was as if her life was encompassed by his. She felt secure in this place. The back of her hand tingled as she evoked the memory of his touch.

How long had he been waiting for her to feel this way? She thought about the everyday events like chatting, eating and seeing each other, but now viewed them from a different perspective. From that place, his actions and words longed for more than friendship. She shook her head. How had she been so blind? Even Caleb's brother Kenaz had made a massive hint at it all that time ago.

It didn't matter now. Eliora was not going to beat herself up over not seeing all the signs. The only thing that mattered was that she understood, and she felt the same way. Love was a giddying thing. She let out a little laugh. She thought that if a guard walked in now, it would only confirm their belief of her madness. This only set her giggling more.

Eventually, the harsh reality broke through. She was slave to the cat room and Caleb slave to the brick maker masters. She gazed out in the direction of the distant pits. She could not see them from here. The palace was far removed from that horror. The Nile was the only landmark that connected them in this moment.

The Nile, when it flooded, must have covered the plain and flowed into the trenches, to allow plants to grow this close to the palace. However, the water was at its lowest level now; it was as low as she had ever seen it and the plants were suffering.

The river banks contrasted her immediate environment. Lush green ribbons of vegetation grew alongside the Nile. Following the flow of life she caught a glimpse of two men, a long way off, who were walking in the direction of the green banks. She recognised her uncle immediately. His stooped form, as if he carried his load of bricks, had straightened a little in recent days, but a lifetime of harsh treatment bent his back. On closer inspection she found that both her uncles were heading towards the river together. What were they doing here?

Further up the river, a light coloured sail moving slowly along the skyline caught her attention. The colours embroidered down the edges were the same as her belt. The royal boat was taking a trip down the river. This was not a coincidence.

Eliora didn't think twice. She dropped to the ground, the reeds scratching and catching on her tunic, and raced to the water's edge. She was careful to check for river monsters before she hid in the greener reeds by the river.

The heat was intense, even this early in the morning, and sweat ran down her back as she crouched down close to the water's edge.

The boat glided through the water. Several people were on board; many of them dressed in a similar outfit to Eliora. They steered, paddled and guided the boat down river. The others on the boat were enjoying the protection of a tent roof stretched above them. Some of the servants were busy herding these smaller occupants into the shade. Eliora suddenly understood. Pharaoh was taking his sons, the royal princes, on a river ride. With this in mind she searched the boat for the familiar face. Standing proudly next to the pharaoh's chair was a tall slender Egyptian and beside him, standing with equal pride was Si.

It was strange to see Si so closely associated with the pharaoh, his father, after all he had said about him. The diverse contrast unsettled Eliora. She did not know this side of Si at all.

Eliora is fascinated by the royal boat. I am with her but I am not to show myself. My comrades, on the other bank are not cloaked like me. They present themselves in full battle armour. My friend stands furthest forward, the sun glistening off the jewels in his sword, behind him the regiment poised. They are stunningly powerful.

The evil one hisses as it spots the welcome reception. Sitting with the king of this land, it has taken on a different image. It resembles one of the creatures that lurk in the depths of the river, the crocodile. Another god created to mollify, but not satisfy the spiritual needs of the human race.

It calls its hordes to do its will.

There are many of them. They clamber for their place. The boat is overrun with dark scaly creatures.

The boat continued to travel toward the place where her uncles waited. Moses leaned over to Aaron and pointed to a place at the water's edge. Aaron carefully made his way down the far bank and Moses followed, losing his footing only briefly and steadying himself with the staff in his hand. They waded through the reeds and up to their knees in the Nile. Waiting until the boat was a little closer, her uncle Aaron cleared his throat and called out across the river.

'The Lord the God of the Hebrews sent me to you saying "Let My people go, that they may serve Me in the wilderness. But behold you have not listened until now."'

Aaron's voice was strong and clear. All the people on the boat gave him their full attention. Eliora felt the air go very still but it wasn't just the tension from the confrontation.

'You will know that the Creator is King here!' declares Release.

The air is full of His Majesty. All is silent.

'You have failed to do as requested. You will now be witnesses, along with all the people you hold, to the supremacy of the Maker.'

Aaron continued. 'This is what the Lord says, "By this you shall know that I am the Lord: I will strike the water and it will be turned to blood. The water will become foul and the Egyptians will find difficulty in drinking water from the Nile."'

Eliora looked for a reaction from Pharaoh, but he was unmoved, so she turned her attention back to her uncles. Moses looked full of sorrow as he spoke briefly to Aaron.

Aaron lifted up the staff, the same one that had eaten the protector snakes, and struck the water of the Nile.

The impact caused a splash and a ripple.

Pharaoh began to laugh.

But before his laughter was fully formed a change was taking place on the river bed. A small swell, of what first appeared to be bubbles, was rising to the surface. As they gushed to the surface they burst open, releasing a thick red substance into the surrounding water. It spread, bleeding through the river, surging through the lifeline of Egypt.

Aaron and Moses climbed up the bank and away from the pollutant.

The stain flowed quickly and soon the royal boat floated on a river of blood.

Several children screamed.

Fish rose to the surface, gasping for air, unable to survive. Eliora heard the canopy on the boat snap with the sudden breeze that had begun to flutter. It chased away the already skittish animals with the strong sent of blood.

Pharaoh rose from his chair.

'What have you done, Moses?' He motioned for two of his magicians to come forward. 'I am not convinced with your tricks. This proves nothing.' He turned to the men. 'Show him the gods can do the same.'

This man has blind confidence. He sees the miracle before his own eyes. His sight is still that of blindness.

One man took an earthen water jug that had sat beside the pharaoh, the other a shallow bowl and placed it on the floor before at Pharaoh's feet. Eliora noticed they did not strut as they had done when they were in the throne room; perhaps they were not as confident as before. They began to chant and shake. Eliora had never seen anything like this. Her hair stood up on her arms, she felt very uncomfortable watching their worship and summoning of their gods. She rose slightly to view what would happen. The man with the jug peered inside and smiled.

The evil one cannot create like this. It sees the challenge for what it really is.

The river is the god of life to these people. The Creator attacks their symbol of life.

The creature, seething with anger, climbs from its high place and pushes aside the creatures at its feet.

It reaches for the jug.

It looks inside and a sharp, tooth-filled smile stretches across its jaws. It thinks we have made a mistake. It sees the blood there and claims it for itself.

'I rule here! You will not take my throne! You will not take my slaves that build my empire. I am supreme!' It shouts over the scarlet river.

He raised the jug high into the air and then poured out the liquid into the bowl at the pharaoh's feet. A red streak of blood flowed from the lip and splashed into the bowl, splattering the pharaoh's tunic.

Pharaoh shifted his feet away from the bowl, looked up and gestured to the evidence before him.

Eliora wasn't aware that she was standing straighter and leaning forward until it was too late. As she tried to regain her balance, her foot slipped on the waxy reeds and she slid a short distance down the bank. The reeds broke under her weight and shook with her sudden movement. She lay still for a moment. Perhaps no one had noticed what with the events on board. Slowly sitting up she peered through the slightly bent reeds.

The pharaoh's attention was captured again by the blood filled bowl. Eliora sighed and relaxed a little. She scanned the rest of the boat. One person had noticed the movement. One person now searched the section of river bank where she sat. His eyes searched for the source and found her.

Eliora faintly heard someone speaking.

'I am the Lord of Egypt!' Pharaoh declared, sat down and turned away, instructing the helmsman to return the barge to the palace.

The boat sailed further down the blood filled Nile towards the palace. Si stared at Eliora, his expression unreadable. She shivered despite the heat. His cold look froze her from the inside.

As soon as the boat was out of sight, she got shakily to her feet and stumbled back to the cat room window. Clambering up to the ledge was difficult, as she seemed to have had lost her strength.

She was alone for a moment. Her heart was racing at what she had witnessed and the fierce glare from Si.

She is not alone. She is never alone. But here, now it may feel that way.

I stay close.

The flash of light behind me signals that I am now joined by Release. This is not a happy reunion as before.

He grasps my shoulder as a bright silver tear runs down my cheek.

Eliora steadied herself, and sat on the stool away from the open window. She felt a sudden urge to close the shutters, to shut out the horror of the event she had seen. Her family had been tied again to disaster, the source of water turned to blood and the calling of the gods. But it was Si's angry glower that made her shiver.

It was too late. Two hands gripped the window ledge and suddenly she was joined by Si, standing large and still, a silhouette against the glaring sun.

Si is not alone. As always he brings his own company into the room.

Anger rolls off him in thick, blood-red waves.

'Ebonee.'

'Si ...'

'I saw you.'

'I know.'

'What were you doing by the river?'

Ebonee bowed her head. 'I'm sorry.'

'So now you know,' Si sneered. 'My father is Pharaoh.'

'Yes.'

'So? What do you think of that?' he asked aggressively.

'I already knew that, Si.'

'What? When?'

'I've known for a while.'

'But you thought you'd humiliate me today.'

'No. No, not at all.' Ebonee confessed. 'I saw my uncles and wanted to know what was going to happen.'

'Uncles?'

Eliora swallowed. What had she done? What had she said? Everything in her wanted to take back all that she had blurted out, but there was no sparing the words now.

'Uncles. Those men are *your* uncles?' Si moved closer to Eliora. She instinctively stood up, moved behind the stool and backed away. 'I guess I should have worked that out. Why would a girl like you have the honour of working in the palace? Of course you had to be related to that traitor.'

'My uncle is not a traitor.' Eliora replied angrily. 'And besides, you never thought it was such an honour to be at the palace.'

'How dare you assume that you know me? My honour comes from by bloodline. I may not be the crowned prince, but I am my mother's firstborn. I may rule one day.'

'You will never rule over me.' She could not hold back her anger at his hypocrisy. 'Me and my people will go free.' Ebonee was unsure from where her confidence came. Perhaps it was a deep-felt assurance that she knew the truth.

Si growled.

The sound startled her. Ebonee stepped back only to find that the wall was firmly behind her.

He moved swiftly. He sprang towards her and punched her across the side of her head. The power of the swing forced her cheek against the wall. Nearly blacking out, she stumbled, put her hand to her throbbing cheek and pushed herself away from the wall and out into the middle of the room. What was he doing? How could she deserve this?

'Si, stop it. Please.' she murmured weakly.

The pain spread across her skull. The sunlight seemed to flicker, and to jump erratically.

He stalked after her.

She lifted her hands to her face to defend herself, but it was not enough. Si had picked up the stool and swung out at her. It broke as it connected with her, across one shoulder. His rage was out of control. She fell to the ground and didn't move.

I want to help. I want to protect.

The prince and the creature seem to be the same being. It only has to whisper the words and he responds. He listens and does not even try to walk away.

Eliora lies still but she is alive. Her words of faith were spoken with passion and conviction. The enemy hates to hear truth.

I knew I would have to witness this act of brutality against this chosen one. That is why Release is here to help and guide me. He knows what the Creator has said.

The boundaries were given. They will not be overstepped.

Boundaries that I do not understand. Boundaries that will allow her to hurt and be defiled. I ask again.

'Please let me step in. Please let me help her.'

'The Creator knows what he is doing. Trust in Him, Faithful.'

I remember Eliora as a child, young and awkward. She would run only to trip and fall. Her mother, who loves her completely, would see that it would happen yet would allow it. Eliora would graze her knee and cry. She would come back to her mother for comfort and it was always given. Eliora would learn about how to run because she had stumbled and hurt herself. This is much more than a stumble and a graze, but I think the principle is the same. The Creator, who loves Eliora far more than her mother, far more than me, sees the hurt, pain and sorrow that she will experience, but allows it because of who she will become. Just as her mother doesn't want there to be pain, the Creator never wanted it for the human race. The human race created that for themselves.

I reach back to my quiver and grab an arrow.

'Careful friend.' Release warns.

'I will not shoot unless that boundary is crossed.'

He allows me to string my bow. I will protect her against what has not been permitted.

The prince rips open her blood splattered tunic.

I see her stir and her eyes flash open.

He stands over her, evil intent inside of him. The creature is leaping about with hideous joy. The prince now acts out his own desires. He will not be merciful. He listens to his heart. This is what he wants.

He forces himself on her.

'No ... No! Leave me alone!' Eliora cries out. She pushes at his advancing body but she does not have the strength to fight him off.

She begs him to leave her alone.

He does not listen. He intends to get all that he wants without a thought for her. He violates her in his act of rape.

Afterwards, tears flow in silent rivers as she struggles to be free from him. I cry for her. She is the Creator's beloved.

I see his hand reach for the stool once more. His intent is to silence her for good. My arrow flies strong and straight. Release's sword swings in a wide arc.

The creature screams as the arrow spears its arm and wails as the blade rips open its back.

A cat hisses and jumps to the prince's face, claws out. He yells, taking him from his selfish actions and seems to finally see what he is doing.

The prince and his host, at his back, flee.

Eliora trembled as she sat up. Her head throbbed but that was nothing to the pain she now suffered. Everything had changed, and she had no power to reconcile who she was last night to the person she was now. Her tainted spirit longed for the innocence she once had. She felt filthy and wanted to scrub Si's scent and touch off her body. She stumbled to the water jug at the stand; she was desperate to clean herself. Gingerly she poured the liquid into the bowl. She gasped as the bowl filled with blood.

Suddenly, despite her ordeal, she was aware that the pharaoh's magicians had not performed a miracle on board the boat, but that God had. Those magicians were frauds. They had no power. Her God had all power. He had turned the Nile into blood; not only that, all the water held in containers was miraculously changed too. God had been in this room and changed the water.

'My God, why have you abandoned me?' She wept as she wished he had stayed there to protect her.

'The Creator cares for you Eliora. He will provide for all your needs.'
I reach out and touch her bowed head.
'This is a gift for you.'
Her tears glint of gold as they fall.

The tears flowed fast and unrelenting. Eliora bowed her head as revulsion for what she was, threatened to overwhelm her. She was no longer pure, but spoiled and ruined. Her life as a Hebrew was over; her customs dictated that much. She would have to remain here, at the palace and belong to him - that selfish prince. She heard the gentle drip of her tears hit the blood-filled bowl. Then a second gasp escaped her.

The blood was being diluted by her tears. No, not just diluted, it was being transformed. The salty tears spread through the deep crimson blood, flowing through it and swirling in clean eddies. After a few moments all the blood was dissolved away, and in its place a bowl of crisp clear water stood.

She did not know what to do or say. God was there. He was here now; he'd been here before. So why had he stood back and watched while she was brutalised?

'I don't understand,' Eliora whispered.

She took the cotton cloth and began to scrub away the dirt and grime she felt was there. Eventually, she gingerly dabbed the cut on the side of her head where her hair stuck to the congealed wound, she winced with the pain. The water stayed clear, no matter how many times she dipped into it.

At last she was finished. She gathered up her tunic and fastened it tight about her. She peered at her reflection only to check her hair suitably covered her wound, she could not bear to look at herself properly. No one would ever know. No one could ever know or she would be banished from her people forever.

12

Healing Ointment

'Aren't you going to see your friends tonight Elli?' her grandmother asked sitting by the fire.

'I wasn't going to,' Eliora replied not looking away from the flames.

'Is something wrong? You've hardly said a word since you got home,' her mother asked.

'Alright, I'll go.' And she turned towards the door and left as quickly as her aching body would allow.

'What is the matter with her tonight?' Eliora heard her mother ask as she left. She would have to be more careful. They were noticing.

She fears for so much now and trusts no-one.

The settlement was very noisy tonight. There was lots of chatter about the blood Nile. The Hebrews were exhausted and thirsty after hours of slaving at the pits, but their thirst could not be quenched until new wells and water sources had been created.

Eliora just wanted to get away from the day. She wandered the busy streets looking for a quiet place to go. She knew the best place, a peaceful place, but at the same time she was hesitant to go there. The gardens would be wonderfully quiet right now but Caleb would be there, and she wasn't sure about seeing him. Her heart ached. Deep down she knew the best place to be was to be where Caleb was.

She came to the garden via another path due to her wanderings. The peace of this place was almost tangible to her, but now just out of reach. Caleb was sat in their spot with his head in his hands. He was looking down the path she normally took.

She stood for a while and just watched him. What could she say? Her heart trembled at the thought that she could lose him. She had to be cautious.

Caleb looked up. 'There you are!' He rushed to his feet. 'I thought that you weren't going to come tonight.'

'No. I'm here.'

He drew close, studied her face for a moment, and then offered his hand.

Nervously she took it, hers shaking a little.

He led her to the wall where they usually sat. 'I thought that maybe ... after what happened you wouldn't be here.'

'Nothing happened,' she replied quickly looking down. She felt his grip on her hand weaken. He had meant something different, what had he meant? 'Oh, you mean last night.' She looked up at him, his face was so sad, 'Of course I would be here.' And she squeezed his hand.

'This is right isn't it?' he said caressing her cheek with his rough, warm hand.

'This is what I want,' Eliora replied. 'More than anything,' she said longingly.

'I'm glad.' Caleb wrapped his arm about her. Eliora winced. 'What's the matter? Have I hurt you?'

'It's nothing.'

'What's nothing?'

'I hurt my shoulder, that's all. I bruised it.'

'Let me put some ointment on it. I have some here.' He looked through his bundle of belongings. 'It really takes out the sting. I use it loads. The results of the beatings are a little bearable with this.' Caleb had produced the small wooden pot and before Eliora could protest he asked, 'Where is it bruised?'

'No Caleb, really, I'm fine.'

'You are not fine. I barely touched your shoulder. You are in pain, let me help.'

She tightened the shawl over her shoulders. But her mood was not playful.

'Please Elli,' Caleb said. 'I don't want you to hurt. You know you can trust me.'

'I do trust you but ...'

'Well, where is the bruise then?' he said standing behind her.

Eliora prayed that he wouldn't say anything.

She lowered the shawl, and pulled carefully at the neck of her dress so that it fell over her shoulder and down her arm a little.

Caleb reached for the lamp. As the light got stronger he gasped.

The bruise spreads from her shoulder and down her shoulder blade. There is swelling and grazing to the surface. Caleb will assume the cause as a beating.

He studies the injury, and feels sick with his conclusion. He has let his mind consider what else has happened to her, but refuses to believe it.

He treats her with gentleness and respect, just as he should.

'Find out the truth Caleb,' I urge. 'She needs you to know.'

She turned to him, begging him with her eyes to not speak.

He understood. Gently he applied the ointment. It was cool on her hot skin. His touch tentative and soothing.

After a few moments he came and sat next to her again.

She adjusted her dress and shawl and stared at the ground. She wanted him to grab her hand, but he didn't touch her. She felt rejected.

The silence was harsh to her ears. He did not want her. She should leave.

Eliora took a deep breath then stood.

'Well Caleb. Maybe I will see you sometime,' she said dejectedly.

'What?' Caleb stood up quickly. 'Don't go.' Suddenly he was tripping over his words. 'What happened to you? Who did that?'

'I fell.'

'I have been around too many beatings, Elli, to see that that bruise is no result of a fall. Who did that to you?'

'Caleb, please!'

'Tell me!'

'Caleb ... I can't,' she sobbed.

Suddenly his arm was around her waist and he was hugging her to himself. He guided her back to the seat.

Kneeling before her, he lifted her chin so he could see into her eyes.

'Elli, who did this to you?' he asked gently. She tried to turn away. 'I want to help you.'

'It is beyond your help. I'm so sorry.' The sobbing came in jerky breaths.

'Beyond? Why are you sorry?' Caleb sat down next to her, one hand about her waist and the other wiping at the tears.

Eliora knew that Caleb was confused, and would draw his own conclusions, even those horrors would not come close to the truth. He was tender with her though. Would he remain so if he found out the real story?

'Is it beyond my help because it happened at the palace? Is that it?'

Eliora nodded.

'Not a guard though ... that prince ... right?'

'You can't do anything about it,' Eliora repeated.

'You can't go back there.'

'I have to. I have no choice.'

'Elli, I wish I could protect you.'

She wished he could too. But it was as she had said, she had to go back. There was nothing that could be done, her slavery would only stop when her people were redeemed.

'What happened?'

She jumped at Caleb's words. He wanted details. 'I don't think you really want to know.'

'Of course I do.'

'It won't help.'

'Elli, I want to be part of your life.'

'But it doesn't matter how it happened. All that matters is he got mad and I got in the way.'

'He had no right.'

'Can we please stop talking about it?'

'I'm sorry. Of course we can,' Caleb said smoothing circles on the back of her hand. Eliora could tell that he still wanted to talk, but she just wanted to forget it.

The insects hummed noisily in the still night. The silence between them seemed to expand. Caleb broke it.

'The masters were shocked when they discovered that the water containers were full of blood today. They blamed us to start with, but how could we all have polluted their water supply at the same time?'

'Can we talk about something else?'

'What do you want to talk about? Whatever I suggest isn't working!'

'Caleb,' Eliora said backing away from him, 'Please don't get cross with me.'

'I didn't mean to frighten you. Are you alright?'

'I'm fine.'

The breeze had stopped and the garden was warm with rich scents of citrus fruits. Eliora could feel Caleb's tension disappearing as the minutes wore on.

Suddenly Caleb spoke with resolve. 'I want to talk with your mother.'

'About what?' Eliora panicked.

'Well, us. If that is alright?'

'Oh,' Eliora said, relieved, 'Yes, of course.'

'This is what you want isn't it.'

'Yes Caleb, I want this. Is it what you want?' she asked nervously.

He got to his feet, offered his hand and gently pulled her up. 'Absolutely! Well there is no time like the present.'

'We're going now?'

'I think so. I want everyone to know!'

Eliora wanted desperately to tell him everything, give him a chance to be free from her. But she battled with her own need to keep him, her own need for security and her need to forget and cover what she had become.

She took his hand. She would not tell him. He would never need to know.

The walk back to her house seemed to take only a moment.

The living space was full of people. Her uncles had come to chat, and their families had joined them. The door stood open to allow the cold night air to soak into the busy room.

Caleb strode confidently into the crowded space. Eliora hovered by the door, her cheeks reddening as each moment passed.

'Jochebed, may I speak with you?'

'Caleb. How lovely to see you. Of course you can. It's so noisy in here, would you like to speak to me outside?'

Eliora's mother was never formal yet here she was. It was at that moment that Eliora knew her mother understood what it was all about.

Caleb walked out the door looking a little grey, followed closely by her mother, who squeezed her daughter's arm as she went by.

Everyone in the room watched them leave and then looked intently at Eliora. She wanted to disappear. So she turned and followed them out to the street.

Burning torches lit the dusty street.

Caleb and Jochebed stood a little distance away for the door. Caleb's face was serious and earnest. Eliora listened as his words drifted towards her.

'... and so as my father is no longer alive, and Eliora's father is also no longer with us, it is my duty to ask you if you would be willing to give your daughter in marriage to me.'

'Caleb. I would be honoured as long as that is what Eliora wants. Although, we have very little to offer in terms of a bride price.'

'With the risk of sounding sentimental, Eliora is all that I want.'

Eliora let out a little hysterical giggle and they both turned. He wanted her? How strange and yet comforting that sounded. Would he still feel that way if he knew? Eliora could see her poisoned future stretched out before her, a loving husband, beaten and battered by the slave masters, devoted to a woman he unknowingly shares with his enemy.

'Well Elli.' Eliora started at her mother's voice. 'Do you want to be married to Caleb?'

'Yes Mama.'

Jochebed took her daughters hand, kissed it and placed it into Caleb's.

'Then I agree.'

'Thank you Mama!' And suddenly Eliora was crying. To her mother and future husband it may have appeared to be tears of joy, but they were tears of guilt.

Jochebed rushed into the house.

'Eliora is betrothed!'

Cheers and laughter spilled out into the night.

Soon, aunts, cousins and uncles were out in the street, hugging, kissing and slapping backs. It was then that the tears of joy came. Everyone was so happy for her, Eliora was overwhelmed. With each hug, her shoulder ached. Even in this, her moment of joy, she was wrenched from the scene and subjected to suffering.

Eventually, the celebrations returned to the house.

'We should speak with my mother,' Caleb said.

'Now? It's so late.'

'I don't think she will mind!' Caleb was energized by the warm reaction from Eliora's family.

He took her by the hand and practically ran home.

'Mother!' He called as he entered. 'Mother!'

'Caleb, whatever is the matter?' came her voice from the back of the house.

'Mother I have some news.'

Caleb's mother came in from the cold taking the shawl from her head. She glanced at her son, noted his hand clasped around Eliora's and began to cry.

'Mother?'

'Oh Caleb! Eliora! This is wonderful!'

'But I haven't told you yet!'

She dashed across the room and embraced them both. Eliora did her best not to wince.

'You, lovely lady, are just what my Caleb has needed. Someone to heal his wounds.'

Eliora's breath caught. No-one would ever need her. It was Caleb who would be her saviour, she did not have the strength to be his.

13

Waiting

Sleep did not come easily. Eliora lay quietly in the darkness, listening to her mother's slow breathing. She tried to concentrate on relaxing her body and mind, but she just felt tense and battered. The last thing she wanted to do was to process all of the day's events but her thoughts returned again and again to different ends of the scale. Complete numbness to complete happiness, the two extremes could not be reconciled.

The moments of complete happiness were rare. If she could start the day again, rearrange and alter the events, happiness would be the natural emotion. But life would not allow her have that gift. She was betrothed. Everything inside her screamed for her to be joyful, but she felt dirty and deceitful. She needed Caleb to want her, even as she was.

She relives the moment over and over again. There is nothing she could have done to stop it.

Memories contrast harshly - the attack and the proposal. She cannot reconcile the two. I'm not sure any human could. There are no vibrant colours here. She is shrouded in murky, grey tinged swirls.

The secret of the shame she feels, has made a way for the enemy to take hold. A dark creature shadows her. It blocks out the light and warmth. It has no distinct form but has a very distinctive voice. It whispers lies. The lies have a root in truth, that is what makes them so believable, but they are lies, all the same.

'You deserved it. You are a slave, it is what you are here for. You asked for it, you never turned him away, you flirted with him. You can't blame him for being that way with you. And as for Caleb, well, what he doesn't know won't hurt him. Why should you tell him what happened anyway, what purpose will it serve?'

I want to help her untangle herself, but she will not ask for assistance.

She was relieved but weary when dawn eventually arrived. She dressed carefully, applied the bare minimum of make-up and refused to straighten her hair. She would distance herself in as many ways as possible from the Egyptian lifestyle, she no longer wanted this way of life.

Eliora ate sparingly. She fidgeted and showed little interest in the warm oats her grandmother had prepared.

The settlement, stirring sleepily, was slowly coming to life. Eliora wanted nothing more than to hide here today. She stepped from the house into the cool fresh air. Above, the sky was tinged with streaks of orange and pink, and the warm rays seeped into Eliora's exhausted body. She turned towards the brightness, closing her eyes, trying desperately to welcome it in. It was such a beautiful morning, one that should bring hope of a new beginning. It mocked her. Her life was so far removed from this ideal that she huffed at the ironic thought.

She jumped at the touch on her hand.

'Sorry,' Caleb murmured. 'I didn't mean to startle you.'

The shadow speaks urgently. 'Don't let him know! He must not know! He'll throw you away if he ever finds out.' The heady scent of musk saturates the air.

'Lies! They are all lies!' I shout but she doesn't listen to me.

Eliora took a few slow breaths.

'I only wanted to say that ... well ... take care today.'

'I will.' She felt the emptiness of her promise even before it left her lips. She had no control over her own care. 'Work hard. Come back to me in one piece.'

'You don't need to worry about me.' Caleb bent to kiss her on her cheek, his rough bristles tickled her. Then he took her hand, adjusted the bracelet so that the star faced upwards and kissed that too. 'I love you.'

'I know. But I don't know why.'

Caleb frowned and opened his mouth but was interrupted by Jochebed who rushed from the house.

'Enough of that now you two. Elli, let's get going.'

'I'll see you in the garden later,' Caleb called.

Eliora waved as her mother guided her away.

Jochebed, who was now Simra, set a speedy pace. They had reached the edge of the settlement quickly.

'You go on ahead Mama. I don't want to make you late.'

Simra smiled at her daughter and rushed on ahead.

Eliora reached the boundary line between the place where her people lived and the Egyptian territory. There was nothing there to mark a line, no row of stones or fortified wall, only a dusty track. There might as well have been a cliff face to climb, because it took all of Eliora's remaining courage to keep on walking.

The open space was exposing. She hurried to the shelter of the brick built structures in the distance. Along the way she could see the freshly dug ditches, filling with murky water. The water underground remained uncontaminated. She had caught wafts of fish as she hurried, but here, where the air moved slowly, caught in the passageways and avenues, it was intense. It wasn't the pleasant aroma of cooking but the stench of rotting flesh, so thick that

Eliora's already unsteady stomach threatened to heave. She covered her nose and mouth with the cloth from her food pack and dashed to the palace.

The air here was clearer. Eliora could pick out the smell of salt and metal as well as the fish. She realised this was the smell of the Nile, the smell of blood.

The cat room was all but deserted except for a few small kittens, which mewed incessantly. Eliora tensed at the thought of having to walk around the palace to retrieve the missing cats. She did not want any surprise encounters. She decided to only go if she was summoned. She placed her cushion facing the window. If he intruded today, she would not be caught unawares.

She stared at the window, twisting the bracelet around and around on her wrist. The appearance of the cat made her jump. Its sleek form, an apparition, leapt into the room carrying a silver fish in its mouth. It slunk to the floor and began to devour its meal.

Eliora could not cope with the sight or smell. She ran to the window, leaned out and vomited. She wiped her mouth, returned to find her water bag and drank the cool water. Shaking her head, she sat back on the cushion and watched the window intently again, purposely avoiding looking at the cat.

The fish had been what had tipped the balance but Eliora knew why she felt so ill. She feared the prince's return and what he would do to her. There was so little she could do. The frieze of paintings around the room, the images of the gods, mocked her. She sat, feeling judged by their looks of disdain, and knowing that she was the lowest of all creatures. She wept.

She went to the bowl to rinse her face, then she remembered. She recalled the transformation her tears had made to the bloodied water, she remembered she had one last hope.

'God, if you are out there, I need you. You came yesterday, you turned the Nile to blood, please keep me safe today.'

She has nothing left but to call on the Creator. She sees His power elsewhere, but not yet in her own life.

She fears for her safety, here, in this room, that holds her nightmares.

The shadow cringes as it hears her prayer. It slinks away from her and cowers in the corner.

I cup my hands and rub them gently together. I feel it blossoming within. Opening them I see a golden, pulsing ball of light. It flickers and sparkles. Bolts of energy intermittently arc. I release the ball and it floats before me. I breathe deeply, air that is clean and free from the stench of death, and blow it towards Eliora's huddled form. The scent of jasmine blends with the sparks.

'Be at peace!' I command.

The ball crackles as it breaks apart, weaving golden streamers of light and calming floral perfume through the air. They wrap around Eliora whose tense countenance instantly begins to relax.

She sighs.

You can sleep little one. I will guard you. You will come to no harm.

It was almost instant. Eliora could feel the tension lift. Somehow she knew she was safe, even in this place. Laying down, resting her head on the cushion, she closed her eyes and drifted off in dreamless sleep.

14

Suffering

I stand guard at the window in full armour. My bow ready in my hand. I will watch and wait.

Every day I have guarded her.

The Nile flows with blood. That is seven days now. Rotting fish have made its banks a repulsive place to be. Small clouds of newly emerged flies swarm over the decomposing bodies, before landing and laying their own eggs, readying the next generation to be immense in numbers. It is all part of the Creator's plan. This is an extremely dangerous place, as crocodiles roam the banks devouring the unexpected feast.

Eliora now curly haired and not painted, except for the kohl about her eyes, has spent her days inside the cat room, undisturbed. The days are empty of any kind of company.

Today will be different, but she is ready. She will face him.

I see him pacing at some distance. His face shines with sweat. It is not the heat of the day that causes him discomfort.

I check on Eliora. She sits sketching. I will not let her be surprised.

I blow on the thin drapes that hang at the window. They flutter in the breeze.

Eliora's attention was diverted by a cool, refreshing breeze which swirled about the room. She got up and approached the window. Then she heard footfalls crumpling the dry reeds. She took a deep breath and realised the Si was striding towards her, but he was no longer her friend, he was Horusisus, the prince. She let out a whimper. What could she do now? Where could she go?

She refused to be trapped in this room again. Trying desperately to slow her frantic heart, she stepped to the ledge and jumped down to the ground.

Horusisus shuffled back at the sight of her.

She stared shaking her head.

'Well, hello Ebonee,' the prince said, quickly recovering.

'What are you doing here?'

'I wanted to see you.'

'And you always get what you want, right? Now you have seen me.'

'Now, now. That isn't very friendly.'

Eliora huffed in annoyance. 'I don't want to be seen anymore.' She wanted to turn and leave but she was a slave girl, and he was an Egyptian, her master. She felt vulnerable and exposed but refused to wrap her arms around her. Instead, she stood as tall as she could, her hands tightly fisted at her sides.

He will not have authority here. Prince Horusisus stands confident, the creature so much larger than before, rests a casual limb over his shoulder. It whispers in his ear.

'Are you going to let her talk to you like that?'

Neither of them have authority here.

I clothe myself in light. Adorned in the splendour my Creator made, I flare into their presence. The air vibrates with the power given to me.

The creature recoils and lets off a string of profanities. They bounce off my armour, useless.

'Who invited you?' It finally asks.

'It is you that needs permission to be here, not me.'

The cool breeze blew across her face once more. She welcomed it. It cleared her head a little, enabled her to think. She suddenly felt that she could walk away from him and that he could do nothing about it.

She turned and walked from the window, out into the heat of the day, towards the shade of the palms near the river, her heart no longer reverberating in her ears, her breathing calm and her head held high.

She could hear him following, but he would not dictate this encounter. She had thought about and played over what she wanted to say to him if she ever saw him again. Now was her chance.

In the shadow of the trees, Eliora could see and smell the blood river as it moved sluggishly along its route.

'You can't just walk away from me,' Horusisus raged.

Eliora looked up at him. His face was reddening. The last thing she wanted was to be the brunt of his anger again.

'Prince Horusisus, what did you come here for?'

He raised an eyebrow at the use of his royal name, but did not correct her. 'I wanted to talk to you, to see you,' he said tight lipped.

Eliora could feel her anger rising. She took in a ragged breath.

'Let's go back inside,' he said, trying to be the friendly person she once thought she knew.

'Us?'

'What is wrong with that?' he asked.

'Do you not remember anything?' she said in disbelief. 'I don't want to be anywhere where you are.'

'Don't be like that!' Horusisus answered darkly.

'Like what exactly?'

'Like you didn't ask for it. It was all your fault. You were the one who made me angry. You only got what you asked for and deserved.'

'I didn't,' Eliora stuttered, 'I didn't ask for anything.'

'Of course you did. Sneaking up and spying on me. Like I said, you cannot go around humiliating princes. Now, let us go back inside.' He began to approach her. 'I promise I won't hurt you if you do as I say.'

'I will not go with you.'

'Yes you will.' Horusisus said, confidently.

Remember the true promises Eliora. "Like the stars of the sky!" That is what He said. "You will live in a land that you possess!" His promises never fail.

Eliora stood firm and shook her head in disagreement.

'I am a prince and you will do as I say.'

'Yes, you are a prince,' she paused. 'But my orders come from someone much higher than you.'

'The queen!'

'No, the King.'

The prince was confused. 'My father would not lower himself to give you orders.' He took a step towards her.

'I wasn't referring to that king.'

'What king then?'

'The King who did that.' Eliora pointed to the river. 'The King who will free my people.'

'You will never be free. You were born a slave and will die one.'

'No Prince Horusisus, named after Horus? Right?'

'Horus, the god of war and victory,' he smirked.

'The god of those things but also prophecy.' Eliora could feel her confidence rising. 'You are wrong Prince Horusisus. My God will free me but you will always be who you are, a slave to your gods.'

'You dare to call me a slave?' His face reddened. 'I will make you suffer for that!' He clenched his fists but remained where he stood.

'You made me suffer a week ago, but you know what, I will be free from you and what you did. But what you do not know, is that you will suffer because of what you did to me. I am a Hebrew and I belong to my God.'

What a revelation! Yes Eliora, you will be free!

He took a large step towards her and reached for her arm. She saw the approach and moved away.

'Don't touch me. Don't ever touch me.'

'I will do what I want Ebonee. You are just a slave.'

Eliora took a step backward, out from the shade of the palms, her heels catching on the plants that grew by the river banks. He followed, a wicked smile playing on his lips. She felt trapped. The river cut off one escape route and there were no people to witness what was happening out in the afternoon sun. How foolish she had been to lead him here and let him trap her again! She continued to back away. Maybe she could make it back to the palace walls? Maybe she could run faster than the prince, but she knew she was not stronger than him especially when he got into a rage.

'Please ...' she begged all her confidence drained and reality facing her squarely. 'God, help me!' Eliora whispered.

'You don't deserve help!' he mocked.

She may not deserve it, but she will get it!

I pull back on the string. That has caught the creature's attention.

My bow hums with power. The light pulsates through its fibres. I turn my back on them. The arrow is already nocked; I pull back and let the arrow soar. It raises high into the air, an effortless arc in the sky. As its trajectory turns towards the ground the shaft sparks and crackles with energy. It enters the centre of the blood Nile, in full view of the creature who hesitates in its incessant ranting.

He took one more step, then stopped, his gaze locked on something behind her.

Eliora took a step sideways, but he didn't follow her movement. She glanced quickly behind her, what had captured his attention?

Steam tendrils rise from the surface as the arrow pierces the blood. Incandescent sparks shoot through the polluted river where it is pierced. The sparks, like lightning, fork across the surface. In their wake rivulets of clear liquid appear. The intensity of the flashes increases. Soon, the whole surface flickers with energy, and in the depths, bright blue sparks transform the river. All remnants of blood are removed and in its place pure, crystal-clear water flows. The conversion continues both down and upstream.

Eliora gasped and turned back to the prince.

His eyes were wide, taking in the scene slowly. Eventually he looked back at Eliora.

'Who are you Ebonee? What kind of sorcery is this?'

'This is no sorcery,' she said emboldened by his fear. 'Don't ever call me Ebonee again. I am Eliora, an Israelite, one who belongs to the only true God and *He is my light*.'

Wonderful! She declares the truth!

She speaks with certainty and from her heart. She stands before me glowing gold. The air around her is enveloped in the creamy vanilla perfume of benzoin. It enfolds her and seals her words. She is secure in who she is. Outwardly, she has put away the Egyptian façade, but this is the true and living transformation. She stands here, knowing who she is!

The creature cannot bear to hear such things.

'Get away from me!' he screamed in pain and covered his ears. He turned and ran, leaving Eliora standing alone by the river.

She slumped to the dry ground. Was it really over? Her breath was ragged with sobbing. Her hands clasped at her chest. Then suddenly, she was laughing shakily. She turned again to look at the river. The sun glinted from the slight ripples, it still flowed with clear water. She was safe. She had been rescued. She looked up to the cyan dome that was the cloudless sky.

'Thank you,' she called.

Getting unsteadily to her feet, she staggered to the shade of the palms. Everything had more colour, more texture. The palms stood tall and magnificent, the rough bark stabbing into her back as she leaned against it. Birds glided overhead, calling to one another before landing on the far bank.

The river was returning to its more natural colour. The water browned with silt from further upstream, its richness restored.

She pushed away from the tree trunk, her legs no longer shaking, and walked confidently back to the window. She was still a slave and had to return to the nasty cats, but she knew that this would not always be the case.

15

Palace

My friends are eager to see this people transformed, as am I.

Everyone in the palace has seemed to overlook the pharaoh's inadequacy. They will be reminded of it soon enough.

I see to it that Eliora is safely back in her room before I set a guard at the door and window. She sits, eyes bright with revelation of who she belongs to and marvelling at the wonder she has witnessed. My companions will not let anything pass. I have received the command to meet with Release at the palace gate.

I clothe myself in battle gear as I streak through the air.

'Well met friend!' I say as I arrive and reach over to hug him.

'We are ready!' Release declares in his deep voice.

Moses and Aaron are hastening to meet the pharaoh. We follow.

I can smell them before I see them. The throne room stinks of sulphur. The creatures line the walls, cramming themselves into the room. There are great numbers here. They have been summoned to try to intimidate us. I am amazed at their show of force but also know our own numbers and strength.

Pharaoh sits casually on his throne, yet he shimmers from insipid green to murky red, showing his discomfort at facing Moses again. The creature flares at his head. It hisses and spits acid at us as we approach. The stench of foul burning sulphur flows unhindered through the air.

'This is my dominion. Get out!'

Release says nothing in return. Inwardly, I smile at his reserve.

Aaron stands straight and makes the request. 'This is what the Lord says, "Let my people go that they might serve me."'

'They will not serve anyone but me, I am the lord.'

'You know that is not true,' Release states simply.

Pharaoh turns to Moses, anger rises in him.

But Aaron has not finished. 'If you do not, the Lord will smite the whole of your territory with frogs. They will be everywhere, on your people and your servants. They will cover your land and be in your houses.'

The creature storms from the throne right up to Release's face. My friend stands firm. It grows intensely hot and the flames roar. The creature changes shape and size. As the flames billow, its frame widens and strengthens. Its torso ripples with muscle and broadens in a show of might. It continues to unravel itself until it towers over Release.

'You are nothing to me,' it bellows as it looks down on us. 'These people are nothing to me, but you will not have them, do you hear, you will not have them.' It reaches over and snatches at a creature that has the form of Heket. It has the body of a woman but the head of a frog and looks pitifully small next to its leader. 'My army infiltrates all of their lives. They bow down and worship me, they will not be altered.' It turns to Heket and signals for her to perform. She bends low to the ground and takes a cruel blade from her belt and cuts off one of her claws. It squirms on the floor for a few moments before reforming into a frog. The creature smirks satisfactory. 'I will not let them go. I am supreme here.'

'Then you will suffer further,' Release answers in a strong but controlled voice.

'It is not I that suffer.'

'But it is.'

'Get out!' Pharaoh shouts.

Aaron and Moses are grabbed by the Egyptian guard and rushed out of the throne room and hurled out of the palace.

'Well that seems to have caught their attention.' Release smiles. 'Moses it is time.'

As Moses instructs Aaron to symbolically stretch out his hand over the water of the palace I see what happens below the surface.

The earthen banks begin to crumble as frogs, which have lain dormant in the damp earth begin to emerge. The soil and sand trickles down to the water. The frogs tumble on the shifting ground to the river and receive hydration. But the river is already bubbling with smooth bodies clambering over each other. Soon the banks are covered with damp, dark, jumping creatures of assorted sizes. The sounds of splashing and croaking fill the afternoon air.

Moses and Aaron walk on to the next pool, the next ditch, the next stream.

Frogs emerge from the pools and ditches. Swathes of what appears to be mud line the edges of the waterways, but it is not mud. Thousands upon thousands of froglets climb from the water and scramble over each other. Their dark bodies glisten like damp mud in the sunlight. They jostle for room and soon spread as far as can be seen. Even here, some are overwhelmed by the numbers and are suffocated. Their bodies will not be wasted as small flies hurry to lay their eggs.

The land no longer resembles Egypt in all its regal splendour, but a dark, undulating land, where evertwhere you look there are more frogs.

I don't know how long they will be able to tolerate it. The people are already shouting to one another over the din of the frogs. They find them in their clothes, in their food, in their beds. There is no escape.

16

Veil

Apart from when she was with her own family or Caleb's, Eliora was treated with contempt. Her own people distrusted her and her mother, and the palace people hated her and her people for bringing so much suffering. Only when she was with Caleb did she feel any comfort, yet even then, her own dark secret cast a shadow over those times.

Her uncles had visited the pharaoh several more times. Frogs had covered the land. She had initially been relieved when she heard that her uncles had been called to the palace to deal with the frogs, not only because she would not have to pick them out of her food anymore but because Pharaoh had said that they could leave for the sacrifices. His word did not stand. After order had been restored, he would still not let her people go. She felt cheated by him. It was his fault that she was stuck between the two worlds.

The Hebrew people cleared out the dead frogs from their homes and piled them high. They were burned in large heaps. The smoke and smell lingered in the unusual humid air.

Away from her land, the Egyptians left the dead animals where they lay, allowing the birds and other wild animals to feed on them. At the palace the cats seemed to be immune to the revolting, stomach-wrenching smell as they insisted on returning with more rotting animals even after Eliora had cleaned the room.

She knew that her uncles were due to return, so gladly left the cats and their repulsive eating habits and watched as they stood outside the palace walls. No-one official came out to see them, but there were plenty of witnesses.

Eliora dared not go near so was unable to hear his words but she saw her uncle Aaron strike the ground with the staff in his hand. The dust of the ground looked to vibrate. She watched in wonder as another plague began.

Release stands outside the gates. Taking out a small scrap of Egyptian cloth from his cloak, he marks the ground.

Moses attention is caught by the sight of the embroidered material.

'Strike here,' he instructs Aaron.

His brother, completely confident, does just as he says.

The ground does vibrate. Eliora is right, but there is more happening here than she has detected.

The usual dry hot air has become humid and sticky. Perfect conditions.

The leaves of plants here are covered in brown spots and they wilt in the heat.

Gnats had laid their eggs here only a few weeks ago. The plants were damaged, right to the roots with the growing hunger of the larvae, but now they are ready to emerge from their metamorphosis. The loose dust of the ground has housed them for long enough. It is time to fly! They take to the air scattering the earth particles as they leave.

Thousands of eggs have transformed into swarms of gnats.

Eliora was fascinated but her fascination turned quickly to pain as the huge cloud of small black gnats filled the air. She found herself itching before she realised what had happened. She retreated back to the cat room and pulled the drapes across the window to try to prevent the insects entering, but they still came relentlessly. The cats mewed in distress, scratching aggressively at themselves and hissing viciously at her, as if it were her fault.

Even in all this, Eliora heard rumours as she went about her work. She overheard the kitchen staff, amid complaints about hundreds of gnats crawling about in their ingredients, talking about the magicians at court. When they had been called upon to perform the same magic that the slaves had done, they had failed. They had admitted that it could not be done, and what was more, they had declared it as the work of the finger of God. When she was seen smiling at their chatter, she was scolded and sent back to the cats without the milk she had hoped to fetch them to calm them down.

She covered her head to stop the irritating bites as she ran home. It was no different here. The gnats swarmed around any remaining dead frogs and attacked anything that smelt of fresh meat. Eliora was happy to see that despite working out in the pits Caleb had come home no worse than her. She had waited inside, leaving a message with his mother that she would be at home tonight, to avoid the gnats as much as possible.

'The mud helps,' he explained as he sat beside her while she stitched. 'I ended up rubbing it over the exposed skin, it seemed to work, well, mostly,' he said scratching his head.

They had found a quiet corner in the house, although it was still busy with family. Miriam sat by the fire, listening to Moses and Zipporah, her mother busied herself making bread and her cousins were playing over at her uncle Aaron's house.

'What are you making?' Caleb asked.

'My veil. I need to do something with my hands or I will scratch my skin off!'

'It is beautiful.'

'Thank you. It's just a remnant of material, but I think it looks transformed. I'm nearly finished.'

'And what about your bridal clothes, are they ready?'

'Yes, this is the last bit to do.'

'So we can get married soon?'

'I'm sure it will be a while yet.'

'Why? I have the house finished. I'm ready when you are.'

Eliora glanced up at Caleb. He was so certain, so self assured.

'There's no hurry.' She tried to joke.

'Sure there is. I want to marry you before we leave this land. Let us start our new life together.'

'But that could be any day.'

'Exactly.' He frowned seeing her hesitation. 'Too soon?'

'I suppose not.'

'Then what is it?'

'I guess I'm just a bit nervous.' She looked down and concentrated on her stitches again.

'Is that all Elli?'

'Of course.'

Eliora could feel Caleb examining her face. 'Then let's make it next week.'

'Please Caleb, don't rush me.'

'What is it?'

'I ... please just give me a little more time.'

'But I thought this is what you wanted,' he whispered, but she could hear the pain in his voice.

'Of course it is what I want. How could you think it wasn't?' She placed her hand in his, took a deep breath, fixed what she hoped was a composed smile on her face, and looked up at him. 'I'm getting myself ready, there are just a few more things that I need to work out. Female stuff. Things you shouldn't worry about.'

'As long as you are sure?'

'Hmm. I'm sure.'

They sat quietly again. Eliora could sense that Caleb wasn't satisfied, but tried to ignore it. She threaded her needle with a blood red strand.

'You've not said anything since the day I asked.'

'What do you mean?'

'The day I asked you to marry me. You don't seem to talk to me anymore.'

'Yes I have.'

'Not really you haven't. I mean more than just the everyday things. I love to hear what you thinking about.'

She smiled, but it quickly faded.

'Has something happened?' he asked in whispered urgency. 'To us I mean. Have I done something wrong? You can trust me.'

'I know I can. You have done nothing wrong at all. It's me. Just me. Please be patient.' She did her best to smile at him but a massive weight of guilt flattened her joy.

'There is something, I knew there was. I'll wait Elli, you know that. But you need to know that whatever it is, I'll stand by you, do you understand?'

Eliora did not know what to say. She wished she could really let him know what she thinking, but was worried that she did, he wouldn't stand by her and understand. Silence filled the gap in their conversation. Even though she was again focussed on her veil, she could tell that he was hurt. She tucked the needle into the fabric for safekeeping and gave him full attention.

'We will be fine, I promise.' She seized both his large, callused hands in her unmarked ones. 'We should fix a date. You are right. Can we give it just a couple more weeks though?' The guilt still laid heavily upon her, but her eagerness was sincere.

'When you are ready Elli, and not before. Sorry for putting pressure on you.'

'If anyone is putting pressure on me, it would be my mother. She has seen the house, knows it has been ready for a while, and has been working hard on organising me to be ready,' at least in the physical sense, she thought, 'helping me with the sewing and reminding me to get on with it.'

'The house has been ready for you for years.'

'Caleb!' she blushed. 'Sorry I have been so slow.'

Eliora rose early. Her head itched and stung from bites. She brushed out the tangles in her hair and decided to wear a headscarf to protect herself. Nothing too fancy or

Hebrew, just plain and dark, so at a quick glance it might even pass as her hair. It seemed an odd mix, one that would never go together, the Egyptian linen skirt and kohl eyes alongside the Hebrew headdress. It was ironic that today she finally looked how she felt. Neither Egyptian nor Hebrew, and not even something between the two. There was no compromise. She could not be both.

Her mother had already left and the house was quiet. The sun had not yet risen above the horizon. She was a little late, but she was not the only one walking towards the palace. Ahead, she could see her uncle Moses striding purposefully.

She felt a little rebellious, maybe it was the Hebrew in her resurfacing, and so decided to follow at a short distance. He did not enter the palace as he had done before but stood waiting at the Nile's bank.

She had been waiting only a few moments, hidden among the reeds, when the two tall, heavy wooden doors in the palace wall were prised open. They moved sluggishly and with great effort. Framed in the opening was Pharaoh, surrounded by officials whose faces showed a sense of relief. The dying chords of a song faded as he raised his arms, welcoming the new sun.

There is a growing hesitancy in the palace.

Rumours have been spreading throughout that perhaps the pharaoh is not all powerful after all. No one dares say those exact words, but it is beginning to formulate in their minds.

Even now, as they watch as this man, believing that he calls the sun to rise, the others around him are relieved to see that he is still able to do so. They have put their hope in him for all their needs, yet their trust is looking frayed at the edges.

The creature cackles at their frail human ideas. It has not changed. It seeks out what it thinks as human weakness and digs in its claws.

This empire, is built on such things. The men that surround the pharaoh reveal their need to have a ruler, one that is in control of the things that they do not understand, one that can bring wealth or disaster.

Humans need a ruler. They have sought the wrong one.

The creature stands idly at the pharaoh's back, soaking in the deception with an almost bored expression. This one has seen this ritual performed over many decades. It knows, as do I, that the sun remains in place and this country, a part of a small but highly significant planet, circles it. It has fed people lies for centuries. It will never change. It has fabricated stories and rites that lead to itself being worshipped. Something it has desired from near the beginning of time. A custom it has grown far too used to.

Now is the time for this to be broken.

Now is the time for them to see who deserves all worship.

For a moment Pharaoh's face was triumphant, and then he caught sight of Moses.

'The Lord says "Let my people go that they may serve me"'

'You! Again!' Pharaoh spat scratching at his arm. 'I will not let them go. Now be gone!'

'Because you will not let His people g,o the Lord says that He will bring swarms of insects on you and your people and on your people's land.'

'What are you still doing here? I have heard enough.'

'But,' Moses called out to him as he turned. 'You should know this. The Lord will not bring the swarms to his own people, he will set them apart.' Pharaoh paused and looked back to Moses over his shoulder. 'This will happen tomorrow.'

Before Pharaoh could speak again Moses had walked away.

Eliora sat open mouthed.

Her uncle was either brave or very stupid. She half expected Pharaoh to send a guard after Moses, to arrest him and punish him for his insolence, but he remained at the doorway. She noticed now, his regality had not protected him from the gnats. His arms and legs were red and inflamed from the irritating bites. His silence was thickening. Red patches rising on his cheeks. His glorious welcoming of the sun had been tainted by a threat from a slave, from a slave's god.

She could see Pharaoh composing his face into one of nonchalance before turning to his subjects.

'Let the day begin,' she heard him state as he marched inside.

'When will you understand that this is my domain?' The creature asks pointing a sharpened claw at me.

'You are welcome to your domain. From where I stand, it crumbles.'

It hisses at me, sickly, grey sulphur pouring from its mouth. It follows its host inside.

I take an arrow from my quiver, and send it high into the sky.

Only moments pass before Release is at my side.

'Are we ready?'

'Yes. Are the host in place?'

As if in answer, a series of flashes of golden light highlight the path some distance behind.

We rush to join them.

There is nothing here to distinguish between the Egyptian territory and the land where the Creator's people live, only a dusty track. But that is about to change.

Everyone is poised, shimmering in glorious golden light. Release stands far on my right at the edge as it sweeps away from the palace guiding those out of sight, another old friend, Liberty, does the same on my left.

I launch into the air, feeling the warming earthly wind against my face. Threads of gold, countless in number, stream from my feet, my hands, my hair, anchored deep into the ground. Each ribbon flows fine and straight until I reach the pinnacle above the very centre of the settlement. The host follow my lead with Release and Liberty reaching me first, while the others fly as if by chain reaction. The sight is graceful.

With a quick smile, I loop my friends and head back to the ground on the far side. My threads cross and bind themselves with others as I penetrate the ends into the ground.

I launch myself again, repeating the process, thickening the golden net. I hear the laughter of my fellows. There is such joy in this part of the plan.

After one more flight I am certain that the job is complete. I look closely at my work. The fine fibres vibrate as if with life. The filaments bound so closely together that air molecules cannot fit into the spaces between. Standing back, the dome rises into the air, higher and stronger than any other structure in this landscape. It is not made to glorify a man, not created to transport a life into another world, not a result of a lie. It has the texture of the finest woven cloth. It is a promise to protect, to set apart a people, a structure made to reveal the True One. A veil of glory, separating this people from their slave masters, a covering for a lost people.

17

War

The new day brings a new horror.

Eliora's sleep is fitful and sporadic. She dreams with images the colour of blood. She cowers from his fist and wakes with a start. The tendrils of darkness that wove about her, fade away like smoke. Sweat glistens on her brow. She will not return to bed. The reality of her dreams cripples her with fear.

Despite my victory at the river, she still lives with the memory of the past. This will be addressed at the correct time. The command to wait has been given. In this I will trust, after all, the Creator's timing is always perfect.

He has planned this event. Everything had been put into place days, weeks and years before. He caused them to sleep. Now He is waking them up.

The sky is yet to change from its deep darkness into the predawn light.

There is stillness in the Hebrew settlement, like the sigh before a heavy rainfall.

Sleep had evaded Eliora again. The whispered conversation with Caleb still played over in her mind. He knew her too well to accept that she was the same. He had seen a difference, one that she had hoped he would equate to their betrothal, but he had not been fooled.

Layer upon layer of guilt. It was unfair for her to have to hide this, but life had drawn her the losing lot.

She dressed quietly, grabbed a chunk of bread and began a dawdling walk to the palace picking at the soft dough, rolling small pieces between her fingers before popping them into her mouth.

The dirt track, hard packed from many feet, produced small clouds of dust as she walked with very little purpose. The lightening sky and the fading of the moon spoke of another day of being trapped.

As the last stars disappeared into the dawn, Eliora found herself back at the Nile's edge where she had witnessed her uncle's challenge the previous day. A mist still clung to the water, swirling in the gentle breeze.

Chanting music drifted out of the palace as the doors were once again shifted open. Eliora crouched in the shadow of a line of palms that stood by the long reeds. Framed again, was the pharaoh, dressed to command the sun to rise. On cue, the sun breached the horizon and sent long shadows skittering across the baked ground.

Eliora, enjoying the first glimpse of the sun was distracted by a humming sound. At first it was a faint, background noise, but the more she listened the stronger it grew. She looked back to the pharaoh, perhaps they had started another ritual, but they were just stood there. Officials in the background fidgeted, disturbed by the unusual sound. They began turning their heads, searching discreetly for the source.

The dead leaves beneath her fingers began to shift. The small hard head of a beetle emerged. He quickly scrambled and climbed out causing the sand to trickle from his yellow and black striped back. The wing casings opened and he unfolded his transparent wings. A gentle thrum of beating wings accompanied him as he took off.

Eliora looked up into the air. Tiny dots were moving above her, constantly being joined by others lifting from the ground.

She rushed over to the palm trees. Small beetles struggled from the feathered gaps in the bark and gathered in clusters before they launched into the air.

Hundreds of beetles had taken flight. The bright morning took on a flickering half-light as numbers increased to thousands in the interrupted dawn.

A human screech caught her attention. Back at the palace doors, an official bent double on the floor groaned. Pharaoh raised his arm one more time and bought the golden stick down onto the man's exposed back.

'But ...'

'Don't answer back!' and hit him again. 'They are sacred. You deserve punishment.'

'Yes Sire!' he whimpered.

'Where are they all coming from? I need to know what this means.' He turned back to the room. 'Summon my magicians.'

His head dropped, watching the floor as he stepped carefully back into the palace.

The noise was intensifying. Eliora had never seen beetles in such numbers before. They flitted about her and scrambled over the ground at her feet. She stood quickly, shaking the jewelled insect from her sandals and rushed to the palace to find refuge among the less creepy cats.

She found no respite. The beautiful polished floors were littered with crawling black beetles that hissed and scuttled to the edges before climbing the walls, clinging to the carved images and defecating on the painted images.

The palace guards and other workers, hostile to Eliora any other day were somewhat comical. The creatures scurried over feet and up bodies, some even perched in the Egyptians' hair. Yet they weren't flicked away, they were carefully and reverently lifted, gently brushed and delicately tip toed around.

'What a ridiculous load of effort!' Eliora said quietly when she finally made it to the room, whilst kicking one beetle and stamping on another. These creatures may have been objects to honour and worship if you as Egyptian, but she was not hoping to be that anymore.

The cats played with and pounced on the beetles that blackened the floor. Eliora didn't mind that they ate them, but the crunching of their shells made her stomach turn.

There was nowhere to sit or stand without the creatures climbing over her. She cringed away from them. She had thought things could not get worse. The Palace finally felt like the darkest place to be.

It was true, when Eliora had first found out that she would work at the palace when she came of age, she had felt special and set apart. For a long time, she had boasted in the privileges of the less manual work, although, quietly, she missed her friends and wished to join them only for their companionship. She had seen them suffer in the baking sun and the slave labour of the pits, and secretly she had been pleased that she was special. If they were to be cruel to her for something that was not her fault, they should get punished, at least a little bit. They may have thought it unfair. They knew nothing. Her being selected was unfair. Her having to be treated with disdain by her own people and by hateful loneliness by the ones she served at the palace, that was unfair. There was no way to win. Then when she thought she had reached the lowest place she had found, what she thought was friendship, only to be cut down more severely than ever before. It was only after that nightmare event that her perspective had shifted. This was a loathsome place to be. Full of fear and hatred. She had nowhere and no-one to help her escape.

This room was a place of horror. It stank of cats, crawled with clicking and creeping bugs and contained only lingering and festering memories of pain and mistreatment.

She tried to recall the moment of freedom she had experienced at the river. She closed her eyes desperate to find again that moment of peace. It had been so real at the time, but now, clinging onto it with such frail threads it seemed like a dream.

'I don't want to be here anymore. I don't want to be anywhere.'

I watch over her. She feels she is at her lowest.
Her hope has faded and she has little strength left to fight her darkest thoughts.

'God, do you hear me?' Eliora cried out, 'I can't do this anymore.' She slumped to the floor, scattering the beetles.

The Creator hears you, dear Eliora. He is merciful.
From the folds of my cloak I pull out a handful of small acid green beetles and place them carefully on the floor.
In the corner, a cat watches a beetle scuttle across towards her.
I push the beetle closer to the cat's tense body.
'It is yours. Go ahead and eat it.'
The cat pounces, catching the bug beneath its sure feet. It bends down and tears off the beetle's head. The cat quickly gobbles the rest down.
I stir the room. I direct the iridescent green beetles, teasing the cats. Sunlight glints from their shells before they are trapped and eaten.
Freedom is coming for you Eliora. You will be redeemed.

Eliora flinched at the touch of creatures starting to climb over her again. She could not stay on the floor and rose quickly to her feet. She reached for the broom and brushed aside the insects that approached. It was an endless and fruitless task. They scuttled across the floor, up the walls and in through the window. Black and bejewelled bugs clung to the billowing fabric, buzzed above her head in flight and gnawed at the wooden furniture. There was no escape from them.
She didn't notice at first that the mewing had stopped and that the rough sound of retching was coming from different places in the room. But soon the noise couldn't be ignored. The cats were ill, and not just one or two but nearly all of them.

Using the broom to clear a path, Eliora approached a lithe black cat hunched over in the corner. It had been sick and was retching once again. She rushed for a dish on the counter, tipped the beetles from it and poured water from the jug. She flicked the floundering creatures out and was about to put the dish down for the cat to drink from. It was too late. The cat lay motionless on the cold marble floor in a pool of blood filled mucus.

Eliora stood motionless. What could she do? What just happened?

The sound of another cat in pain caught her attention. Turning, she saw that this deadly illness was sweeping the room.

She rushed to the door and flung it open.

'Help, you've got to help!'

The guard turned in surprise.

'Come quickly!' she urged, grabbing his arm.

Suddenly his dagger was at her throat. 'Don't touch me you accursed Hebrew.'

Eliora drew her hand back slowly.

'You don't understand. The cats. Something has happened to the cats.'

He peered into the room. The floor littered with furry bodies that at first seemed to be moving. Eliora ventured in and picked up a body. It was already teeming with beetles.

The guard paled.

'Are any alive? What did you do to them?'

Eliora knew he would assume it was her fault. 'They will all be dead unless you help me right now.' Eliora scanned the room. 'Some are still alright. A couple over there, one on the counter. Those kittens seem alright.'

'Gather them up and come with me.'

She cleared a small basket and grabbed the animals, scattering beetles in her wake.

The guard looked down the corridor.

'Here, use this,' Eliora said, handing him the broom. His face reddened with anger. 'Well you can hold the cats if you like and I'll sweep a way out of here.'

He snatched the broom from her and marched ahead, clearing a narrow walkway between the teeming beetles.

Eliora hurried along behind him, before her path was littered again.

With her hands full, all Eliora could do was shake her head to dislodge the insects. Thankfully, if she stayed close to the path swept by her guide the beetles couldn't get close enough to climb her.

The colourful images that lined the corridors were obscured by creatures and the thrum of wings filled the usual serene silence. The palace workers were trying to go about their work but were finding it difficult. Eliora looked into rooms as she passed. Each one the same. Each one infested and each Egyptian, that caught her gaze, glared back in hatred.

The guard led her to an ornate door, inlaid with gold and flanked by two muscular sentries. He knocked twice.

A familiar person answered the door bowing low.

'Mother!' Eliora whispered.

Her mother looked up anxiously, her eyes wide.

The guard completely ignored her and marched in, Eliora followed. Dread began to fill her heart.

'Simra, shut the door before any more come in.'

Eliora turned, and saw her mother quickly obey.

The queen lounged on a couch while her ladies rushed about brushing aside the beetles that had made it into her chamber. They collected them up and gently released them out the window. It seemed a pointless task, as more entered each time the curtain was opened. The queen however, sat comfortably beetle free and regally dressed. A cat that Eliora had never seen before purred loudly from the queen's lap.

'What are you doing here? I didn't call for you.'

The guard had bowed low, Eliora, quickly followed suit.

'Your Majesty. This girl has set death on your cats. These are the only ones left.'

'I didn't kill them.'

'Silence!' Eliora bowed lower under the authority. 'My cats have died?'

The guard turned and roughly pulled the basket from Eliora. 'These, I rescued, your Majesty.'

The queen inspected the cats. The cat on her lap sat up and peered in.

Her freedom is nearly at hand.

I bend down and place the acid green beetle where it can be seen.

There you are little one. Do you see this? It is for you. Eat up now.

Seeing a beetle scuttle across the basket, the royal cat leaned in and ate it. 'Clear the beetles from this basket.' She instructed handing the basket to one of her ladies. 'And get rid of that half chewed insect too.' The cats hissed. 'You, what is your name?'

'El ... Ebonee, your Majesty.'

'You are Simra's daughter.'

'Yes, your Majesty.'

'Simra!' the queen called. Eliora's mother, dressed as Simra, rushed forward carefully avoiding the beetles around her. 'Your daughter has killed my cats.'

'If you please your Majesty,' she said bowing low, 'She would not dishonour you that way.'

'Did you kill my cats?' she asked Eliora suspiciously.

'No your Majesty.' Eliora looked up at the beautiful queen. 'I would never do such a thing. I have taken care of them.'

'So what do you suppose has happened?'

'I don't know.'

'You were looking after them?'

'I was trying to, but the beetles are everywhere. I was trying to stop the cats from eating them.'

'You failed at that. There was a specimen in with the ones left.'

'Yes your Majesty.'

'You there,' she said to the guard. 'Go back and collect the poor creatures. Their souls must be set free. Take them.'

The guard left quickly.

'So what do you suppose I should do? Your people have caused us a great deal of trouble.'

'Not my people.' Eliora replied quickly. Simra took a sharp intake of breath.

'Do you disown them Ebonee?'

'No your Majesty. I am not disowning them. What I mean to say is that it is not my people who are causing the trouble. The pharaoh has angered my God, so it is my God that has been working for us.'

Simra gave a stern look to her daughter, but the queen held up her hand.

'Do not worry Simra. Your daughter is only relaying the facts.' She turned again to Eliora and studied her face. 'You are right. Your god is actively working here.' The queen's face paled. 'Yes, your god does seem to want something.'

'He wants us to be free to worship him.'

'You will never be free.'

'Then you will never be free from trouble.'

The queen looked down at her cat. It was coughing and spluttering. She stroked its head gently. 'What is the matter little one?'

The cat convulsed then threw up in her lap.

She jumped to her feet, and the cat landed awkwardly on the floor, still in pain. It retched again, blood seeping from its mouth. The queen screamed, and the doors flew open and the sentry guards rushed in.

'My love, my poor love.' The cat made a hideous gurgling noise then collapsed to the floor. 'Is she dead?'

A lady rushed forward, but hesitated before touching the body. She nodded up to her queen.

'You will never be free from trouble. My God has gone to war,' Eliora whispered.

'Get out!' the queen shouted. 'Just get out! I never want to see your disgusting Hebrew face again.'

The guards grabbed Eliora roughly and dragged her from the room.

Her mother looked on in shock. She recovered quickly, grabbed a linen towel and carefully draped it over the dead cat. As Eliora was taken away she could hear her mother singing a beautiful lament, and the hysterical screams dulling to a gentle sob.

'Please keep my mother safe,' Eliora prayed.

'You and your Hebrew god. Just leave us alone!' The guard threatened at he threw her outside the palace.

Eliora almost laughed, had it not been for the rippling muscles on display. He was frightened of her. She got up and shook the dust from her clothes and shoes. She turned away and never looked back.

With each step, she relished the crunching of the beetles. It was because of the beetles and the death that they had brought that she was able to put to death her life at the palace. She was free.

The Creator is merciful. He brings freedom to the oppressed.

The sun blazed and the heat coming off the ground shimmered and danced, but nothing could scorch Eliora's mood. She broke off a number of reeds, settled herself in the shade and hastily wove them together. As she worked she sang quietly to herself, occasionally laughing out loud. Before long she had made a fan and was on her way home.

As she entered the settlement's boundary she noticed the lack of crunching underfoot.

'Where are the beetles?' she questioned. The ground was completely clear. The path beyond the boundary still crawled with creatures, but here, on her land there was nothing but dust. Her land was free from the death beetle.

Eliora stopped short. Suddenly the realisation hit her. She was special, her people were special and they had been set apart from the Egyptians. Her God was indeed at war and He was on her side.

18

Belonging

Eliora used to listen to the tired and hushed return of the slaves when she was little, but today, as they entered the settlement, their spirits were lifted, and an unusual hum of excitement filled the air.

There was a deep sense of joy as the workers returned home. The battle line that had been drawn between the Egyptians and the Hebrew settlement did not go unnoticed.

Miriam, Eliora's grandmother, whose quota had been taken on by more able bodies, was no longer sent out to work at the pits. Instead, had worked hard at the settlement all day. She had cared for her youngest grandchildren, baked what little food they were able to harvest, and cleaned. Eliora arrived home by early afternoon and joyously told her grandmother of the distinction between the peoples. She changed out of the Egyptian clothes and proudly put on her own. She threw herself into helping with the chores and now sat in the doorway while her grandmother sat inside and dozed with exhaustion.

She caught sight of her old friend Dinah, who was sun darkened and dusty from work with straw sticking to her outer garments. She tried to smile kindly, and received a hopeful and friendly response. The thought of joining her team seemed a little less terrifying. Because that is what would happen now. She could not stay at home with those that were too frail to slave for the Egyptians, she would also go to the pits.

Jochebed, still dressed as Simra, dashed up to her and pulled her close.

'I was so worried!' she whispered. 'I didn't know what would happen to you. Are you alright?'

'I'm fine,' Eliora reassured her mother. 'At least I will never have to go back. What about you? Did you get punished for it?'

'Well,' she said as she looked into Eliora's eyes. 'The queen was frantic. She kept asking what she had done to displease the gods so badly. She couldn't think of a way to appease them. Finally she was silent for the rest of the day. What happened really shocked her, so I got away without punishment.'

The mood of celebration continued into the evening. Families and neighbours sat outside and the sound of laughter filled the settlement.

Caleb arrived and spoke quietly with Eliora. 'Come to the garden with me. We haven't been there for a while.'

She slipped her hand into his and he led them away from the bustle of noise.

'You were right you know,' Eliora said as they walked.

'Was I? About what?'

'The gods.'

'What about the gods?'

'That they are being stripped down.'

'So it appears.' he smiled sadly.

'But it is good.' She squeezed his hand. 'This means I no longer work at the palace.'

'Are you sure? Can't you do a different job?'

'You want to send me back there?'

'I don't want you working at the pits.'

Eliora felt the tug at her heart. Everything was happy at the settlement except her. Caleb had wanted to come to the garden, he had said he didn't want her with him in the pits. Had he found out? Was she going to be rejected and thrown away? Fear bubbled up to the surface. Eliora swallowed hard. She was free of the palace and the prince, or so she had thought, but even now, in her world, he still controlled her.

They walked on in silence finally reaching the garden. Eliora didn't sit down but lit the lamp and began to pull up weeds. Perhaps she could put off the inevitable.

'Elli, what have I said?'

'Nothing.'

'Stop that. Talk to me. What is wrong?'

'You said you didn't want me working in the pits. What is so wrong about me working with you?'

'Working with me is not the point. It is the place of work that is the problem.' He bent down to catch her hands. 'Did you think I didn't want you? Is that it?' Eliora straightened but didn't look at him. 'How can you think that Elli? I want to marry you more than anything in this world.'

'Why would you not want me with you?'

'I want you to be where it is safe, where you can't get hurt. The palace is the safest place for you.'

Eliora let out a twisted laugh. If only he really knew. Than a shiver of fear shocks her, he must never know just how dangerous a place that was for her. 'I'm not going back there,' she eventually said.

'I know. I just don't want you to have to see what I see and be what I am.'

'But I am what you are.' He led her to the low wall in the garden and they sat down. Eliora brushed the dirt from her hands.

'I don't ever want you to be what I am,' he said quietly.

'Why?'

'Because you are too precious,' he said sadly. 'I don't want you to be ordered around, to be beaten and hurt, to be made to feel as if you are worth less than nothing. I want to protect you from all that.'

'You can't protect me from that.' She sighed, no one had ever been able to protect her from that.

'Everything in me wants to.'

Eliora battled. Caleb was so sincere, how could she continue to live with this lie between them?

Tell him, little one. Tell him.

She has built walls around herself, but they will not protect her.

Even now she backs away. Even now that lie has power over her.

I hate to see it twisting about her, serpent like, just like that first lie. It lives to torment and torments to kill. It leaves a bitter taste in the air.

It has no place here.

I will not banish it, but I can give her the weapons to do it.

I take the cloak from my back. The fabric is thick with tightly woven threads, it offers protection from the cold, yet light enough to carry.

I drape the garment over her shoulders.

'This is courage, little one. This will protect you from the cold.'

She stood suddenly. 'There is something that you need to know.'

'So tell me then.'

'Please hear me out.' She looked down into his confused face. 'Then I will be gone.'

Caleb shook his head. Eliora felt her heart racing. This would be the end of it all. She would lose him. She almost stopped but felt a whisper of courage envelop her. But if she was going to lose him, or set him free, she wanted him to at least know the reason why.

'A while ago,' she began turning her back to him. 'Do you remember the time after the river of blood.' She paused, 'Of course you remember the blood.' She rushed on. 'Well, I got hurt, you know that, but it wasn't just the bruise on my shoulder.'

'What do you mean?'

'Please Caleb, if I am to get through this, I need you to just listen.' Eliora waited, but he didn't speak up again. 'The bruise was the easiest part of it for me to tell you about.' Eliora stopped. How could she relive that moment? How could she reveal her own filth? She took a deep breath and began.

'He didn't just hit me. He attacked me. It wasn't my fault, but he said it was, so maybe it was. I found out who he was, that's all, just saw him on the boat. But he saw me. He was so angry. So very, very angry. There was nothing I could do. He's a prince and I am only a slave.' She paused and looked down at her clenched hands. 'He ... he raped me... I'm ruined ... we're ruined.' She hung her head. There came no reply. She slumped to the floor. Her breathing stuttered as she tried to control the sobbing that threatened. Then she noticed the silence that said she was alone, Caleb had left quietly, just as he should have. There was no use in feeling sorry for herself, she had known the outcome before she had begun. It would be better for him to be without her. It was a kindness she had offered. She knew now that she loved him far more than she had ever thought, to give him freedom. She loved him enough to let him go.

The stench of vomit floods through the air as she relives the event in her mind.

A spindly creature weaves itself into her hair, its limbs bound tightly to the strands. It seems very settled, however, that is not the case. It will not stay here much longer.

Caleb sits fixed in place. Flashes of vermillion clash with the underlying background of mustard. Rage fills him. His beautiful Eliora has hidden this truth from him, but his anger is at her reluctance to tell him before now.

'Peace Caleb.' I touch his head and my hands drip with aloe. 'Put yourself in her place. View it from her position. Would you have spoken about something so horrific?'

The flashes subside.

His colours intensify and purify. His rage becomes directional. It moves away from Eliora and moves outwards towards Egypt. Just as it should. But there is more here. I smell dirty smoke. He is burning himself over what has happened.

She pulled at the sleeve of her tunic and wiped her eyes. She had to face her bleak future. Gathering up the hem of her tunic, she got to her feet and brushed off the dust. She turned.

'What? You're still here!' Eliora exclaimed. 'Why?'

Caleb was sat exactly where she had left him, but his shoulders were hunched over and he was staring at the ground.

'I thought you had gone,' her voice quivered.

Suddenly he was looking intently at her. His eyes were fierce. The remains of tears glistened on his cheeks.

'I'm so sorry Caleb,' Eliora whispered. 'I free you from your promise to me. I won't think badly of you and I won't let others think badly either. I'll tell them, maybe not the truth, but something. This won't come back to you, I promise.'

'Why didn't you tell me earlier?'

'Because I knew this is what would happen,' she said, brushing away the silent tear. 'You would need to leave.'

'I sent you back in there.' Caleb clenched his fists. 'I sent you back to that ...' He stood quickly. 'Did he, has he... touched you ...again?'

'No.' Eliora closed her eyes. 'He got what he wanted the first time.' She looked at him again and she saw what she had never seen before. Her Caleb was sure to be lost to her.

Caleb trembled.

'You don't have to stay. But Caleb, please, let me be the one to tell my family. Please, can you give me that?'

'What do you mean, I don't have to stay?'

'You won't want me now.'

'It wasn't your fault. You didn't ask for him to ... Elli, you can't think this is what you deserved?'

The question hung in the air. She would remain honest.

'Perhaps.'

'Perhaps? Elli, you are not taking the blame for this. I just want to go in there and kill him.'

'No! He'll kill you.' Eliora could see the battle waging inside Caleb. 'It is all my fault. Don't let your death be my fault too.'

'How is this your fault?' Caleb questioned. 'That prince is nothing but the lowest form of life, taking what doesn't belong to him, just as his father has done for years. He had no right.'

'But I am his property.'

'No.'

Eliora shook her head as she wrapped her arms around her body, holding her confused and vulnerable self in.

Images pour from Caleb. Acts of violence and revenge against the prince.

'Stop him Eliora!' I urge. 'Stop him before his plans form.'

'Promise me you won't go after him.'

'Are you protecting him?'

'Promise me Caleb!' she pleaded.

'I can't believe you are protecting him!' Caleb hissed.

'It's not him I want to protect.' She reached out to him. 'Please Caleb, promise me you will let this go.'

'He deserves to die.'

'Yes,' Eliora wept, 'but not at your hands.'

'We don't belong to them,' he said through clenched teeth. 'They contain us, they rule us, but we are more than just a physical thing. They cannot own us. Elli, you are not owned. Your life is free to give to whoever you want to give it to. They cannot take you, no-one can.'

'But I couldn't stop him. He took everything. And now he is taking you too.'

The garden was still, poised for another life to be destroyed by the mighty nation.

'Elli.' Caleb approached her slowly. He gently placed his hand on her cheek. She watched as a solitary tear ran down his face and into his stubble. 'I promise.' And then she understood.

'You aren't going to leave me?'

'No.'

'But...'

'I made a promise to you,' he said, 'If you still want to share your life with me I will gladly, willingly and wholeheartedly accept it. I love you.'

The creature is losing its grip. Its weak limbs are struggling to cling onto her. Caleb has accepted her and declares his love for her. This creature's power is diminishing.

'You cannot send me away, I belong here!' it whines.

'I will not drive you away yet. Believe me, you will know when you are no longer welcome here!'

It cringes from the golden bolts starting to spark from Caleb.

'But what about ... what happened?'

'Will you forgive me for letting you go back to that palace?'

'I had to go. That was where I worked.'

'No. I could have done something.'

'There was nothing you could have done.' She rested her hand on his cheek. 'There is nothing to forgive.'

They stood, each touching the other's face, barriers down at last.

'You are my Elli, nothing can change that.'

The couple are connected by the swirls of gold encircling them.

At last the foundations of their relationship can be built upon.

He receives her acceptance and forgiveness for not protecting her and she experiences his true love for her without the looming darkness of the secret that had surrounded her.

19

Warning

The settlement sleeps after an evening of rejoicing.

It has taken them a long time to see their favour with the Creator. It is good that they are finally coming to the realisation that this is what He chooses to do, and they are the chosen ones. His timing is perfect for a remnant in the grip of a foreign land.

Eliora sleeps peacefully. Her heart unburdened and her soul reassured by Caleb's words.

Her family rests too.

Release stands guard over the house. He is suited for battle but his sword hangs in his scabbard at his side.

'It has been an important day for these people.' Release says.

'Certainly has!'

'This will give them hope for the trials ahead. The Creator knew right from the start that the Remnant would be surprised by their distinction.'

'Yet He chose to continue because His mercy is beyond anything.'

'Indeed,' I agree.

We stand, silent and still trying to grasp this unfathomable concept, yet it escapes our understanding.

'Are you off then Faithful?'

'I am indeed. I should be back before dawn.'

'I'll be here. There will be no call for war tonight.'

'I don't know about that. I have a battle to fight!'

Release smiles and waves me away.

It is not far away so I decide I will walk, I want to savour the atmosphere in the settlement tonight. It is as if a great burden has lifted from their shoulders. They know that they will head back to the pits when morning comes, but hope, smelling of almond blossom, floats on the breeze.

The veil above me glimmers in the moonlight. The night is clear and the temperature has dropped.

My task for this evening is to give a warning. It is a warning that I will repeat over the next few nights.

The house is cool and quiet. It had once been a busy place full of family noise. Parents, two boisterous boys and one equally demanding girl. Now only Caleb and his mother live here.

This house has been the scene of such happiness and sorrow but the darkness holds no secrets. Even before the physical deaths occurred, this place stank of death. It had been welcomed in like a true friend only to attack the structure of this family from the heart.

Other gods had been introduced to his home. They were subtle and alluring. Caleb's wife had bought her carved images with her that had lain hidden but she had also introduced and encouraged self-pity and judgement. Caleb had been lost for a while, wallowing in his own mire but the Creator knows him best and knows how to rescue.

It had taken a few words, harsh at the time, from none other than Eliora, to shake him from his sleep. She had seen the change in him, she had missed his positive attitude and his faith at what he was called to do and be. His awakening had been a sudden one.

The events that followed were questioned by many. Caleb's life had been judged by others as first his father, then his wife and newborn child died. But now he is fully awake. He has thrown out the idols. Cleared the rooms of images and cleaned his heart out of unrighteous motivations. He has answered the judgements with repentance and forgiveness.

Caleb had found his strength in the midst of the trauma. It was the birthing of the man I see now.

People had seen the miraculous change in him. He is now a source of encouragement and a lifter of heads.

His life is not unnoticed!

The Creator has plans for him. Plans to give him a future and a hope. Plans that need him to find the originator of his strength again so that when he is tested he will stand firm.

That is why I am here. That is why I must give him the warning. He will know that he is not alone and that he can trust the Creator no matter what.

Caleb sleeps peacefully. He has worked so hard, taking the burden of his team on his back. His quota gets filled day by day. He doesn't know how, as there should be no possibility of completing the task the Egyptians set, but complete it he does.

I am about to interrupt his sleep.

Caleb is so exhausted by the end of the each day that he rarely dreams. This is about to change.

I capture his interest with Eliora.

She stands in the shimmering heat, head covered by an unusual green scarf. She turns and smiles.

Caleb's heartbeat reacts. I have his attention.

He watches as Eliora is suddenly transformed from her Hebrew self into her Egyptian form and collapses to the floor.

He rushes forward, only to find his way blocked by a red Egyptian staff thrust into his path.

Caleb wakes suddenly, his eyes wide in the darkness and his heart hammering in his chest.

I wait.

Eventually he calms, shakes his head and drifts back to sleep.

Eliora is once again before him, then enslaved in her Egyptian uniform and collapses onto the floor. The suddenness of the red staff jerks him awake a second time.

He remembers the dream in detail now.

I let him rest. I will be back tomorrow night and the night after that.

I have visited Caleb for five nights now.

Tonight he climbs into bed worried about the dreams that will inevitably come. But he is different.

'Please,' he whispers in prayer, 'I don't know what you want me to do. Please show me.'

I spread a wave of peace over him and he quickly drifts off into sleep.

The dream begins as before.

Eliora smiles, transforms, collapses. The red staff plunges into the ground but doesn't wake him. Now he will have his answer.

For the first time, Caleb realises that he wears his cloak, even though the heat of the sun beats down upon him he is not hot. He takes off his cloak and approaches Eliora. The red staff suddenly bursts into flame and is reduced to ash before his eyes. He is able to approach Eliora unhindered. He lays his cloak carefully over her. She stirs and sits up. The cloak falls open and she has been restored to her Hebrew self. Caleb feels happy. The cloak drops further. In her arms, a small baby sleeps. Eliora looks up, she is scared. Caleb wraps his cloak firmly around her and lifts her to her feet.

Caleb wakes.

He sits on his bed barely breathing. The image of the baby fixed solidly in his mind.

'Take care of them Caleb!' I shout as I flare into light and go.

20

Sickness

She is exhausted. I inject the air with the scent of nutmeg to lift her energy levels. It has only been a little less than one week, but her back aches and her hands are sore.

She pulls at the green headscarf to cover her exposed forehead.

Eliora's role is to gather straw from wherever she can find it.

She has quickly learned to look down instead of up. Slavery does that.

She knows that this task is essential to keep her people safe. She feels the responsibility. Without straw the bricks cannot be made. Without bricks, her people, the Creator's remnant, get punished. She works hard for Caleb. She doesn't want him punished any more than she feels she has done to him already.

Release stands with me, sword sheathed. The battle here has not yet begun. We are observers. His eyes pierce the scene.

'She works hard,' he says after studying her. 'She thinks it is her job to save them.'

'Regretfully, yes.'

'Does she know?'

'Not yet.' Compassion fills me.

'She will be led through this Faithful,' Release says confidently.

I know that he speaks truth. 'But she will stumble.'

'As they do,' Release states. 'You have been given instructions. The Creator knows her best.'

'Yes, very true.'

'She will be safe here.'

I glance up and see the host patrolling through the slaves. They are relaxed. They bend here and there, helping to take the heavy loads, pointing out hidden resources of straw.

'We need to go,' Release says capturing my attention. 'Are you ready?'

I nod and we both flare into light and are gone.

A moment later we stand at the boundary. The woven protection glimmers over the Remnant's settlement behind us. It remains firm and undamaged.

I can hear the voices of two men approaching, and can see their shimmering forms through the heated air. They wear the uniform of the palace and speak the Egyptian language.

'We should let them through,' I say to Release. 'It is essential that they gain evidence.'

Their voices give the outward appearance of official business, but I see the underlying currents. They are inquisitive and a little fearful.

As they draw near, I see the short blades at their sides and the whips curled at their belts. They have come armed and accompanied. The dark shadows that follow them have seen us and they spit at the ground where we stand.

The humans pause, looking at the sprawling squat houses of the Hebrew nation.

'You may enter,' I say to the shifting creatures. 'But be warned, you will not be permitted to touch a single soul here.'

'You are no match for the power of Ra!'

Release smiles. He knows the truth as well as I do. And if these creatures would admit it, so do they.

'Be that as it may, not a soul, do you hear?' I instruct.

'We hear,' one hisses. They cry out as they cross through the veil.

The men continue, their voices lower and more secretive than before.

It is not long before they are shaded from the sun in the alleyways and pathways between the houses around the edge. They continue to skirt the settlement. The shadows pale in the light coming from the veil.

The very young and very old look on suspiciously at their unannounced visitors.

A small child runs along in their wake.

A creature creeps towards it.

'What you here for?' she says boldly to the men.

'None of your business!' he replies harshly and raises his hand.

The shadow yelps as I bear down on it. 'You will do no harm!' I command.

The child runs to the safety of an open doorway.

'Enough, we have work to do,' the other man states.

They wander, they search and they find.

Their response causes Release and I to smile.

'Hanif, how is this possible?'

They walk around the sheep pen and up to the sparse land where the livestock are kept. Goats, sheep and their young are fit and healthy.

'We must report back.'

'How exactly? I don't know that I want to.'

'We can't stay here Osahar.'

'When he finds out, what will happen to us?' Hanif asks nervously.

'It's not our fault that their livestock are still alive,' Osahar states, trying to convince himself as much as Hanif.

The shadows are uneasy. They are reading the situation with much more clarity now.

The spies have little choice. We follow as they inspect further flocks throughout the settlement, each time more hopeful that the animals are dead. They turn and head back to the palace. Their report will be given that even though the Egyptian livestock has perished, the Hebrew livestock lives.

'I don't think that will go down so well with their Ra.' Release laughs.

Days have passed since the spies returned with their report.

Eliora watches as her two uncles fill small sacks with the soot from the empty furnace where the Egyptian animals were burned. The smell of burning flesh had filled the air for several days. But the pharaoh still holds her people here. He has seen the destruction of the livestock, and instead of letting them go he stands hardened to them. The people have traded with lands near and far to gain back the lost wealth of animals and are indifferent once again.

Eliora, Caleb and her people set off to their unceasing work, while Moses and Aaron head in the opposite direction. Release follows them, while I stand guard over Eliora.

She is struggling today.

The heat felt relentless, even this early in the morning.

Caleb quietly worked at her side. Eliora noticed the dark shadows under his eyes. Maybe he was worrying about her being here, but even now, he must see it as the lesser of the two evils. A sharp pang of guilt raked through her stomach. She watched as he took another handful of mud from the trough and threw it into the mould. The measure was perfect as he pushed it into shape and smoothed the top with his knuckles. He lifted the wood to reveal another brick in the long line already made.

Eliora stood chopping the straw into manageable lengths. It was a welcome change to foraging, although some Egyptians seemed intent on giving straw to the Hebrews in the past few days. Perhaps they felt that by sparing her people a little of their work they would be overlooked in the disasters that were falling on their own people.

Each time Eliora finished and scattered the chopped straw into the mud treading pits she had thought that she could take a short break, only to see a fresh delivery of straw. The heat was so intense.

She reached down and grabbed a handful. Standing up, her breath caught and the view spun around her before she collapsed to the ground.

She woke to the sound of harsh shouting and cool water dabbed on her face.

'Get back to work!' came the ruthless Egyptian master's voice.

'Please, let me just see that she is alright,' Caleb begged.

'Get back.'

Eliora opened her eyes and saw the guard raise his rod to Caleb before he struck him across his back. Caleb doubled over then slowly rose to his feet.

'It's fine Caleb. I'm fine,' she said struggling to sit up.

Dinah pulled at Eliora's hand to help her stand.

The guard made to strike Caleb again, Eliora signalled for him to hurry back to work.

'You don't look well,' Dinah whispered.

'I'll be fine. I just need some water.'

'Here.' Dinah pushed the water skin into Eliora's hand.

Before Eliora could drink, she crumpled to the ground and vomited.

'Get that girl out of here!' the master commanded.

Dinah tilted back the water skin and let it trickle over Eliora's face. 'Any better?'

'Thanks.'

'Lean on me. I'll get you home.'

'But I need to work.'

'Let someone else do it.'

Eliora turned to see Caleb hesitate, his brow wrinkled with worry.

The slave master showed little mercy and hit him again.

'It's no good you being here,' Dinah said as she ushered Eliora out. 'He'll only get beaten more.'

She couldn't argue and leaned on Dinah to lead her back home.

Eliora welcomed the coolness of the house. Her grandmother was out on some errand, so Dinah sat her down in the shade.

'You don't look well Elli.'

'I haven't been feeling well for the last couple of days.'

'Maybe you just aren't used to being in the sun.' Dinah called from outside as she ladled some water into a beaker. 'Do you think you are going to be sick again?'

'It will pass,' Eliora said quietly as she thought about the pattern of the past few days.

She became incredibly still as a terrible thought took root.

Dinah walked in and held out the beaker. 'Here you are,' she said impatiently.

Eliora was shaken from her horror. 'Thanks.' She took the drink and tried to smile. 'You had best get back, I'll be fine, I guess.'

'If you like. I'll see you tomorrow.'

Her companion poses as a friend. There are outward signs of care but I can see the depths of her heart. She is glad Eliora suffers. Firstly, she feels Eliora deserves punishment and secondly, she can stay away from the pits for the rest of the day, Caleb would not discipline her for her absence.

Eliora does suffer, no matter what Dinah feels.

She has pieced together the facts and feels violated and angry.

'How s this fair? As if what he did to me was not enough.' She weeps bitterly in defeat.

Now sits feeling lonely and hurt. But she is not alone, she is never alone.

'It can't be true, it can't. That is just cruel,' Eliora mutters to herself.

She tried to recall when she last bled. Could it really be six weeks ago? 'This cannot be happening to me.' She retched.

She felt disgusted at the thing that was growing inside of her. An act of such violence could not produce anything of value or beauty.

'Why is this happening to me?' She thought about Caleb. How would he take this news? He would surely leave her now. How could she escape this?

'Why are you doing this to me?' she cried out.

There came no reply.

'Well if you refuse to help me, I'll sort this out myself.'

Eliora dashed out of the house and headed for the Egyptian border.

I follow after her. Her plans are to harm, but the Creators plan is for good.

I watch as Release follows Moses and Aaron.

They walk with confidence towards the pharaoh's procession. He is inspecting the large monuments engraved with his image.

A hush falls over the crowd as Moses and Aaron draw near.

The creature flames with fury when it sees them. It stands tall and powerful, towering over the pharaoh and all other living things. It has lost the look of mild indignation it once had. It sees the threat but will not stand aside.

A long clawed hand rests on the pharaoh's shoulder. It increases its grip as the men stop a short way off.

'What now?' It hisses exasperated and throws its arms wide. 'I will not let them go. You seem to think that I will give them over to you. I am not as weak as you.' It steps forward, pushing aside the humans. 'You have such little power. I have gained so much. My choice has made me great. The whole nation bows to me. I control what happens here and there is nothing that you, your so called host and your feeble humans can do about it.'

'Go ahead Moses,' Release gently instructs.

Moses thrusts his hands into the bag and lifts out two fistfuls of soot, Aaron copies.

Without a word, Moses and Aaron throw it into the air.

The creature begins to laugh.

I see Release breathe deeply, and then he blows.

The air spirals and swirls, causing the robes and tunics to whip and flap. The soot rises, a dirty funnel against the blue sky.

He stops blowing and the soot ceases to twist, but spreads out over the land of Egypt, like a thin mist, bleaching the colour from the sky, turning it grey. The dust begins to float down. The tiny particles glitter as they fall.

'Is that the best you can do?' The creature taunts.

Release stands, unmovable, unshakeable.

The first flecks of dust land on in the crowd. Then the cries of pain turn heads.

Angry red welts rise on the exposed skin.

Release encourages Moses to leave and they move away from the confused crowd.

'Get this stuff off me.' The pharaoh's voice rings out. 'Cover me over. Don't let that dust touch me. Get me back to the palace. Bring me my magicians.'

Eliora knows the place she needs to go. She rushes towards the streets of the Egyptian people. She is so self occupied, she doesn't notice the lack of interest in her. The market is nearly deserted and the streets are unusually quiet. She asks an old man, quickly clearing away his stall for directions.

She finds herself standing outside a heavy wooden door painted with a hieroglyph of a rounded vase, what looks to be an upturned bowl and stick.

She hesitates.

Even she is unsure now.

Again she thinks of what it is growing inside of her and fear grips her.

She knocks on the door.

An irritated reply comes from inside and Eliora enters.

The room was cool and cramped.

A long wide bench stood against the far wall and shelves were littered with bowls, tubs and wooden images. The floor had woven rugs scattered over it and the edges of the room were lined with reed baskets.

'I told you to go away.' A voice came from the back of the house. 'There is nothing I can do about the sores.'

'Excuse me,' Eliora said quietly. 'I need your help.'

A woman hobbled into the main room, leaning on a stick. Her long dark hair streaked with white and clothes daubed with dirt. Her arms were inflamed with red pustules and her face was caked in drying mud.

'Help?'

'Yes.' However, Eliora looked at her filth and began to think otherwise.

'And why would I help you? Child of the god of the plagues.'

'You make people well again?' Eliora asked in her basic Egyptian.

'I used to,' she said bitterly, and scratched at her arm, then winced. 'I've never seen this skin complaint before, and it appears I can't heal this.'

'I need you to get the baby out. I don't want it.'

'How are you not covered with boils?'

'I don't know.'

'You are one of them!' the woman accused. 'Why should I help you?'

'I have treasures. Things of value.'

'I don't want anything that you could offer me.'

'What do you want then?'

The old woman approached her and wagged a sore covered finger in her face. 'Your people are nothing but trouble to us. I ought to rip it out for you, it would be one less to hate. But why do you want it gone?'

'It is there by mistake.'

'Oh! You are not married! You are ashamed are you?'

'No, I'm not married. I need it gone.'

'If you had come yesterday, I would have helped you.'

'But now?'

'I will not help you now. It is better that you suffer. We suffer because of you and your kind.' The woman took her stick and began to push Eliora towards the door.

'Please!' Eliora begged protecting herself. 'Please! I need your help.'

'I will not help you. I will never help you.' She prodded and pushed. 'Get out! Get out!'

I bend down and offer my help. I push with the old woman.

'Eliora, get out of here.'

Eliora gives up and is forced outside the house. The door closes with a firm bang. She is not welcome here.

I leave the infected house and follow Eliora closely. She pays no attention to where she is going.

The streets are deathly quiet, but even if they were bustling with life, no one would approach a girl with such a wild expression.

Guiding her back to the settlement is hard work. She wanders and will not focus.

It was late afternoon by the time Eliora reached her home. Her lips were cracked and her mouth dry. She wandered into the house and ladled out a beaker full of water. The liquid was tepid and quenched her thirst, but brought on a new bout of nausea. There was nothing for it. Eliora retired to bed where she quickly fell asleep.

21

New Life

Eliora could hear voices from the other room.

There was a gentle rap on the door before it was opened a little.

Her mother appeared. 'Caleb is here. He wants to see you.'

'I'm not feeling very well.'

'I told him that. He is being very persistent.'

'Tell him I'll speak to him when I feel better.'

'Elli, please! I want to talk to you.' Came Caleb's voice from the other room.

'Eliora, what harm will it do for him to see you? He doesn't have to stay long.'

'Fine. Just give me a minute,' Eliora said, straightening the blanket and adjusting her shawl.

Her mother left the room and pulled the door to.

The nausea had passed as she had slept, but Eliora had stayed in bed for the rest of the evening, hoping for some time alone to think. Barely any time had passed before there was an urgent knocking at the door.

Eliora took a deep breath to steady herself. 'Come in.'

Caleb pushed the door open and walked slowly towards her, his urgency lost. He had changed from his muddied work clothes and had washed off the day's work. He carried a small wooden plate with a barley roll, a bunch of grapes and chunk of goats' cheese, in his other hand was a beaker.

'Well hello there!' he smiled. 'Glad to hear that you are feeling better. What's so wrong with seeing me then?'

'Nothing.' Eliora quickly thought of an excuse. 'Just thought you wouldn't want to see me ill that's all.'

'You forget. I saw that this morning.' He approached her raised bed and perched on the side. 'Your mother thinks you should eat something,' he said handing her the plate.

'Thanks,' she said but she set the plate to one side.

'You look a little sunburnt. Do you want some ointment?'

'I'll be fine.'

'I didn't think you had been out in the sun that long today.'

'I went for a walk,' she said defensively.

'I thought you were ill.'

'Are you angry at me Caleb? Because I'm really not well enough to argue.'

'No. I just thought you were coming home after this morning.' Caleb frowned. 'Why are you angry with me?'

'I'm not feeling well Caleb, that's all.'

Caleb sighed. His posture relaxed as he reached for her hand.

Eliora looked down at his hands clasped around hers. They were strong and very warm.

'Caleb ...'

'You know, you really should eat.'

'I'm not hungry.'

'But you need to keep your strength up, especially now.'

Eliora pulled away her hands and stared wide eyed at Caleb. His face was calm and peaceful.

'What?' she questioned.

'It is important that you take care of yourself.'

'That is not what you said,' Eliora accused.

Caleb reached over to take her hand once more. She reluctantly let him hold it.

He smoothed his finger over the bracelet at her wrist.

'Lots has happened since I gave you this.'

'I know,' she replied sadly.

'Things will never be the same.'

Eliora nodded and her eyes began to sting with tears. How was she ever going to let him go?

'I still want to marry you.'

Eliora sat very still. 'Why do you say that?'

'Just so that you know.'

'I don't think that you do want to marry me. Not really.'

'Then you know very little about me. I want to marry you, the sooner the better.'

'I think you should wait. At least for a little while.'

'Maybe you think I should wait eight or nine months.'

'Caleb, what do you mean?'

He pressed her hand to his lips. Her breath caught.

'Elli. We both know.'

'Know what exactly?'

He paused. 'The baby.'

How could he know? She searched her memory for anything that would have told him of the dreadful thing. There was only the vomiting at the pits today, there were no other clues. She had only just worked it out herself. 'How?'

'How do I know?'

Eliora nodded.

'I dreamt about it.' She shook her head. 'All this week, I've been having the same dream. What happened this morning, with you collapsing, has happened every night this week,' Caleb stated. 'I know that I am to take care of you and the baby.'

'But this thing,' she said pointing to her stomach with disgust, 'is ...'

'Is innocent.'

'How can you say that?'

'You are innocent of what happened Elli, just as the baby is innocent.'

Eliora considered what Caleb had said. It was true. This baby had not asked to be, yet it was part of the evil act.

'But you don't want it,' she said, and I certainly don't want it, she thought.

'I want you Elli and that baby is part of you.'

'It is also part ... Egyptian,' she admitted shamefully.

'I know.' Caleb smiled sadly. 'I would have planned things differently.' He lowered his gaze. 'I would have planned never to have children at all.'

'No children?'

'I think so. I hadn't really considered how I thought about having children until the dream on that first night. All I know is I would not want to lose you. I'm confident that this will be so different to before. I trust that you will not want anything Egyptian interfering.' He watched as she lowered her gaze. 'I'm here now. I will stand with you. This baby will be our child.'

'Are you sure?'

'I'm certain.'

'I didn't want it,' Eliora whispered. 'I went to get rid of it.'

'What did you do? But you didn't, I mean the baby is still alright isn't it?'

'That doesn't make up for the fact that I tried.' She began to sob.

'Well, we just need to move forward from here.' Caleb tried to reassure her.

'I'm not sure I want to move forward. I don't want this baby.'

Caleb frowned. 'I'm not going to leave you alone.' Then added gently. 'Please Elli. Trust me.'

'I do trust you. But you can't want this.'

'I want you.'

'What about the baby?'

'I want that too.'

'Someone else's child?'

'You can't punish this child for what happened. Anyway, I would be its father in every sense that really mattered,' Caleb replied confidently.

'You do want it, don't you?' Eliora said, shocked at his heartfelt response.

'Yes, Elli, I do.'

'How can you be so sure?'

'I've already had a week to think this through. I'm certain this is the right path for us.' He gently placed his hand over her stomach. 'For all of us.'

22

Power

The brothers walk through the shimmering web and on towards the gloom of the palace. They plan to meet Pharaoh at day's break.

It is still dark, but the day has already begun for Moses. He is readying himself as is my friend, Release.

'I think we will need some support. Will you come along too?'

I look down at Eliora. She sleeps soundly at last. Her day will be difficult, but she will not be alone. Caleb will be here soon.

'Gladly,' I reply.

They walk briskly, Moses sharing the message that is to be delivered.

The river slithers past the palace grounds and all appears quiet and peaceful. But we know that the palace is restless.

'You haven't been at the palace for a while. The reception has become increasingly hostile each time we arrive.' Release warns.

'But they must see that they cannot continue to hold on.'

'You see that and I see that, but their stubbornness may not be all it appears to be.'

I frown.

'Just wait. You will see.'

Moses and Aaron wait at the doors where Pharaoh welcomes the new day. The sky is lightening and activity is spilling out to greet us.

Several large creatures burst through the walls in an attempt to intimidate. They stand, swords drawn and eyes blazing. Their putrid breath hangs in the morning air mingling with the feeble mist.

The ceremonial doors open and Pharaoh steps out. He looks weary. His arms and legs are covered in angry red sores and his chiselled features are obscured by a layer of ochre cream.

The beast cloaks his human host with its body. It twists around his torso and towers over his head in an act of superiority. The flames that once resembled a bird and then a crocodile now have another animal form, but this is one of myth. An image from one of their tales. It is long muzzled and fierce. The flames no longer burn lazily but have energy.

Before the pharaoh even opens his mouth, we have been seen.

Suddenly the space between us is swarming with obsidian bodies, snarling and cursing our presence.

'Get back!' Their commander shouts and Pharaoh steps forward.

'You! Again!' Pharaoh starts, pointing an accusing finger at the brothers in our care. 'What now?'

Aaron steps forward and begins to deliver his message. 'The God of the Hebrews says ...'

'...Let my people go! Yes I know what he says.' The creatures cackle with one another and the irritated reply from the human leader.

The creature conducts the chorus of laughter with its own. It is not moved.

'There is more,' Aaron adds bravely. He stands firm as the creatures creep towards him.

'Really? Enlighten me!' Pharaoh mocks.

'He says that he has allowed you to remain so that he may show his power to you and to the people. So that all would know of him.' Aaron is unaware of the hissing that accompanies this message.

'I will not let your people go!' The pharaoh replies in a bored voice and turns away.

'He also says,' Aaron continues and the pharaoh stops moving away, 'that as you continue to exult yourself against his people by not letting them go he will send another disaster upon you.'

'Any specifics in that?' Pharaoh replies angrily.

'Yes. About this time tomorrow there will be the heaviest hail this land has ever and will ever see. You are to bring in your servants and livestock. Any left outside will die.'

It amazes me that even in this exhibition of hatred for their self-sufficiency, the Creator is still willing to be merciful and gracious. He still wants to give them the opportunity to change and to trust in Him instead.

The pharaoh is consumed with anger. The creature at his back is furious.

'I am in command here. I exult myself because I am superior. I am god.'

Then I see it, the slightest flicker of fear, the smallest understanding of defeat on the horizon. I recognize that tone, yet have not seen it within the ranks of demons before. It has the flavour of the work of one of the host. Is there a friend among all these foes? If I look closely, I can see the slight glimmer of gold on the occasional wing, the shimmer of a speck floating in the air.

Release raises his eyebrows as I glance at him.

They know nothing of it.

These creatures, once used to worshipping in glory have resorted to worshipping in a lesser, reflected glory. They do not see their intruder or the doubt that crossed Pharaoh's face and the terrified fear that is shaking him from the centre of his being.

But it is there for such a short space of time. He rapidly adjusts to be the god of his people and any people he subdues. He will not be shaken and the Creator will be glorified.

'I will not let your people go,' he declares, marching back into the palace and out of sight.

The army of creatures hiss and scream at us as they leave. Only two of the largest creatures stand guard, ensuring we do not follow. But there is no need to follow. We already have our presence in the palace.

When we are alone, on our way back to the Remnant, I ask about what I thought I saw.

'Many lives will be affected by the coming events. The things that are seen and experienced will turn some misplaced lives to the Creator, only as of yet, they do not know it.'

'But our friend was within the enemy ranks.'

'True. But the Creator will turn all things to good, even if it isn't clear to begin with. The plan must be completed. Pharaoh's heart must be hardened.'

Moses rises early. It has been almost a full day since his encounter with the king of the Egyptians. He stands at the edge of the settlement and stretches out his hand toward the sky.

Great cumulonimbus clouds are forming, swirling and bubbling above the land not too far away, rising ever higher. From a distance the billowing shape appears soft, but internally it is anything but friendly.

The minute water vapour particles begin to collide and join to make water droplets. They would fall if it were not for the updraft. Instead, they ascend higher into the cloud, all the time moving through colder air. The temperature drops below freezing point and gets increasingly cold the further the ice pellets travel.

Moving sometimes at high speeds and other times more slowly in the changeable wind, the pellets grow; layer upon layer of condensation sticks to the freezing surface, trapped by the chill.

The frozen water droplets, varied in size, collide within the cloud and cling to one another forming larger masses the size of small stones and rocks. Still the updraft carries them.

Higher and higher they are carried. Howling wind passes them through super-cooled temperatures. They continue to grow.

The updraft struggles to keep them aloft. The mass of the ice is too heavy to bear. They fall at increasing speeds, free from the cloud, gathering more pellets to their surface even as they fall.

But this is an exceptional case. A larger cloud awaits, a much stronger updraft catches the stones and carries them through the process again. The stones grow to massive proportions, layering with freezing vapour and smashing together.

The billowing cloud expands and spreads. Moving quickly with the south easterly wind, the storm passes harmlessly over Goshen and approaches the land of Egypt.

The heat of the day quickly chills as the sun is obscured by thick, dark clouds. For the people living here, the sight is a warning. The weather changes so little day to day, that the threatening appearance sends rivulets of panic through the land.

The updraft cannot hold the ammunition any longer.

The collected ice is expelled from the storm, falling rapidly from the cloud, increasing in speed, slowing down for nothing. The hailstones slam towards the ground. Whatever stands in their way is pounded and crushed.

Young plants are shredded and flattened in the onslaught. Fields are decimated and trees broken and shattered. Imported cattle, donkeys and camels, that are unprotected, stampede for shelter; their young have no chance of survival. The hailstones show no mercy. Skulls are crushed and bodies are broken.

Egyptians that had not found shelter when the dark cloud loomed, shield their heads with their arms and rush to escape the battering. They were warned. Those that escape huddle together in the chilled air, nursing bruises and cuts. Wet clothes add to the numbing of their bodies.

The chunks of ice pound the ground, bouncing and splintering on the hard packed dust. Crashing vibrations shake the earth in the relentless and building storm.

All this time, the cloud has been building an electric charge. The charge is now so intense that it is affecting the earth's surface, repelling electrons deeper into the earth and causing the air to break down. A path for the electric current to flow is forming, glowing purple within the cloud. The current is finding a route of least resistance.

On the ground, objects begin to respond to the cloud, invisibly reaching out for it, waiting patiently. But it is the current in the cloud that reaches down and makes the connection.

It forks this way and that, flowing through the cloud before it touches the ground. The overwhelming current explodes through the air with a brilliant blue white flash; the heat so intense that it melts the sand where it strikes.

The screams are engulfed in the deafening thunder as the shockwave radiates away from the strike. Anything still left standing nearby is shaken by the energy before it flows away.

Lightning strike after strike pummels the ice laden ground as fire and ice, opposing forces, work together.

The howling wind, shaking ground and ear-splitting thunder rouse the Remnant from their beds.

The people of Goshen watch the show unfold.

They are protected. The cloud does not cover their land.

They are observers at the edge of disaster. Many climb to their roofs, searching out a better view.

Celebrations are heartfelt but muted. They see their oppressor's land being battered by the Creator while they enjoy the warmth of the sun. They believe that surely they will go free now.

Eliora stands at the boundary line. She watches the dark clouds swirl and dip to the ground. Hailstones land repeatedly a short distance from her feet but never cross to Goshen. Caleb stands with her, his strong arm wrapped around her. They do not speak, they only observe. They see the justice in the attack and are glad for it.

Behind them Eliora's family gathers. From the oldest to the youngest they regard the scene, each feeling something different; elation, sorrow, relief, fear, superiority, insignificance.

Through the blurry landscape I see figures approaching; two men crouching beneath a wooden board accompanied by an old friend. As they draw closer, I can see my friend leaning over the men as they run through the pounding hail storm, protecting them. The hailstones sizzle and smash at my friend's back. The wooden board is dented and split.

They speed to the boundary, shivering and panting.

As soon as they cross the line, the warm sun greets them. The heavy thumping of the hail stops and they look up, wide-eyed.

'Well met friend!' I say as I clasp my dear friend's broad hand.

'Hunter, for this mission.'

'Well Hunter, it is so good to see you again.' He hugs me then moves over to grab Release.

My tall friend wears dark clothing, in contrast to mine. His skin is dark in tone but there is a dazzling translucent quality to it. He has startling golden eyes.

'I didn't know you were here, I haven't seen you.'

'But I have seen you! I have been at the palace.'

'That was you yesterday?'

'Indeed. I am hunting out those who can be saved.'

'Dangerous mission.'

He nods.

The men that are with him are wearing the royal colours of the house of Pharaoh. Eliora backs away, but her mother offers them water. They guzzle down the drinks then they approach Moses and Aaron.

'My lord Pharaoh wishes to see you. You are to come to the Palace at once.'

Release shelters the brothers as they leave the safety of the settlement. Hunter does the same for the messengers. They have changed in the few minutes rest with the Remnant. New colours surround them and there is a scent of sweet perfume. I understand now, why Hunter accompanied them. These two are part of the Creator's harvest.

23

Decimation

Eliora gazed out at the aftermath of the storm. The fields of the Egyptians previously filled with barley and flax were destroyed by the pummelling of the hail. There was no grain to harvest. But there was hope for the nation. The wheat and spelt were still in the early stages of growing. With a little care, the young plants would still produce a crop.

She compared it to her own garden plot. The vines were heavy laden with grapes, the herbs strong and rigorous and the juicy fruits ripening more each day.

Her uncles had gone with the messengers and by late afternoon the storm stopped. There was no wind to carry it away, it just ceased to exist, fading in a moment. The abruptness unnerved Eliora.

Today, her uncles had gone again to the palace while she worked alongside her people in the pits. The heat was intense and she found little relief in the warm cup of water. Her stomach still felt unsettled and the sickness had not passed. Caleb kept a close watch on her and had given her the easier task of collecting straw for the bricks. The straw was plentiful now, after the storm had crushed the barley. Eliora didn't have to travel far. The wet, damaged stalks smelt strongly of mould. They had been ploughed from the fields and left in vast bundles. The Egyptians were not supposed to help the Hebrews, but the onslaught of catastrophic events had made them fearful of the Hebrew god. They did not want to anger him further by causing more suffering.

The smell wafted as she grabbed a handful to stack into her basket. The reek stirred her stomach and she was sick.

Eliora leaned back, eyes closed and took a deep breath. She wiped the sweat from her face with the shawl that was protecting her head. When she opened her eyes, Dinah was watching her intently.

'You're not still ill are you?'

'It's just the smell. That's all.'

'It isn't that bad,' Dinah scoffed frowning at Eliora.

Eliora rubbed her aching stomach, but left her hand to linger. Dinah's eyes widened and she gasped.

Eliora saw that Dinah was focused on her hand caressing her belly. She quickly dropped it to her side. But the damage had been done. Dinah straightened her stance and shook her head. Eliora could feel heat in her cheeks.

'I would never have thought it of you!' Dinah said. 'You are a disgrace to the Hebrew nation!' She turned to walk away.

'Dinah!' Eliora begged. 'Please. It's not what you think.'

Dinah looked over her shoulder. 'Really? You are so "look at me, I'm so special!" Had to go one step further and get yourself pregnant did you?'

Eliora looked at the ground.

'You make out that you are so much better than the rest of us. But just look at you!' And she marched off, head held high.

Eliora picked up her nearly full basket and ran after her.

'Dinah!' She called. 'Wait!' Eliora caught up. 'Please Dinah. Don't say anything.'

Dinah gave her a revolted look. 'You don't want Caleb to look bad?'

'It's not his,' Eliora said before thinking.

'Not his!' Dinah exclaimed. 'You are disgusting! You can't just do that to him.'

'He already knows.'

'Of course he does! That is why we all believe he really is going to marry you!' she said laden with sarcasm. 'No one will marry you now. He is probably trying to think a way out of it. I guess if he leaves it long enough, he won't even need to explain.'

'People don't need to know,' pleaded Eliora.

'I'm not talking about people, they'll find out soon enough. I'm talking about Caleb.' Dinah looked down her nose. 'If he already knows, it won't make any difference if I tell him then will it?'

Eliora slowed her pace letting Dinah strut off ahead of her. Maybe she was right. Maybe when the news was out Caleb really wouldn't marry her. He had said he had wanted her, but not children. Eliora's mind became muddled. What was the truth? Dinah's argument made so much more sense than Eliora's memory of a promise. Maybe Caleb really was just going to wait until her shame was on full show for everyone to see. Silent tears ran down her cheeks.

That foul spindly creature is taking hold again. Its weak limbs are strengthening with the words of a so called friend. It clings to Eliora's head like a crown, Its thorn-like spikes digging into her scalp drip with rejection. Its crooning voice whispers lies.

Eliora approached the cutting floor. Dinah had already emptied her load and was lingering near her group of friends at the water container. Eliora begged for pity with her eyes when she caught Dinah's attention, but Dinah just turned away.

Knowing that it was too late to change her friend's mind, Eliora began to unload her basket. She had placed two handfuls of the foul smelling stalks on the cutting floor when a sudden gust of wind caught the loose stalks and threw them up into the air. The wind whipped at her headdress and flapped her clothes. It stopped only briefly than began once again.

Blowing from an easterly direction, the wind carried dust and sand making it difficult to see. The slave masters, knowing what a sandstorm could do sent the Hebrews back to Goshen and fled back to their homes themselves.

Caleb wrapped his cloak over Eliora and huddled her close to him as they stumbled home. The fierce wind was in their faces, pushing them back.

Dinah hurried up to Caleb's other side.

'Isn't this cosy!'

Eliora sighed and drew closer to Caleb.

'There is something you should know about your, how shall I put it, your prospective bride, Caleb.'

Caleb looked down at Eliora. She tried to look strong and fearless, but she knew she had failed when Caleb's brow furrowed with worry.

'She isn't what you think. She isn't pure. She is pregnant by another man!'

'Yes Dinah, I know.'

Even in the roaring wind, Eliora could hear Dinah's shock exclamation.

'Was there anything else you wanted to tell me?'

Dinah didn't say a word. She let the strength of her fury carry her forward and toward the crowd heading home.

'She won't keep quiet you know,' Eliora said sadly.

'How does she know?' Caleb asked, raising his voice over the howling wind.

'She worked it out when I threw up on her shoe, just like everyone else will eventually.'

'Let them come to their own conclusions. Time will teach them what really happened. We know the truth.'

He held her firmly to his side. Eliora couldn't have run away from him if she had wanted to, which she didn't. She was safe.

I see the truth behind Caleb's words. He knows human nature enough to guarantee that there will be those who jump to the wrong conclusions. That Eliora and himself will be the subject of discussion and gossip. That there will be things said and spread through the people that he wants to protect Eliora from. We both know that when this baby arrives that they will have to take back what was judged upon this precious couple.

Eliora is safe.

She needs to listen to the truth. Caleb will not reject her and neither will the Creator. She is allowing the creature to have a foothold in her life. Truth declares that she is accepted as she is. I am named Faithful for a reason. Her Creator is faithful and will continue to be faithful.

Continue to show her the truth Caleb.

My attention is drawn away. The host are busy. I see a multitude on the eastern horizon, ushering the wind. Many look as if they have travelled some distance, their clothes and skin dusty.

There are many more yet to come. They will not arrive until morning, travelling on the wind, with their cargo, keeping it moving. We will wait.

I send word to the guard of the golden mesh to check for damage. The report comes back that the settlement is secure.

The last of the Remnant are through the barrier. The guard station themselves around the perimeter, swords sheathed but ready.

All through the night they have travelled and they are hungry. The swarm is buffeted by the wind. It swirls in a dark mass, blocking out the hazy sunrise.

It reaches the edge of the mighty land of Egypt and the wind drops to a gentle breeze. The friends that have contained them give them free reign.

One after another the locust drop to the ground. Exhausted and hungry they devour the green shoots of wheat and spelt, munching through the drooping leaves. The ground is swathed in the mass of locust bodies. They spread to the left and to the right, marching over the dry ground and buzzing over the water canals. Anything that has any tender growth is targeted; trees and scrubby bushes that are trying to recover from the hail; huge areas sectioned off for crops. The thick band shows no mercy. In their wake, stalks are bare.

Farmers rush in with sticks, shaking the locust from their crops, but they are hopelessly outnumbered. Small clouds of locust rise into the air but they do not go far. They land on more green feed, and tuck in.

Messages are sent into the city. It is not long before the Egyptian people are aware of the attack. And this is how they see it now. This is a persistent attack on them, and they are fearful of the Remnant's God.

Many are sent out to the fields with beating sticks. They are trying to protect their future harvest.

There was no work for the Remnant. The slave masters did not come for them to work at the pits.

Eliora and it seemed the whole settlement welcomed the unaccustomed break in work. She had climbed to the flat roof, stepped over the grapes drying in the sun and stood squinting into the sun. She saw the black swathe across the Egyptian land. She watched it rise and then fall to the earth again. The green banks of the river looked different, upstream they had faded from lush fresh growth to a diminished hint. She knew that the insects, having attacked the crops, were now eating their way through the reeds.

Her attention was caught by the giggles from the street below. Voices drifted up to her.

'No! Where did you hear that?'

'I can't say,' said a female voice in hushed tones, 'but let's just say that it comes from a reliable source.'

'Well, that surprises me.'

'She never did say why they threw her out of the palace did she.'

'I thought they said the cats had all died.'

'Well, I heard that they found out she was expecting. You know, they banished her mother until she had given birth to her way back when. Went back with open arms when the time came though.'

'But she isn't married yet. That Caleb!' exclaimed the shocked voice.

'He has been tricked by her.'

'He'll have to marry her now.'

'Well, I heard he isn't even the father.'

'No! Well which of our men has she seduced then?'

'I blame the mother,' came the loud reply. 'They always have thought themselves to be special.'

'Maybe since Moses came, she feels she needs to draw the attention back to herself again.'

'Well, she certainly has the attention now that she's pregnant!'

There was a fit of giggles and the gossips were gone.

Eliora felt sick, but it wasn't morning sickness. She knew her mother was inside the house, unable to cross to the palace because of the strong winds and sandstorm. Why did they choose to have their conversation outside her house?

'Elli, is it true?'

Eliora could hear the pain in her mother's voice without the need to turn round. 'Yes Mama.'

'How could you do this?'

'It isn't what they said. It's not like that.' She turned, desperate for her mother to understand. She saw the fresh tears running down her mother's cheeks.

'Would you like to explain?'

'I'm not sure you want to hear.'

'I want to hear whatever you have to say.' She approached and sat in the shade of the wall at the edge of the roof. 'Sit with me.'

Eliora sat quietly for a while, but her mother waited patiently. She stared down at her feet as she told the whole story. Not once did her mother interrupt, not once did she look up.

'So Caleb said he would still marry me, but I'm not sure he will now, not when everyone else thinks I'm some kind of ...' She huffed.

'That doesn't sound much like the Caleb we know.'

'You really think he will still take me?' Eliora asked facing her mother for the first time.

Her mother nodded. 'Are you all right? I wish you had told me sooner.'

'And what would you have done if I had?'

'That's a good question. I don't know.' She smiled sympathetically. 'Maybe hurt that prince. Maybe the same as you. Maybe I would have tried to get rid of it too.'

'I can't do that Mama.'

'I know sweetheart. I wouldn't ask you to,' her mother said gently and put her arm around Eliora, she felt like a little girl again. Her burden seemed to lift slightly.

'I've raised you. We can raise this little one.'

'What about me? Caleb said standing on the roof.

'Caleb! What brings you here?' Eliora's mother asked.

'I've come to see my bride.'

'I wasn't expecting you until later,' Eliora said, sniffing.

'I wasn't expecting the settlement to be buzzing with our news and I thought you might need some support.'

Jochebed looked Caleb full in the face. 'We need to know what you are going to do Caleb.'

'I'm going to stand by your daughter. I love her and will not let some loose tongues change how I feel. I am going to marry her and raise this child like my own, and hopefully one day, have more children.'

'I am glad to hear that you are the man we know.' Jochebed said as she got to her feet. She turned, took Eliora's hand and helped her up. She led her daughter to Caleb. 'She is yours. I know that you will treat her with the love and kindness she has never known.' And she placed Eliora's hand in his then returned to the house.

'You really mean that?' Eliora asked.

'It is no good is it. You will not believe me until we get married!' Caleb drew her closer to him and wrapped his arms around her. 'We need to stop this news dead.'

'I'm not sure that is possible,' Eliora said miserably. 'Everyone will have an opinion of me.'

'And whose opinion matters?'

'I know I should say you, but I care what other people think.'

Caleb stared over at the locust fields. Another large dark cloud was landing nearby.

'We just have to hold up our heads. We have nothing to be ashamed of. We know the truth Elli, and so does our God. The people that care about us will fight our battles with us. Let other people think what they like. Let them devour whatever information they want, they are just like the locust, when all the juicy greenery is gone, they'll go too.'

Eliora looked out at the fields too. 'But there are so many locust.'

'But there isn't much to feed on is there?'

'I know, but what little there is they will decimate.'

'They can only eat what is above the ground. We need to give them reason to leave us alone.'

'It is going to hurt Caleb, especially you.'

'I can cope with it. Don't you go worrying about me. What does it matter what people think?'

Eliora huffed.

'No really. The more upset you are by them the more power you give them. Answer me this, do you still believe you will be free?'

'They can't keep us much longer. Everything they have is being destroyed.'

'Well, the same goes for us. When the rumours are destroyed by the truth, not that we have to tell it, they will see the truth eventually, just like the pharaoh, and have no choice but to set us free.'

'I'm not sure I want to be ravaged by plagues before that happens.'

'Some lessons are painful.'

'I know.'

'I am going to marry you Elli, I promise. Are you ready for it?'

'Everything is done.'

'That is not what I asked! Are *you* ready?'

Eliora paused. In her mind it was the clearest path. She looked up into Caleb's expectant face. 'There is nothing I want more.'

24

Darkness and Light

The locust had been allowed to ruin the Egyptian crops. Pharaoh had been stubborn and had watched as their scarce food source was rapidly devoured. Vast, dark bands of locust invaded the Egyptian land, houses and palace hunting eagerly for their next meal.

Her uncles had been summoned, and within couple of hours the westerly wind had picked up and carried away the locust swarm and drowned them in the sea.

The wind, however, had not carried away the gossip. Eliora was aware of the whispering and sudden silence when she walked past her neighbours. She tried to hold her head up.

She spent more time inside than out. Her uncle Moses didn't walk round with an air of triumph, but seemed almost sorrowful.

'He wants a compromise,' Moses offered as an answer to Eliora's mother. 'He will allow some of us to worship, but not all.'

'He can't hold on much longer. The whole nation will be ruined.'

'He will wait,' Moses said as he paced.

'It seems he is not satisfied with the damage,' she suggested.

'It isn't that. Our God knows when we will leave. There is still work to be done with us as well as them.'

'But we are ready to go,' Eliora said from the corner of the room.

'Are we?'

'I am. I can't wait to get out of this place, to be away from them,' Eliora replied quietly, frowning.

Moses looked over at her. 'There are so many things we fail to understand, Elli. You will have justice, but it will be on God's terms not yours.'

Eliora felt like she had been scolded and got up to leave. How dare her uncle judge her like everyone else?

'Caleb is quite remarkable. He understands these things. He knows that God's wrath is much more effective than a woman's, or any human's.'

'What is that supposed to mean?' Eliora stormed.

'Elli! Don't speak like that,' her mother reprimanded.

'You have in your mind exactly how you want this played,' Moses said, continuing despite his niece. 'You can't run away from the things that hurt you. I learned that,' he said sadly, 'because one day you may just have to face them again, and believe me, facing them when you are older and somewhat wiser in your own eyes may not be pleasant.'

Eliora huffed.

'Elli. Face your fears. Deal with them now. Trust in the love Caleb has for you, because he trusts in the Lord and there is no better place to be. Just look at Pharaoh, he trusts in himself and the false gods, that all incidentally point to him too. His misguided trust will only lead to destruction.'

She sighed. Her uncle had a point. Caleb trusted in something much bigger and more powerful than himself. This being, Caleb's God, was working for their freedom. This being, the God Caleb knew, continued to show mercy to them by protecting them while attacking their captors. Caleb's God could turn a river into foul blood, pour frogs, flies and beetles over the land until it crawled like a living thing. He could bring disease, fire and hail at his will. He could bring locust until the sky was darkened. It was his miraculous persuasion to get the right thing accomplished. He wanted to vindicate his people, to rid them of the evil false gods. But he could also be patient and willing to see change. Each time Moses and Aaron had been summoned, Caleb's God had stepped in and bought relief. It wasn't out of stupidity that he ceased the punishment, he knew that Pharaoh would not give them up. He saw Pharaoh's heart.

Eliora was suddenly aware of a God that was willing to show awesome power but also be interested in a heart attitude. Her heart attitude must be of importance too. If she were to examine it what would she find?

She smiled as convincingly as she could then swiftly left the house.

She wandered along the busy streets, only taking notice of the path she was taking and not of the looks from her neighbours.

What did her heart look like? It was a question she had never really considered before. She should be honest about it, after all, nothing was hidden from Caleb's God. But was he her God? If he was, what would he make of her heart? She thought of the things that she had once held dear. Of her status in her tribe, of her special role away from the pits, of her pride. It was pride, she recognised it now. She had been proud of the fact she was part of the Egyptian culture, she never corrected the idealised view others had of her role, she let them believe she had been special. She had embraced the idols and gods, she had accepted them. She was once happier to be part of the Egyptian people than to be a Hebrew. What else was in her heart? There was fear. Fear of what was to come but the greater fear was what others thought of her.

Hatred. Hatred was a big one. She hated Horusisus, what he had done to her and the damage he had caused. Her hatred for him was like a chasm deep within her.

She hated her uncles for causing her trouble, although, when she lingered on that, it wasn't really their fault, but it was God's. Caleb's God had made it worse. It was his fault.

She stopped suddenly.

How could she think such a thing? Was it God's fault? The bad things that had happened to her were a reaction to the punishment he had poured out, but it was the pharaoh and the Egyptians that were the slave masters. They had taken God's people, enslaved them and refused to let them go. She had suffered cruelly at their hands. It was her God who was going to free her. It was her God who was showing her mercy, even now, by leading her to him.

She had reached the garden. It was empty of people, which was a welcome sight for Eliora. A solitary tear rolled down her cheek. She realised, all this time she had been depending on other things: her grandmother's role being passed down to her mother then to her; Horusisus giving her status in a palace that detested her; Caleb being her rescuer. She had never considered Caleb's God to be her God. She had never depended on him like Caleb did, like Moses did, and yet he had been there for her, he had been faithful even when she hadn't.

As she sat among the herbs, the image of the bowl of clean water came to her mind. He had provided clean water.

'I'm so sorry,' she whispered. 'My heart is a mess. Please, I need you to help me. I can't do this on my own. I want you to be my God.'

I raise my hands high above me. Joy fills me completely and I laugh.

'Hallelujah!' I shout.

The creature hisses and cringes away from me. Its thin body shakes in fear.

'You have no place here! She will never be rejected by the Creator. She is His precious Remnant, adorned with beauty and grace,' I declare, grabbing the lithe body and snapping in in two.

The creature lets out a strangled squeal before it is silenced.

Gold dust twists and turns on a lavender scented breeze. It swirls on the eddies before it settles on Eliora's head.

Her sincere expression breaks into a wide smile.

Peace eases through her body and she stays here for a long time.

The Creator knows the plans He has for her. His timing is perfect.

She is a different person leaving the garden. Nothing looks changed from the outside, except maybe her head is held a little higher, but on the inside she is changed. Caleb has spoken words of truth over her, yet it is not until her Creator speaks over her that she is changed.

As she approaches her street, the neighbours watch. Her head drops a little.

'Look up! You belong to the King!' I encourage.

Her chin rises and a gentle smile lightens her face. Their comments will not determine her character any more.

As she approached her house, she saw people on their roof tops. They were looking towards the city.

She climbed the stairs and joined her mother and grandmother on the roof.

Eliora looked out and it seemed the land had just disappeared, and all there was left was a mass of blackness. The darkness swept across the land. The sight was so strange. Where once the river shone and sparkled – nothing. Where the tall palms and rushes lined the water – nothing. Where the distant shimmering buildings and statues stood, where the fields and irrigation channels criss crossed the land, where the brick making pits lay empty of workers – nothing. Nothing but darkness.

She frowned at her mother.

'The next plague, Elli,' her mother explained.

The darkness seeps from the ground. The pores of the earth open, and tendrils of impenetrable darkness swirl and creep over the ground like an erroneous morning mist. As the darkness steals across the land the light is being drawn from above. Beams of light, replaced with the absence of any light at all. Black rods of darkness, dotted here and there are soon joining making immense patches of deep shadow where no light exists. The darkness spreads with increasing speed across the land of the Egyptians until there is not one place where light can penetrate.

Screams and cries of help issue from the land. Labourers in the fields are lost and have no way of finding home. Mothers call for their children, searching with their hands to find doorways and safe passages. Many frantically attempt to light their night time lamps, but this is futile. This darkness cannot be banished by some will of a human, it is not weightless like the night but it has a mass, a heaviness that is other worldly. Even for me it is dark and difficult to navigate.

The palace is in uproar. Pharaoh shouts to his officials, demanding light. They cannot obey. He commands his magicians to do their work, but they are unable to mix potions in the darkness. There is muttering behind the scenes. Pharaoh is unable to bring the sun, he is unable to banish the night. He has lost his powers to the Hebrew god.

The creatures that inhabit the palace thrive in the darkness. They consider the environment one of celebration.

The darkness is thick with sulphur as the creatures cackle and shout out their approval. The rush of enthusiasm is sickening. Flapping wings stir the stench through the air as they speed to find a victim.

A horn sounds in the Hebrew settlement, but Eliora was distracted by the absence of light in the distance.

Eliora doesn't notice as Caleb joins them on the roof.

She was startled to hear his voice and turned.

'Jochebed,' he says formally. 'I have come with my bride price. I wish to marry Eliora today.'

Eliora felt heat rising in her cheeks. The horn was sounded for her. He has come for her today.

Caleb held a folded woven blanket in his arms. 'There are two goats, which make a rich cheese and a dozen sheep in your fold if you will accept them.' He looked longingly at Eliora and the colour in her cheeks darkened.

'That is an acceptable bride price Caleb,' Jochebed said, taking the blanket. 'She is yours.'

Eliora's mother wrapped her arms around her daughter and squeezed her tightly. 'I hope that you have finished those wedding clothes of yours,' she whispered.

'Weeks ago,' Eliora replied.

Caleb led them from the roof to the ground where a crowd had formed. They were cheering and waving scarves in the air. Eliora studied their faces. Where she had once seen disdain and judgement, now she witnessed joy. She could not help but laugh in response.

Eliora hurried inside followed closely by her mother and grandmother.

'Oh Elli!' Miriam said weeping.

'Mother! That doesn't help. Come on, get her comb and sort her hair out.'

'Jochebed, I am allowed to weep. She will leave us today. They are not sad tears, but happy ones. Caleb is a good man.'

Eliora unfolded her garments. Her dress was of simple design. A full and long sky blue skirt and fitted bodice, with a brightly embroidered shawl tied around her waist.

As they all changed into their wedding clothes Eliora's mother sang and her grandmother joined in.

When they were all dressed, Eliora's grandmother combed and teased her granddaughter's hair, twisting and tying it at her nape. Her mother approached to apply some make up.

'No Mama. I want to go as myself. I don't want anything Egyptian.'

Her mother nodded in approval. 'Of course Elli.' She lifted the veil and fixed it into her hair before gently pulling it over her face. The delicate flowers that Eliora had stitched framed the edge.

'You will need this,' her mother said gently pressing a small object into her hand.

When Eliora looked, she found the gold band that her father used to wear.

'I can't ...' she began.

'Yes you can. It will seal your own marriage. I want you to have it.'

Eliora felt the prickle of tears before they flowed down her cheeks. 'Thank you Mama.'

Jochebed took the corner of her headdress, lifted the veil and wiped her daughter's tears away before dabbing at her own.

'Enough tears. This is a happy day,' her grandmother whispered.

'That it is!' stated Eliora, laughing.

'You look so beautiful.' Jochebed smiled. She bowed her head, raised Eliora's hands and prayed the prayer of their ancestors. 'Our sister, may you increase to thousands upon thousands; may your offspring possess the cities of their enemies.'

Eliora left the house with her mother holding one hand and her grandmother holding the other.

The street was filled with colour. More people had gathered to see the procession to Caleb's house. They cheered and laughed, the small children danced and ran alongside the three women.

Caleb stood in the street a few houses away from his house. He was surrounded by many men and the tribe elder. As Eliora approached, he held out his hand and Jochebed and Miriam each placed the hand they were holding into his. In this way Eliora was led forward to the covered porch of Caleb's house.

The tribe elder stood before them and the crowd hushed.

'You are consecrated to me with this ring,' Caleb said in a clear voice as he slid the band from his smallest finger and placed it onto Eliora's. It was not cold, but as warm as Caleb.

Eliora's mouth was dry. She swallowed then taking the worn gold band her father had owned, she opened Caleb's hand and eased it down his finger. 'You are consecrated to me with this ring.'

The elder filled a goblet with wine and handed it to Caleb. He drank a little of it then offered it to Eliora. She stood, just staring at him for a moment. This was the moment. This is what would seal their lives together. She reached out and drank from the cup.

The crowd clapped, cheered and shouted. The air vibrated with jubilant noise.

Suddenly Eliora was surrounded by familiar faces. Women reached out to kiss her cheeks and children pushed through the gaps to cuddle her. Through the bustle, she did not let go of Caleb's hand. She could feel his tight hold of her and was glad of it.

As the crowd moved around, family came to join them.

Her relatives stood around them smiling and laughing. Then there was Caleb's mother, who reached over and kissed their clasped hands, and Caleb's brother and his wife. These were her new family, the people she was to live with. A small part of her ached for her own family, and she wanted to live there still, but there was so much to distract her that the feeling went almost without notice.

The families went into the house where the table was laden with a feast. Roasted meat, stew in rich gravy, granary breads and sliced fruit, spiced vegetables and stuffed salads. Caleb had raided his allotment to provide such a spread. There were cakes covered in pomegranate seeds and delicately scented morsels. Eliora caught her breath.

'Who did all this?' Eliora asked and looked to Caleb's mother and Martha, his sister in law. They smiled. 'Thank you so much! You must have been preparing this for days.'

'Kenaz and I gathered the supplies,' Caleb added.

'It's amazing!' she said and squeezed his hand. 'Thank you.'

The contrast is so strong; the settlement bathed in sunlight and the celebrations under way compared to the horror in the darkness.

I have seen Eliora walking into her destiny today. She sees the Creator as her God and not just the god of the people. She has come to such an amazing point in her life. She is safe here.

The wedding feast has begun and it is time for me to join the host.

I flare into light and am transported to the boundary line. My friends stand, swords raised and bows ready. At the edge of the darkness I can see the movement of creatures. They are already not satisfied with what they have. They come to the edge looking for more victims. We will not let them through.

I approach Release and report on the festivities in the settlement.

'It is good that they will have time to rejoice,' he says.

'I have not seen Hunter in the ranks,' I state as I look up the line of the host. 'Is he still inside?'

'His mission is to stay hidden. He seems to be doing fine. See for yourself.'

I take a deep breath and concentrate on my absent friend.

I see the scene that is unfolding before him.

The darkness is so thick within the Egyptian compound that all colour has been eradicated from his sight. He sees everything in grey hues. Two familiar men, dressed in official Egyptian clothes sit hunched together against a palace wall in the darkness. The men are the ones who had visited the settlement in the hail, not so long ago. There is a scream from a corridor some distance away. They turn to the sound but see nothing. Their pupils are dilated not just because of the complete lack of light, but out of fear.

'Did you hear that?' The one named Hanif whispers to the other.

'Of course I did.'

'Not the scream, the scratching sound.'

They sit very still for a moment, listening intently.

A creature covered in spines and drooling comes around the corner, its claws scratching on the polished floor. Nose in the air, it sniffs.

'That … did you hear that?'

'Shhh!' Osahar urges and pulls himself tighter to the wall.

Their heartbeats race and the gleam of sweat covers their faces. They listen once again, but the noise has stopped.

'What was it?' Osahar finally asks.

'I don't know.' Hanif replies. 'But I'm not sure this is under control anymore.'

'May Ra help us.'

'Ra? I don't think he cares, I'm not even sure he is powerful at all.'

'Don't say that. We will be damned.'

'Think about it. What have our gods done for us since the slaves' god has been doing all this stuff to us?'

Hanif is greeted with silence.

'Well, I'll take it that you have no answer. I think that there is something about their god that is worth taking note of. That is all I'm saying.' Even the shadowy creatures that once came with them into the settlement and find the darkness so welcome seem to be paling in the growing faith this man is showing.

I know Hunter smiles because this conversation was meant to be.

Hunter takes the point of his sword and scores a line in the ground around the two men. Golden sparks shower the polished surface and the creature that was ready to pounce, backs away as the fiery particles sizzle on its skin.

'You are not welcome here. Go and spread your fear elsewhere.'

The creature eyes the sword and the glimmering line.

'I don't care about those two. I have plenty to choose from.' It turns and scuttles off.

'But if their god is more powerful than our gods …' Osahar begins stealthily.

'What do you mean "if"? There is no doubt in my mind.'

'What is the point in serving our gods then?' he whispers even more quietly.

'I don't think there is a point,' Hanif says in a low voice. 'But what option do we have? Stay here and be slowly tortured to death or go to them and live in slavery?'

'You saw them. They have some kind of immunity to all this deadly stuff.'

'Yeah, I know, but they are still slaves, aren't they?' Hanif murmurs.

Hunter stands tall then walks away. His stride is purposeful.

The corridors and rooms he looks into are infested with foul smelling creatures. Their callous laughter floods through the palace. Humans stay huddled together where they have found companions. Some have secured makeshift weapons hoping to defend themselves but they will be useless against the creatures that will haunt them for the next few days.

From the corner of his eye, Hunter spots the ambush. He spins round and slashes his sword through the air, striking the nearest creatures. Yelping and screeching they move away, acid dripping from their wounds.

A larger creature rises to its full height and bars its jagged teeth. It spreads its wings to reveal poisonous barbs and hisses as it approaches.

'What are you doing here?' It snarls. 'This is our domain.'

'Your domain has been given to you. You are only here by permission.'

'Get out!'

'I will not leave.'

'Then I'll make you!' The creature leaps high into the air and then falls with great speed towards Hunter, its barbs aimed dangerously towards him. Hunter has quick reactions and dives to one side. He raises his sword in such a swift movement that the darkness is cut open. A shaft of blinding light pours onto the creature and before it can land on Hunter its skin burns and blisters. It lets out a deafening squeal and fades away.

'Anyone else want to tell me to leave?' Hunter asks calmly.

'We want blood!' they demand.

'You will have it,' Hunter says sadly. 'But whoever I mark, you will not touch. Do you hear me?'

The creatures shiver. They hear the authority ringing through his every word, an authority given by a far higher being. Satisfied with their prey, they pull away from my friend and scuttle off to the darkness they feel comfortable in.

Hunter moves on. He searches the whole palace. When he discovers one that belongs to the remnant, he lowers his sword and creates sparks in the ground. The golden flecks remain on the skin of those he marks.

When the whole of the palace has been searched, he turns towards the houses and fields. He sets out focused on the task ahead.

25

Face to Face

For three days the darkness has covered the land.

Eliora, Caleb and their families have celebrated together, while the Remnant enjoyed a rest from their labour.

The land of the captors is imprisoned in darkness. Some of the host are stationed at the palace. The place of glory and honour has been reduced to a crawling, scratching people. The highest officials, hidden in the corners of rooms and under furniture that was close at hand when the darkness fell, are now being summoned. Their ears opened to hear the mighty Pharaoh shouting for their attention, his voice hoarse from screaming and demanding assistance. They scramble to their feet, feeling along the walls for guidance.

The corridors buzz with the activity of the enemy. Creatures, fat from their feasting on fear, celebrate in their victory. They do not see the bigger picture. They explored their earthly domain, attacked the human population, but do not accept the truth that this was given to them. It was handed over to them for a short while but they are not the ones in control.

The leader struts about the throne room. My friend Hunter, watches cautiously but not fearfully. He sees flickering flames licking the curved snout and square ears as the creature flexes his muscles under the adoring gaze of his horde. Hunter remains hidden as he guides the two messengers that cling to each other. He is outnumbered in this room.

I see their noses crinkle at the smell. Urine and excrement make the polished floor slippery. The messengers do their best to walk humbly, but as they can neither see the mess or the pharaoh they stop only a few steps into the room.

The one named Osahar bows low although no one can see if he honours his king or not. While Hanif covers his nose and mouth with his hand.

'Great Pharaoh?'

'Bring that Hebrew trouble maker to me.' Pharaoh demands.

The room fills with the sound of cackling, the creatures enjoying the sight of the helpless king. Their leader however, growls at the request and a brief flicker of anxiety crosses his face. He sees the wisdom in summoning Moses, the Creator's mouthpiece. Their rule of darkness will come to an end. Their reign will be threatened once again by the one true God.

Hanif and Osahar's expressions are plain to see. They mirror each other even in this thick darkness. There is contempt for their so called god and king. They are safe in the shadows, from rebuke and punishment.

Hunter leads them through the darkness, guiding their steps. They are led through the maze of corridors, across the fields and are approaching the settlement border.

They step from the lonely darkness into the warmth of the sun. Osahar winces and Hanif covers his eyes. They both shy away from the daylight, squinting even behind their hands.

The shadowy creatures, which follow behind them, fade in the bright sun and they back away to be engulfed in the darkness once again.

It takes a long moment for them to adjust.

Hunter stands strong and upright.

'Well met friend!'

'Indeed!' He grasps my hand and pulls me into a hug.

'You have been busy,' I laugh.

The men stumble forward. They are ill adjusted to the light but feel the urgency to move away from the darkness. Hunter and I follow.

They wander through the streets, marvelling at the sound of joy and life. They wear many layers of clothing to keep themselves warm, but here, in the sun, the heat reddens their faces, and sweat runs down their backs.

Eventually they reach the house where Moses stays.

The normal behaviour for an Egyptian is to just walk in, take what they like and leave, but this duo hesitate.

Hanif raises a fist and taps politely at the door.

I am amazed at the difference. It is not respect that causes their manners, but fear. What they have seen and experienced by crossing the border has sealed in the doubts they had about their own beliefs. The Creator God, the God of the Hebrews is more powerful and cares more for His people than all their gods put together. Their gods cannot set them free from the darkness, but have enslaved them.

Moses and Aaron walk with the messengers. Release and I walk with Hunter.

Both Hanif and Osahar slow as we reach the border, and they tremble. But Moses is bold and with Aaron at his side they step into the darkness. As they walk the thick membrane of shadow pulls away from them. With each step it flees.

The messengers stand in awe. Hanif screams and falls on his face in the dust.

'Oh mighty one. Do us no harm!'

'Get up,' Moses says as he bends down to help the young man to his feet. 'It is not me that banishes this. My God, the only God, goes ahead of me. In him there is no darkness.'

'What must I do to show honour and worship to your incredible God?'

'Leave your Egyptian life and be one of us.'

'But you are slaves.'

'And what are you?'

Hanif has no reply. He frowns at the question.

Moses does not wait for an answer and moves on towards the palace.

As the darkness recedes the creatures yell and scream at us to leave. They continue to hide in the shadow, their place of safety, but they cannot refute the power that is on display. Many rush towards the palace, no doubt to warn their leader of our arrival.

Light fans out behind the men of God as they walk with faith. It pushes the thick darkness away.

Mist rises from the cold ground and swirls about the human feet. The sweet smell of life begins to stir as the warmth of the sun touches the deprived earth.

They walk in silence. Moses and Aaron, have already discussed what is to be said and are contemplating what will happen next. The messengers are unable to speak because of what they see before them.

As they reach the palace entrance, light falls on the imposing structure. Guards and other Egyptians stagger into the light. They are filthy but ecstatically greet each other, celebrating the return of the sun. Many praise and thank Ra for returning, but are stopped mid flow when they witness the Hebrew men walk past. The light clearly goes before them. Celebration is quashed and fear returns, but now the fear is that of reverence. Joyous voices become hushed and respectful.

Vast pillars rise up out of the darkness but they go unnoticed by the small band of men. Moses knows where to find Pharaoh. Release directs him.

The sunlight pours from the high windows to the corridor below. The towering doors to the throne room stand ajar, beams of light revealing the warm grain of cedar. Our charges do not hesitate to enter.

This room has the stench of human waste and sulphur. The creatures hiss and recoil as the light streams in. Palace officials that have made it into the throne room cower in the brightness, shielding their faces and breathing with relief. But still Moses confidently walks on.

The beams spread throughout the room leaving a small sphere of darkness, of nothingness, at the far end.

The walls brighten with their gaudy paintings and the people present slowly adjust to the blinding light. They get to their feet, watching as Moses approaches the place of darkness.

Suddenly, the light falls on the throne. A cowering man, crouched into the corner of the seat squints towards the men we accompany. His skin is sallow and eye sockets sunken. His robe is soiled and his posture is that of an animal trapped. The creature surrounds him, caressing him with flames and whispered lies. It screeches as the light burns into its skin, drawing back only a little.

I smile sadly. This is a man who was made in the image of the Creator, yet destined to be separated from Him forever. He has been reduced to this.

He quickly recovers his poise and sits squarely on the throne, but the moment of perceived power is lost. Everyone witnesses the scene.

'Go and serve your Lord!' Pharaoh spits. 'I see no harm in your going,' but then he smiles cruelly. 'Only your livestock must remain here.'

Moses nods to Aaron and sighs. Still the pharaoh refuses to let them go. Moses is saddened by what must come now.

'No, not one animal will we leave behind,' Aaron replies. 'Our livestock comes with us. We will need it for the sacrifice to our Lord.'

Release, Hunter and I know that our time is now. We flare, and appear to the enemy forces, swords drawn and bows strung.

My clear arrow is trained on the beast on the throne.

'You!' It accuses. 'You have no right here. Get out.' It signals to the horde available and the room bustles with activity.

The creatures draw in closer to their leader. They face us, teeth barred and muscles flexing. Many of them carry their own weapons. Obsidian swords, curved knives, long spears and sharp claws glint in the light.

'You are outnumbered!'

'Be that as it may, you will not battle with us now. You are not ready,' Release states calmly.

The fiery creature hisses and spits. It knows its forces are too widespread and distracted to come to its aid now. We know that this will be quickly remedied. We must be ready for their attack.

'Get out! The next time you see my face you will die!' the creature growls. The others raise their weapons menacingly but retain a distance from our sharp blades.

'Get out!' Pharaoh shouts angrily. He gets to his feet and rushes towards Moses, Release blocks the way and stands firm with his sword raised. The pharaoh stops right in front of him. 'The next time you see my face you will die!' Moses can feel the stagnant breath and spit on his face.

'I will never see your face again!' Moses replies calmly and takes a cleansing breath before continuing to the stunned crowd. 'You have called a greater plague onto your people. The Lord is the King and he will protect his own, but with you and your land there will be such a crying out that no one has ever heard before and will ever hear again. Watch for the night for it will strike down every firstborn in your kingdom. Everyone will be affected, right from your own royal family line to the family of the servant girl, even the cattle will die. It will be so awful that your own people will bow down and compel us to leave.'

Silence fills the room. No one moves, not even the wings of the creatures stir.

Pharaoh stares wide eyed, and the fiery creature, dumbstruck by the power of truth, stand fixed to the spot. Moses, hot with anger, and Aaron turn and leave.

Release walks before them, Hunter and I follow.

26

Substitute

Eliora felt that she was finally adapting to her new life. She had been married for just over two weeks. Everything regarding her slavery was the same. The pits were hot and exhausting but at least the comments regarding her pregnant state were now subsiding a little.

Home life had the biggest contrast. The house was not as busy as her mother's, but now she had a bigger role in serving and had a brother and sister to consider. Kenaz had ceased in his teasing and now treated her with respect; an attitude, she thought, bought on with his wife's encouragement.

Martha, although somewhat older, enjoyed spending time with Eliora. It seemed that they had both longed for a sister at some point in their lives. For Eliora, any sibling would have been a wonderful gift, while for Martha, the only girl in a large family of boys, a sister was something to be treasured.

She missed the noise of uncles and cousins, and felt lost without her mother.

The constant through this unsettling time was Caleb.

His smile still left her with a sense of wonder. He completely accepted her for who she was and didn't push her to be something she couldn't. He protected her when they were hard at work, pulled her into his family with ease, gave her confidence in her abilities and loved her even in what she persisted in calling her ruined state. It was being with him that made all the anxiety worthwhile.

She straightened, having deposited the last of the straw loads to the cutting mats, and rubbed her aching back. The sun was low in the sky and the signal to head home was given. The masters had ignored the steady stream of Egyptian citizens visiting the pits and handing bundles to the slaves all day, and now, as it was time to leave they gave away packages themselves. Caleb carried two such bundles.

Caleb rushed over, still dripping from washing off the worst of the mud, and placed his gentle hand at her back.

'Are you in pain?'

'No more than usual,' she replied planting a kiss on his hot cheek.

'There will be no more of this,' he whispered excitedly into her ear.

She smiled. His faith was unwavering.

He had been the same on the day of the congregational meeting.

The tribes had gathered, ready to listen to her uncle Moses. Many had stood up to object to the instructions. Tethering a sheep outside the house was a defiant act, and many were scared that punishment would come soon after. Caleb had taken his turn and spoke to the tribe of Judah, he had recounted the disasters that the Egyptians had faced and asserted his faith in the God of Israel.

'My father, Jephunneh, saw that the true God was the God of Israel. He left his own people and became part of this nation, even though it was set for slavery. His faith is not wasted. His faith lives in me. He taught me to follow the true God. It would be foolishness to turn away now.' His authority in his tribe, now her tribe, shook her. Despite his history, many looked to him for wisdom.

That evening Eliora began to understand her husband better. He had never taken his identity for granted. He had been grafted into this nation. He knew the mercy and acceptance of God. It was because of this that he was able to accept her and her child.

Her new family were just as unusual as her old.

'Have you looked inside that yet?' Eliora asked, pointing to one of the packages Caleb carried.

'Not yet.'

'You won't believe it when you do!' Eliora giggled and showed him the tied red cloth at her waist. 'This woman came over to me in the field and literally thrust it at me before she left as soon as she could.'

'What is it?'

Eliora gently tugged at the knot and opened the fabric. Inside were gold rings, bracelets and necklaces, a silver statue and chunks of incense in folded parchment.

'Looks like we finally got paid!' he laughed.

Caleb held her hand and walked with an unaccustomed spring in his step. She was sure, had it not been for her he would have run home.

The Remnant is returning. They will no longer be forced to work at the pits.

They wash and brush off the dust of the day, the signs of slavery.

The Host watch over them as they follow the instructions closely.

There is a stillness in the settlement.

I keep watch over Eliora. Her household have had the lamb secured for four days, so now it is due for sacrifice. The men of the houses either side join Caleb.

The blood is collected in a bowl and the meat shared between the families.

Eliora returns from the allotment with the handcart burdened with grain, vegetables and fruit. There is nothing left growing in Caleb's plot.

'Have you harvested your mother's too?' Caleb asks taking a bunch of hyssop from the top.

'Yes. I took it over before coming here.'

'Are they well?' he asks tying the stalks together.

'Yes. Their house is full of people, but looks bare already.'

'You should go inside. There is a lot to do.' Caleb kisses her tenderly. 'But try not to tire yourself.'

Eliora goes inside while Caleb shakes the hands and hugs his neighbours as the bowl is handed to him. He dips the tips of the grey leafed bundle into the blood and applies it to the door posts and lintel of the door. The uprights and across the top are smeared in blood.

The scent of sacrifice mingles with the cleansing, minty hyssop.

Caleb hands the bowl to his neighbour, cuts through the curtain of fragrance that clings to the entrance and goes inside. The tendrils of aroma stir and reseal.

A blameless lamb has died. The substitute has been made.

The sun drops behind the horizon. The evening is drawing near.

There is a holy stillness in the settlement.

No one walks the streets, gathers at the corners or wells. Families share their meals in the safety of their homes, protected and covered by the sacrifice of the lamb. Its death has given them life, their death substituted by the lamb.

The fire spat as the fat dribbled over the meat and into the flames below. The smell of the meat made Eliora's mouth water as she set about packing together their sparse possessions.

Caleb had increased the height of the cart's sides with the use of the shutters from the windows. Eliora had neatly packed the family belongings safely inside. Jars of oil sat next to woven reed containers full of the Egyptian treasures. The food stores were placed between layers of blankets to prevent damage.

Nothing had gone to waste. Wood from the bed pallets, rugs, clothing and anything that could be carried were bundled together and waited in organised piles by the door.

It was a relief, that the instructions that were to be followed, allowed little preparation for a meal. The bread was not able to rise, the herbs not seasoned in a way that removed the bitterness, the lamb just left to cook quietly while the household busied itself to leave.

Having witnessed the disasters sent to plague the Egyptians, Eliora's trust of her uncle had increased. He had heard from his God and had declared what was to happen. There was, however, a small knot of fear that this would not be the end of their captivity. How many times had the pharaoh changed his mind? How would this hope of freedom destroy her if she fully trusted in it?

'Do you need to rest?' Caleb asked gently seeing Eliora hesitate as she slowly attempted to fold the large woollen blanket.

'I'm fine.'

He took the edge dragging on the floor and opened it out in his outstretched arms, folded it in half then walked towards her.

'You're worrying about something,' he said as their ends met. 'Don't deny it.' He gathered up the bulky fold that had dropped to the floor.

'What if we don't leave?' Eliora whispered as they met in the middle once again.

'We will leave.'

'I know you think that.'

'I know it. Trust me.' He smiled and kissed her on the nose.

Blood, mint and now the spicy smell of cedar stir the air. Sacrifice, cleansing and faith. Crimson, sparkling white and green pulsate in the room, weaving together in a striking pattern. A beautiful combination.

27

True Light

Life looks no different to human eyes, but even if I were human there are signs of something about to happen.

The Remnant settlement is peaceful. The sound of voices rise and fall from the houses as I pass by, telling me of family gatherings. The streets are deserted. The host are travelling to the border, eager to follow their instructions.

The golden latticework that we put in place has served its purpose and must be removed. It is almost time to move on.

Several of my friends circle the topmost part of the dome, while others stand at the base. With drawn swords they slash the glittering mesh. It tumbles slowly and gracefully in the evening air. Then slowly the threads rise on the warm current and float into the sky.

The settlement looks oddly bare in the darkness. I am thankful for the glimmering doorposts, silvery in the moonlight.

Release calls me forward with a wave of his hand.

'Hunter has asked for assistance.'

'Count me in!' I know the Remnant are completely safe. They are in the hands of the Almighty One.

'Somehow, I knew you would say that,' he laughs.

I focus on Hunter, poised for action at the entrance to the palace. Release flares and is gone. I am quick to follow.

'Where do you need me?' I quickly ask as I see Release dispatched to the houses nearby.

'The town and farmland is covered. Others are waiting there. The Palace is the most closely guarded. If you are willing, I could do with some assistance here.'

'By all means.'

A flash of light distracts me. The source comes from the Remnant settlement. I recognise the light. It is the most beautiful light there ever will be and it springs from the Creator.

It will not be long now.

I follow Hunter. He has his sword unsheathed and is ready to tackle whatever comes at us. I have an arrow ready to cover his back.

The palace workers continue in their usual night time activities. They sweep the dusty floors, polish the golden statues and prepare food.

We move to the living quarters, the gathering room of the royal family.

Many are here tonight, both human and the horde.

Pharaoh is entertaining. The remains of a banquet are being cleared away by servants. All of the sons of the pharaoh are here. They are seated with mothers and sisters in the main room and adjoining room. The informal and relaxed atmosphere will not last.

Bright flames lick at the pharaoh's back. The creature, unaware of our entering, laughs at the expense of a lesser beast pinned to the floor by the claws of another.

There is one face here that is very familiar to me.

The handsome features are distorted in the jealous scowl on Horusisus', the prince's face. The creature that sits with him has grown in stature, but in this room, surrounded by others, it is still relatively small. It whispers into the prince's ear.

'You are so much better than them! Make your father notice you. Once he sees that you are superior he will find favour with you.'

The fire burns blue at Pharaoh's shoulder.

'I can't believe you are still playing that role!' the creature laughs spitting out sparks. 'You will never make him greater.'

'You wait,' it stumbles.

'Wait for what exactly?' asks the clawed creature, releasing its captive and moving slowly towards Horusisus.

'All I meant was … I was just saying …' The creature shrinks at the towering threat approaching. 'Never mind. I didn't mean anything.'

'Know your place!' admonishes the flamed creature, its eyes burning with obsidian flames. 'Here you are the lowest of the lows.'

The small one snarls back at the reproach, and glances around at the others now fixated on the conflict. It does not consider itself the least among them, but does not have the courage to say so. It will not launch into a fight here and now.

The pharaoh meets Horusisus's, ill disguised, angry gaze.

'Was there something you wished to say to me … young man,' the pharaoh asks trying to recall this one's name.

'No father,' Horusisus offers.

The pharaoh's lips thin as he grimaces and turns away. The prince looks at his feet with shame. Wafts of stagnant water flow away from Si and towards me. What could have once given life, the fresh water of love and acceptance, has become sickly and diseased. It has poisoned this young man and has murdered him.

Horusisus sits in brooding silence as the others chat, but what I watch for are the natural movements like breathing and blinking.

'We should show ourselves.' Hunter says, shaking me from my thoughts.

We flare, showing our readiness for battle in the weapons aimed at the pharaoh's captor.

'Watch for the night for it will strike down every firstborn in your kingdom.' I echo the words Moses had said and realisation flickers over Pharaoh's face.

It happens in a moment. The humans gathered here all blink in synchronisation except for those that are the firstborn in their families. They see it. Their Creator stands in the room.

His awesome light shines. It reaches everyplace in the room, every corner is set ablaze. The darkness and its creatures cannot stand in His presence. The small creatures cringe to the floor hissing, their scaly bodies sizzle. The larger creature that holds the court pulls its wing in front of its face, its flames surpassed by the true light. It screams out in agony. The light paralyses its movement and the smell of burning flesh fills the air.

I watch Horusisus, closely as he looks on the face of the Creator. In that miniscule moment the world shifts for him. He sees the dirt of his life. Physical acts of worship to idols, both statue and self made, stink like rotten fish. Operating out of an idol-obsessed heart, selfishness, pride and anger feed like flies. The destruction of what could have bought life is eaten away by giving into temptation. Darkness seeps over all that he considers good in his life, nothing is good in the light shining now, all of it has a motive that does not worship the Creator. Layer upon layer of darkness falls. The stench of mildew and mould are finally overwhelmed by the beautiful fragrance of frankincense cutting through and cleaning it away.

There will be one exception in this plague. One firstborn son will remain unprotected yet will be spared. All firstborns belong to the Creator and this firstborn, the king of Egypt, his time has not yet come. He must see the awesome power of the true Lord.

In that tiny human space of time, the blink of an eye, the firstborn humans have looked on the face of the Creator. No one can survive such a thing.

The next moment the firstborns slump. Young children and adults alike suddenly collapse. Trays of food clatter and pitchers of wine smash on the cold floor as servants fall down lifeless. Those around them go briefly silent before panic breaks out.

The pharaoh gasps as his oldest son, eyes fixed and wide lays unmoving on the floor. His firstborn is dead. His heir gone.

Bodies of the sons of the king litter the floor. For a moment he stands, confused at the sight. Why have all these other sons died too? Then suddenly the room becomes busy as mothers panic and dash from one room to the next, rush to their children and begin to cry. He has other sons, many are the firstborn of their mothers.

Horusisus's body is motionless. He was never the pharaoh's first born, but the only child of his mother. Her tears flow down her face on bitter tracks. 'My son!' she wails. 'Bring him back to me,' she begs.

The room is in confusion. Many women lay prostrated over their sons. Some are being consoled by younger siblings but there is little that can be said or done to ease their grief.

Through the wailing the creatures rejoice. They have turned the Creator's judgement into a celebration of the loss of human life.

The sound repeats throughout the palace and spreads into the houses and fields. Family after family scream out. The streets are full of panicking citizens. Every household suffers. A chorus of sorrow rings out across the land.

Our work is nearly completed.

I hear the whisper of my friends. They speak to the broken, they are ushering in the promise.

'Moses spoke of this,' says Release in his deep voice.

'This is the work of the Hebrew's God.' I hear another suggest.

'No power in Egypt can stand in a place where their God stands,' I state in truth.

'What else can be destroyed?' Another voice joins the throng.

'Will this be the last thing that falls on you?'

'Will this ever end if they remain?'

'How can you look on them knowing that your future died because of them?' Hunter says quietly to the pharaoh.

I watch through Release's eyes. He stands in the street, following the people as they are quick to join with one another, united in their grief and desperation.

'They cannot stay here.'

'This will never stop as long as they remain.'

'We must send them away, and if they refuse to leave, drive them out before we are all destroyed and they take our place, and we take theirs.'

They band together, gathering items of value along with weapons. If they cannot convince the Hebrews to leave with gifts, they will have to fight, yet in the light of the power of the Hebrew God, no one really believes they would survive such a battle.

Back in the palace, we wait for the order.

'Get them out of my kingdom. NOW!' Pharaoh screams.

The message passes quickly.

The messengers, Hanif and Osahar, who are so familiar with the settlement and the favour of the Creator to the Remnant are dispatched. Hunter and I are sent with them.

They are not heading straight to the settlement.

'What do we do now Hanif?'

'Get your children,' he pauses, 'the ones that are safe. Collect Suma and bring them to the gate. I'll meet you there.'

'Why?'

'We can't stay here Osahar,' he whispers. 'We need to go with them. It will be better to be with their God than with ours.'

'What if they don't take us?'

'I don't know.'

They stand silently for a moment. Osahar then smiles nervously.

'I'll meet you at the gate. Don't be long.'

The two men split up and run to their houses. I follow Osahar and Hunter trails Hanif.

'Meet you at the gate then?' Hunter says with a little laugh before he speeds away.

Osahar's house is just like every other Egyptian house. It is filled with sorrow.

As soon as Osahar enters his wife, Suma, is upon him.

'Badru, my baby!'

Osahar rushes to the bedside of his first born son. He is still and cold. A single tear runs down his cheek.

'Suma!' he calls as calmly as he can. 'We need to go. Pack up as many things as you can. Get the other children. We leave very soon.'

'Go? Where exactly?'

Osahar looks sadly at his dead heir. 'We go with the Hebrews. They will be leaving, or could even be leaving as we speak. We need to go with them.'

'But Badru? He must be buried to ensure his rebirth.'

'What has all this trouble taught you woman? Our lives have been built on lies. Whose god would you serve? The useless idea of Egyptian gods that will not act for a devoted people or a Hebrew God that has actively shown them favour?'

'I can't leave him. I can't leave my life behind.'

'We have no choice Suma,' Osahar says thrusting a basket into her arms. 'It is time for us to go.' He starts to throw bundles of food into the basket.

Suma is shocked.

Osahar will need her with him. The children will need their mother. It will not be an easy thing to do. It is full of unknowns.

I rub my hands together and form swirling bubble of fragrance. I move my hands away and see it suspended in the air before I blow it to the centre of the room.

It bursts sending out a beautiful aroma. Ginger and cinnamon overlay the scent of fresh rain.

Suma softens. She begins to hurry about, picking up essential items, bundling them together in linen. The children, three remaining, gather the things they want to take.

The house looks as if someone has ransacked it. Where it was once neat, things lay toppled over and out of place.

Suma bends down and kisses Badru. Her tears shower his face.

'We must go!' Osahar urges as he takes her hand and leaves, with her still weeping beside him.

Hunter waits at the gate. Hanif, his wife and all their daughters wait with him. Hanif fidgets nervously but as soon as he catches sight of Osahar he settles.

'I am so sorry for your loss my friend.' Osahar says realising that Hanif no longer has a son.

'And I yours. Badru was a good lad,' Hanif replies.

The women and children group together, huddled in the late night.

Hunter and I shield them as they rush towards the settlement.

Many Egyptians are making their way there. I see a few of them, packed up and ready to leave guided by friends, but mostly they come with gifts and extreme anxiety to see the Remnant leave.

Moses waits at the border. The Egyptians flood into the settlement forcing riches onto the slaves. Telling them they are free. Desperately urging them to go.

Hanif and Osahar approach Moses. 'Pharaoh commands you and your people and all you have to leave.'

'Thank you.' Moses turns away.

'Only,' Hanif asks capturing Moses attention, 'Can we come with you?'

'We have witnessed what your God has done for you.' Osahar adds, 'And we want to join you, wherever you go.'

'Join us and be one of us,' Moses replies. 'It is time to go!' he shouts.

The Remnant responds instantly. They are ready.

Moses leads the way, his brother and his tribe follow.

Men, women and children, livestock, carts and foreigners flow away from the settlement in an almost endless line. There seems little organisation. Bands of the Remnant flow out of Egypt. Even in watching I can see the fulfilment of a promise. They look as numerous as the stars above.

28

Journey

'What is wrong?' Eliora asked Caleb.

'The tribe elders are worried. They do not know where to go. None of us have ever left the city.'

The people were everywhere. It seemed like chaos to Eliora but it was slowly becoming organised.

The Egyptians had literally forced them to leave and now the redundant slaves had begun to gather outside the border. Here they could breathe again. They were removed from the land just far enough to regroup. The darkness of the night was fading in the lightening sky and allowed the people search one another out.

Moses had led them out quickly on a route that was familiar to him. At the rallying point the tribes began to organise themselves. Eliora could make out the familiar Levites with her uncles. Caleb was from Judah, so Eliora now grouped with them but she longed to be with her mother in the excited bustle.

Little children who had been carried out were now beginning to wake but even with their playful laughter the mood did not lift.

'Uncle Moses will lead the way, won't he? He knows where the mountain is.'

'We are waiting for word to get back to us. Messengers have been sent out from each tribe to find out what to do now.'

Suddenly silence fell over the nation.

The Remnant have been freed but it is not safe for them to stay here. They have a long journey ahead of them.

Release accompanies Moses with the tribe of Levi. He is ambushed by panicking messengers. They are desperate to know where they are going.

Moses does not need to answer. The Creator hears and acts.

The morning sky is ripped open and a plume of cloud rushes towards the earth. It plummets at great speed. Its highest point is lost in the sky above and the lowest tip dips to the height of a man. There is no wind, yet the vapours swirl and twist. The white puffs billow as if there were a storm raging within.

The Remnant are silent, lost in the awesome sight.

The host begin to bow, one after the other. Release remains the closest to the cloud and he has covered his head with his wings as he waits.

Inside the cloud the particles shimmer and spark. They shoot about with vigorous energy, leaving fiery trails in their wake.

The cloud begins to pulse with life.

Suddenly, in the midst of the cloud there is such holiness that I have to draw my wings before my face.

I can feel the heat pulsing over my back. A powerful intensity of deep love. I have never witnessed anything like it. Cinnamon spikes the air and ribbons of freesia wrap themselves around the Remnant.

The Creator is here, He will lead them.

Eliora stood silent alongside her people. The cloud poured out of the sky, east of the place where she and Caleb waited. She gripped Caleb's arm and staggered back, hiding behind him.

The hush began to transform as the people realised that the cloud posed no threat to them. A few nervous laughs tinkled through the crowd, then a gentle splattering of applause. Soon the people were cheering, shouting and jumping around.

The messengers came sprinting back through the rejoicing to the elders nearby.

'Moses says we are to follow the cloud!' Eliora overheard. 'We are to keep the tribes together and to move on calmly.'

'What about rest for little ones?' an elder asked.

'No instructions were given.'

'Well, they have families too. Let's just see how it goes,' suggested another.

'Alright. Send word throughout the tribe.'

Caleb turned and looked down to Eliora. 'Are you ready for the journey?'

'I think I've been ready for this journey for a while, I just didn't realise it.'

Caleb laughed and bent to kiss her tenderly. 'You completely amaze me.'

'What do you mean?'

He pointed to the cloud. 'Doesn't that frighten you?'

'It would have done, but now, I don't know, there is something quite comforting about it.' She cupped his hands in hers. 'A year ago, I wanted more than anything to be as distant from this people as possible. I desperately tried to fit into Egypt but never quite managed it.'

'There were times when I thought I had lost you,' Caleb admitted.

'You almost did.'

He raised her hands to his mouth and kissed them.

The people around them began to move. The tribes were setting out for the place of worship that had been denied them for all this time.

The cloud went on before them.

Sand and rocks shifted under the feet of the nation of Israel. The quiet but free chatter of many voices was interspersed with the creaking wheels of carts and bleating of sheep and goats. Children ran ahead of their parents playing games of chase, their energy seemed boundless to Eliora whose weariness was creeping up on her.

Just as she felt she could walk no further the people in front began to lower their belongings and settle on the ground. The cloud had stopped moving except for the billowing of the vapours in the unfelt internal storm. The shadow it cast spread out over the people bringing them shade from the incessant sun.

The people stretched out over the void landscape. They were the only point of interest among the scrubby bushes and boulders. To Eliora everything was a shade of brown or yellow. The lush banks of the Nile were far behind and here life was harder on the plants, animals and nomads. The air was dry and dusty.

Word was sent through the camp that there was time for proper rest and sleep.

Caleb set up a makeshift tent using the cut branches of the bushes and some of the larger blankets. Eliora was relieved to find the space sheltered from the crowd and she quickly fell asleep curled up next to Caleb.

The sun had already set when she was roused by Martha holding a bowl of steaming broth in one hand and a plate of flat bread in the other. The sound of voices floated into her tent.

'I let you sleep,' Martha said, seeing the redness in Eliora's cheeks. 'Caleb insisted on it. You need rest. You may be young but you need to think of the baby.'

'Thank you!' Eliora said rubbing her eyes.

Martha smiled, leaving the food on the ground next to Eliora.

It was only when the smell reached Eliora that her stomach rumbled. Dipping the bread into the broth, Eliora savoured the bitter taste of home.

Caleb crept in beside her, sucking the remains of the broth he had just finished off his fingers.

'Good huh?'

Eliora nodded.

'We are breaking camp. I hope you have had enough rest.'

'But we can't travel at night.'

'I am quite confident we can!' Caleb said laughing a little. 'You should see this.' He took the empty bowl and pulled her to her feet leading her outside the tent.

It was not until that moment that Eliora had realised that he had no lamp and that no lamps were lit anywhere in the camp, yet there was light.

The cloud that had been leading them was transformed in the darkness. From inside the cloud a fire burned. It was not like the weak flickering flames she was so used to seeing. Rather, these flames of gold and silver shimmered and danced within the billowing vapours of the cloud.

The expression of wonder on her face makes me stand back too. She sees the visible and is awestruck, I can see the invisible and it is so much more.

By the day it was hidden from the people just how majestic the cloud really is. But now that their source of light has faded, they can see that this source of light is spectacular. Flames of gold and silver lick the air inside the cloud, but multihued sparks are contained deeper within. They pulsate and rumble as if they were breathing and yet it is soundless.

The floral scent of primroses mixes with earthy walnut. This fire is one of protection.

No beast or other creature can come close. The presence of the Creator sets a boundary around the Remnant.

The journey through the wilderness took almost a week. The people had travelled to a plateau.

The cloud would guide by day and by night, letting the people find rest and refreshment when it was needed.

Wild animals stayed away, and any other travellers put distance between themselves and the multitude. They were safe and protected.

Ahead of them there was the crescent edge of a large body of water in a gentle sloping valley. To the south was a steep sided mountain pass.

The cloud turned towards the mountains.

Eliora heard the murmuring of the people.

'Why are we going this way? Surely the plains are a better route.'

She had to agree and looked to Caleb. He half smiled.

'What do you think?' she asked.

'Our God knows where he wants us to go,' Caleb said, but then added more confidently, 'We should have faith and believe this is a better route.'

Eliora gave one last longing look towards the easy route of the open and gentle plains they were leaving behind. She had learned to trust but this was a conflict for her. The wide expanse of easy travelling compared to the closeness of the mountain pass. She felt squeezed in the shadow of the mountain. But to her credit, and to the credit of the other doubters, they pressed on with faith into the twisting valley.

The temperature dropped in the valley. The people were reduced to walking in a narrow column due to the rocky path. Happy voices echoed off the mountain sides as the people confidently followed the cloud ahead.

The small flocks of sheep and goats banded together as they made their way up the slopes looking for food. Shepherding the flocks seemed a difficult task. Eliora watched the men so used to working in the pits climbing over boulders and chasing the strays to ensure that they stay together.

Helping to wheel the cart was enough of an ask for her. Caleb pushed while Eliora guided, occasionally adjusting loose belongings.

They had stopped to refill their jars and skins. The water bubbled over the rocky bed turning the dull and dusty rocks into sparking gems. Eliora drank deeply. She was glad of the trickling mountain springs flowing down to her below. The fresh water was cold and sweet and soothing on her aching feet.

She smiled as she savoured in the taste of freedom, sitting for a moment as her feet dried on the warm rocks. She was so glad of the rest after a full morning's march.

The mountains were majestic and solid. The peaks high above tried to pierce the sky. The landscape was completely unknown to her. She had never been anywhere other than the plains of Egypt. Here the rough and craggy mountainsides out shone anything that she had witnessed. Nothing had been graven, no garish paint covered the walls yet this place was beautiful.

The host have been flanking the Remnant for several days. It is exciting to see their confidence grow.

At the turning point, a battalion have been set to turn back those who would not follow the route assigned.

Eliora, fresh in her faith is being tested once again. She sees the easy path and longs after it, not knowing where her future lies. Broad is the road that leads to destruction yet narrow is the way of life. I encourage her, and she moves on.

As the last of the Remnant are enclosed in the shadow of the mountain valley a trumpet sounds. We were waiting for this.

I flare and join Release at the rear of the company.

Hunter rushes to us.

'They are coming!' he announces. 'The pharaoh has rallied his armies. He wants the Remnant back. His workforce has disappeared.'

'How many?' Release asks.

'There are six hundred of the select chariots, but many more have also joined him,' Hunter reports. 'The horde stirs up trouble and is aiding them. Their number has multiplied. Their leader seems to be stronger then ever.'

'We were told this would happen. It is in His plan.'

'But we cannot be complacent,' I say.

'You are right,' Release states grasping my shoulder. 'Send out a scout.'

'Let me go,' Hunter urges.

He is dispatched.

For now the people move on in peace. 'It will not be long before they find out that they are being pursued,' I say quietly.

'Moses already knows. He was told some time ago, yet did not lead the people along the route he was familiar with. Now that is faith!'

'Indeed!'

'Position yourselves along the pass,' orders Release to the host. 'We are to be on our guard. Attack is imminent.'

29

Trapped

Her dream shattered as a scream far behind them spread through the valley. It was quickly joined by others.

Eliora stood silently with her tribe, listening, trying to determine the danger.

'What has happened?'

Soon there was a young man running, red faced and dodging the people. Questions were fired at him as he ran.

It was only when he had passed on the message to the next runner and was caught by one of the elders that the news spread.

'The Egyptians ... they are coming after us!'

Everything changed.

Panicked voices called out to children and family. Sobbing and cries of fear echoed through the people. There was a rush to gather up and leave. The cloud moved on slowly, far too slowly, surely this was the time to run, to flee.

The orderly column became ragged and dangerous. People pushed and argued their way past each other.

The messenger needs to reach Moses, yet he already knows that his people are being pursued.

The valley hems the Remnant in.

There is no escape from it.

Only one way in behind them and one way out lies ahead.

A few of the Host line the peaks, swords drawn and arrows ready. The enemy are still a long way off, but from their vantage point, my friends see the dark band coming ever closer.

Many friends stay with the Remnant, helping and reducing the risk to the people.

Release stands firm with Moses as he listens to the puffed out report from the messenger. He does not show fear, only sorrow.

Caleb was drained of colour yet Eliora felt peaceful.

'We need to move,' Eliora ushered him. 'We can't get left behind.'

'But where will we go?'

'We are following the cloud. Through the valley and out the other side,' she stated calmly.

'We are trapped.'

'No Caleb,' Eliora said taking his face in her hands. 'We are free. Our God will not abandon us, I am sure of it.'

Caleb looked down on her as if he had never seen her before. She felt him search her face for answers. Slowly a wide smile spread over his face and his eyes sparkled.

'Thank you!' he said as he kissed her firmly.

Hunter calls for assistance. I flare and go to his side.

From our hidden vantage point I see the lines of chariots. The dust stirred up by the horses and wheels cannot hide the oncoming army. The captains ride in richly furnished chariots with the section at their command in close formation behind them. They stretch out in a long stream across the flat landscape. Thousands of men armed with battle axes, spears and sickle shaped swords are chasing after their slaves.

I can hear the shouting and hissing of the multitude of creatures even from a distance. The foul fiery one has rallied a massive army to attack the Remnant. The sky is darkened by their bodies as they rush towards us.

They are angry beyond words.

The torment of the pharaoh's mistake in letting the Remnant go has only fed their leader. It will not part with the nation that was under their domination for so long.

'Kill them. Destroy them. Wipe them out from the face of the earth!' It screams. The flames rage about its body. The pharaoh grimaces in the grip of the razor sharp claws clamped on his shoulders.

'What do you need me to do?' I ask.

'We need the pharaoh to believe he has won this.'

'He looks fairly convinced of that already.'

'No, I have been in closer and see his motives. The creature that gives him so much guidance just wants the Remnant destroyed, we need to work on his pride.'

Hunter shares what needs to be done. We both flare and station ourselves near to the turning point that overlooks the gentle valley below. We are both dressed as nomads, our camels laden with goods. Being hidden in the human world makes me smile. Not even the creatures will recognise us here.

The army approaches. It is vast and spreads out over the plain. An official approaches.

'You there!' he shouts out, calling us to him. It would be foolish, as a human not to obey. I feel the rebellion to ignore him but do not give into it!

'Yes my lord,' Hunter says using his native tongue.

'You trade with Egypt?' he asks.

'Many times my lord.'

'Come with me.'

We follow the official. His crisp white linen is stained with dust and his skin is dry in the heat of the plain. He leads us straight to the pharaoh.

The fiery creature looks down in disgust at us, but does not see what we are.

Pharaoh sneers.

'They are traders with our land, O mighty one.'

'Traders?'

'Yes my lord, the king,' Hunter says as he bows down low. I imitate him.

'Then you would serve me now.'

'It would be our pleasure my lord.'

'We have been pursuing a large band of people. It is obvious that they have been here.'

'Yes my lord. They have been wandering about. They seem without purpose. Weren't we saying that just a few hours ago?' Hunter says turning to me.

'Yes we were. They travelled so slowly and looked to be lost. I don't think that they even noticed the valley ahead. Maybe they have been without food or water too long. They turned back on themselves and entered the mountain pass.'

'They can't be that far along my lord,' his captain adds.

The pharaoh smiles at his captain next to him.

We have done it. The air reeks of burning oil. The danger of acting on this pride will set two nations in different directions.

The creature acknowledges the emotion, and is happy to let it fester.

'That is right! You are the almighty one. What harm could lost slaves do to you? You must bring them back to serve you, to make you even greater, or kill them, which will not be hard since their god has no idea how to look after them.'

I want to cut its throat.

'Thank you for your information!' Pharaoh states generously. 'Be sure to visit the palace and you will be rewarded.'

'Thank you my lord.' Hunter bows again and nods to me.

'Yes my lord. Thank you for your mercy, but may I be bold once more,' I add bowing lower.

'Of course,' he replies.

'The mountain pass may not be suited for an army such as yours.'

The pharaoh stands quietly, thinking it over.

'There is an alternative route,' I press on. 'It is longer, but flatter and wider. And I am sure that with your speed you will be able to cut them off at the other end.'

'Which route do you suggest?' the captain asks.

'Down to the edge of the water and along the shore.'

'Can he be trusted?' the pharaoh asks quietly.

'As a trader, they will know all the routes,' the captain admits. 'It is sound advice.'

The lines of chariots turn away. They move away from the mountain valley and towards the easy road along the shore. As soon as all eyes are fixed on the path ahead, Hunter and I flare and are gone.

Eliora looked ahead eagerly as she walked. Her back ached and swollen belly occasionally cramped with pain. The cart bumped and rolled over the rocky path. The valley's steep sides hemmed the people in. Even in their panic they could not run from the path set before them.

It seemed endless. The cool shadow of the mountains twisted and turned. Finally a different view greeted them.

Rugged angled sides were contrasted with a flat horizon. The end was in sight. Eliora noticed how the flat horizon glistened and shone.

It had been a difficult and long journey. They had only rested for very short times and were exhausted.

Eliora remained positive.

'Chariots will not find that road an easy one.'

Tribe after tribe arrived at the wide beach. The evening air was moist but warm. It felt good to Eliora, to be able to see the darkening dome of the sky spanning from one side to the other. But the people did not notice the sky, they did not look up, all they could see was the far reaching water of the Red Sea, the mountain pass behind them and the shore line route.

The view of that route sent ripples of fear through the freed slaves. The dark advance of a full army was making its way towards them. Their masters were coming for them, and they were going to be punished.

Shouts of despair and screams of fear rang out over the water. Some collapsed where they had stopped, weeping. Others began to run in circles because there was no escape. Vast crowds flocked to the place where Moses stood.

It did not take long for panic to take hold. Life was impossible. On all sides they were trapped.

'Why did you bring us here?'

'Weren't there enough graves in Egypt for us?'

'You should have left us alone.'

Fear became anger and the people were set to turn.

Do they really believe it is better to die a slave than to live free?

They turn their anger towards Moses, but it is focused on the Creator who has shown them the greatest kindness of all.

When will the Remnant see clearly?

The cloud still remains with them, have they forgotten to look at it?

Who is bigger than the Creator, the maker of all things, the one that has taken them this far?

30

Redeemed

Caleb and Eliora stand silently. They do not panic. Their faith is like the mountains here, immovable. I hear their desperate murmurs.

'Save us God. You have done it so many times before. Don't let our enemies, your enemies, have victory.'

'You have been merciful, I know that, please be merciful again. I know that you do not change. You have promised something better for us.'

Moses speaks up and the nation falls silent. 'Are you afraid?' Moses asks. 'Why do you tremble at the sight of this army? Our God has not led us here to die, but to bring us freedom. Look up. The mighty one of Israel is fighting for us. Do not fear!' I hear the words and can see Moses' conviction, but the people are not convinced. 'Stand still and see the salvation the Lord has for you. You will never see these Egyptians again. The Lord will fight for you.'

In his heart the prayer rings out solid and sure. He has encouraged them not to be inward looking, trying to work out how they will save themselves, but to wait on their God and do what He asks. He is right. If the Creator brings someone to a place of difficulty, He will lead them out.

Then other voices begin to sound out. Their fear is leading them to pray.

These silent prayers are more effective than the cries of fear.

The Creator is set to move.

The nation was silent. In the distance the sound of horses whinnying and cracking whips could be heard. The army was advancing.

Eliora gripped Caleb's arm. The cloud that had led them to this place began to retreat into the sky. It remained there for barely a moment, then, where the beach met the shore line route it touched down with great speed and force. The rocks on the near mountainside cracked and rolled down onto the path.

The nation remained silent.

The Egyptians' path was blocked. The cloud was blazing giving light and warmth to the people.

A sudden wind whipped Eliora's hair and skirt. Sand from the beach swirled.

Peering through the dust storm Eliora saw her uncle standing at the water's edge, staff raised, the wind buffeting him and churning up waves.

There still seemed no way of escape.

The fierce wind caused the tribes to regroup, huddling together to keep safe.

But the cloud did not move and the wind continued. In the roar of the storm the people sheltered at the base of the mountains and rested. They were exhausted.

Hour after hour through the night, they were unable to move on. The pass was filled with the howling wind and the shore line blocked.

The light coming from the cloud played strange tricks on Eliora's vision. She turned away from the scene without really investigating what she was seeing. She was so weary that all she wanted was to fall asleep.

I watch with excitement as the host fulfil the Creator's instructions. They sweep down the valley on the head of the wind dragging the air in their wake.

As the wind travels along the valley it intensifies and focuses.

Bursting out of the mountain pass the velocity of the air forces the dense water to move aside. There is no chance for the water to recover before more wind rushes in. It gets pushed further onto the deep body of water either side.

Further and higher it mounts up.

The water sinks in the middle and builds to a windswept wall either side.

But there is a creative work happening below the surface.

The ground bubbles and churns below the water. Pebbles, grit and sand begin to multiply in huge quantities, being raised up, layer by layer.

The ground rises and the water parts.

The sight is amazing but my attention is drawn elsewhere. This is Eliora's time.

Caleb laid out some blankets on the rocky floor and pulled the cart in close. He secured other blankets over the top to offer some protection. Eliora wearily lowered herself to the half tented shelter. Her knees had barely touched the ground when she gasped, curled over her bump and tensed in agony.

With one hand on her underbelly and one supporting her weight, she crawled to a more hidden corner.

'What is it?' Caleb asked anxiously as he rushed towards her.

Eliora lifted her skirts only to find them sodden with warm liquid. She whimpered.

She could not answer. Eliora was aware of Caleb rummaging in the cart to her side, then suddenly there was flicker of light from a small oil lamp. He turned and she could see the panic in his eyes.

'I need ... my mother,' she panted.

Caleb scrambled to his feet and she was left alone.

Torturous aches ran over her bump and down her back, deep, humming pain that only intensified.

She shivered in her wet clothes, but felt unable to move even to pull a blanket towards her.

It was only a few moments before her mother sped through the gap between the cart and the makeshift tent.

'It will all be fine. Take short breaths,' she said calmly as her hands moved swiftly over Eliora's belly.

'I'm not ready.'

'You are ready enough. When a baby wants to be born, there is no stopping it.'

The howling wind outside filled Eliora's ears. How could this be the right time? This baby was not due for at least another month and this was not how it was supposed to happen.

Caleb appeared at the entrance. 'Is she alright?' he asked in panic.

'It is all progressing very quickly.'

'Don't talk about me as if I'm not here!' Eliora complained as the pain subsided a little.

'I'm sorry,' her mother said kindly. 'How long have you been having pain?'

'Just now.'

'Are you sure? No other pain at all?'

'I've been having cramps, but that was only all the walking.'

'That explains how you are so far on.'

'Far on? What do you mean far on? How far? What does she need?' Caleb worried.

'You need to calm down,' Jochebed warned her son in law. 'We need hot water and any clean linen you can gather.' Caleb crouched, wide eyed. 'As quickly as you can,' she urged.

'Get out Caleb.' I push at his shoulders, removing him from the shelter. He is unaware even of such close contact. All around him I smell the smouldering stink of damp wood. It clings to him and his clothing. Before, where there was such faith that the Creator would rescue them, the spicy scent of cedar swirled about him, now all that is gone. He reeks of smoke.

Caleb stands outside the tent.

His fear has rendered him incapable of moving.

'Martha!' I call. 'Caleb needs you.'

Only a few moments pass before Martha comes looking for Caleb. She looks at him nervously. He is normally quietly confident, a different man stands here.

The fierce wind tosses his hair in and out of his eyes and whips at his tunic.

'Do not fear!' I say as I wrap my arm around his shoulders. 'The Creator is with you.' His tension eases a little.

Martha rushes forwards. 'Caleb? What is it? Is everything alright?'

'Eliora ... I need hot water and linen,' He repeats the instructions.

'I'll get them,' Martha answers with understanding. 'She needs you to be strong. Go back to her.'

Martha dashes away.

Caleb turns back to the shelter but does not draw near.

'What is it Caleb? What do you need? The Creator will hear you,' I whisper.

The smoky smell intensifies, then accents of rosemary weave through the bitter aroma. Cleansing is coming. He is working it through.

'I have no right to ask ...' he silently prays.

'Yes you do, you are made in His image. Ask and it will be given to you.'

'Please,' he begs, 'keep her safe.'

'And the baby?' I ask. 'What about the baby Caleb?'

'Keep the child safe.'

The child is for you. Your request has been heard.

Cedar and smoke mingle together as Caleb goes back into the shelter.

Eliora sat propped up against the cart wheel. She looked up as Caleb came back in.

'Where is the water, the linen? Caleb, get out of here!' Jochebed commanded.

Eliora watched as Caleb's eyes widened.

'No Mama. I want him to stay.'

'This is no place for a man!'

'It is. I want Caleb here,' Eliora said as she stretched out her hand to him.

He rushed over, took her hand and crouched next her.

Jochebed tutted.

'Martha is getting all you asked for,' Caleb said to his mother in law without taking his eyes off Eliora. 'Are you sure you want me here?' he whispered.

'Certain,' she grunted as another contraction began.

Eliora could feel the gentle wipe of a cool cloth over her forehead. When the pain retracted once again she opened her eyes. Caleb sat poised with the cloth in his hand but his face seemed aged with worry. Suddenly, that worried face was hidden once again as the lamp flickered in the breeze when Martha rushed in.

Eliora wanted to tell him it would all be fine, but she was not certain. She wanted to reassure him, to stop the contractions, get some time and talk through all the complications. There had been no time, no right time, to prepare themselves. They should have had weeks to discuss what could happen. This was too soon.

Nothing was going to stop this from happening.

It will not be long now.

The Creator's timing is always perfect. This child will be born very soon.

Eliora is in safe hands. Her mother has helped several women over the years and Martha has assisted with her fair share. I am here to do the will of the Creator.

She worries about Caleb, yet the intensity of labour is helping her to focus elsewhere.

Extending my hand, I release ribbons of peace into the shelter and wrap them around Eliora and Caleb's clasped hands. The gentle aroma of rose fills the little tent. It swirls in elegant green patterns and the tendrils reach into the far corners.

I hear the collective sigh of the family.

Eliora noticed very little about her surroundings. She could feel someone pulling her into a squatting position and her mother telling her to push when she felt like she wanted to. She didn't want to move, it only hurt more when she did. Caleb was the only person clear to her. Her mother barked some other instructions, but they were just noises that blurred with the howling wind outside.

'Elli, come on, do as you mother says,' Caleb said in soothing tones, yet she was certain that he was suffering, be it emotionally, by the expression in his eyes.

'What?' she slurred.

Caleb's strong arms wrapped around her and lifted forwards into a squat.

Eliora gasped.

'I'm sorry,' Caleb whispered, still supporting her. 'Are you sure this will help?' he asked, and Eliora knew he wasn't speaking to her.

Then it came. An urge that could not be ignored.

'I need to push.'

'Then do it!' Jochebed ordered. 'Go with it.'

'I need to!'

'Caleb, she's not listening.'

'Elli, sweetheart, that's good, it's time to push.'

Eliora needed no further instruction. Her whole body wanted to do this. She closed her eyes tightly, took a deep breath and pushed.

The physical pain was like nothing she had ever experienced. It was sudden and sharp. Then there seemed a lull for a moment. Then again the urge took over again and again. Finally it was gone.

Eliora lay back exhausted. The tent flapped wildly in the screaming wind, but inside the tent there was no screaming. Silence, deep and dark, filled that space.

Something was wrong. There should not be silence.

Eliora opened her tired eyes and leaned forward once more.

At her feet lay a baby. Grey and still.

'Do something!' she yelled.

The baby is motionless; the cord tight around the neck.

Jochebed is quick to act. She frees the child but still the baby does not breathe.

'Do something!' Eliora yells at her family.

I cannot intervene until I have the command.

Caleb is as grey as the infant. He smells of decay. He hates all that this baby stands for.

'She's my baby, don't let her die!' Eliora reaches for the child.

She is Eliora's baby.

Caleb looks into his wife's face and sees pain.

'I can't do it!' he prays. 'This baby will only remind me of what that beast did to her. Let it die.'

Eliora takes the limp child into her arms and begins to weep.

'Why is she so upset? Is this really what she wants?' he asks himself.

Caleb is consumed. The stench of burnt flesh seeps from him. He loathes the baby. His hatred is directed towards this child.

I reach into the folds of my tunic and pull out a sprig of lavender. Quickly, I strip the dry flowers from the stalk and rub them into the palms of my hands.

The oils cling to my skin, but will not stay there long. Gently, I spread my hands over the baby. The oil flows from me to the child, coating its body in the perfume of innocence.

I break through the shield. 'Remember the dream Caleb.'

I flash the image of his cloak wrapped around Eliora with her sleeping baby in her arms. It is a shocking contrast to the real life before him.

'What have I done? If it is your will, let this child live.'

I hear the command.

'Take the baby, Caleb.'

Caleb reaches for the baby with shaking hands.

Eliora sees him through the tears and offers her baby daughter to him.

The baby is cold.

Caleb tenderly folds his cloak around her still body and pulls her close to him. He opens her mouth, hooks out a wad of mucus and blows gently into her. He can feel her chest rise and fall. He breaths into her again.

'Please Lord. Don't let my anger cause Eliora more pain.' He prays silently as tears roll down into his stubbly beard.

He rubs small circles on the baby's chest and wills her to live with his breath a third time.

'You have bought me life, when I do not deserve it. This child is innocent of the crime that caused it to be. Please don't punish this little one.'

The Creator hears his heart and responds.

Eliora's vision was blurred. She had a baby daughter but her joy was crushed in the still grey baby in her arms. Her daughter had tiny hands and feet. Her face was peaceful but lifeless.

Eliora could feel the crushing sense of pain rushing for her.

Then she noticed Caleb's outstretched arms. His hands shook and he looked uncertain.

She gazed into the still face of her lifeless daughter, someone who was already so precious, before she offered her up to the man she trusted.

He could hold off the pain. He was tender with her vulnerable baby. He was kind to her. He nestled her into his cloak and touched her face and mouth. He kissed her.

Tears flowed endlessly down Eliora's face. Why had she feared this moment? Caleb was kissing her daughter. Caleb was kissing his daughter. Caleb was kissing their daughter. She saw the tears flow down his cheeks and drip onto their daughter. Her own pain was his also.

Eliora thought she had imagined it, but in the flicking light of the lamp she thought she had seen the baby's hand twitch. Suddenly, there was small splutter followed by a welcome cry of a newborn child.

Fresh tears streamed down Eliora's face as Caleb lowered the baby girl into her arms.

'Thank you,' was all she could manage to say. Her daughter wriggled, pink and warm in Eliora's arms.

Caleb's smile was weary but his kiss was sweet on her lips.

He turned away quickly.

Eliora heard a rush of sound. In the advance of her pain everything had become insignificant and disappeared into the background. Noises were obsolete, but now her ears were open once again. Her mother and Martha were squealing with happiness amid hugging one another, the wind outside whipped at the make shift tent beating it like a drum and Caleb's breath was punctuated with stuttered sobs. Most of all, Eliora loved the sound of her daughter who no longer cried, but made gentle sucking noises on her fist.

31

Walls

Early morning arrived and still the wind persisted.

Eliora felt a gentle nudging at her side. She opened her weary eyes and could not help smiling. The small baby lay snuggled up to her on the blankets wrapped in a shawl. Eliora was fascinated by her baby's perfection; her tiny fingernails, downy hair and fine eyelashes. The morning light just made these details all the more beautiful.

Caleb had been sleeping next to her throughout what had remained of the night. She reached out and felt for him behind her, but he was not there.

Eliora stretched and looked towards the shelter entrance and out to the brightly lit cloud firmly set in place between them and their pursuers. The tribes were coming to life again. The sound of voices were muffled and confused by the wind.

'I was just coming to wake you,' Caleb said as he crept in. 'You have got to see this!'

Caleb shifted a little as Eliora slowly moved away from the baby, leaving her peacefully asleep.

'Look Eliora! Look!' Caleb pointed and pulled her further onto the shore.

The water that had lapped at the beach had been pushed away. A path led out in front of them with a wall of water to either side.

People were waking their neighbours and getting to their feet. Groups were making their way towards the land bridge.

As Eliora and Caleb approached the wind howled at their backs. Caleb pulled Eliora close to him and wrapped his cloak round her. The dry land looked to continue into the far distance, the walls pushed back and wide.

'We need to be ready to move,' Caleb said, 'How are you feeling?'

'Sore,' Eliora stated and winced, 'And tired.'

'Let's get back to the ... tent,' Caleb hesitated, 'and get things packed up.'

Eliora leaned heavily on Caleb.

'Take it slowly, my love, we won't be left behind.' He helped her lower herself to the ground just outside the shelter. 'I'll fetch the baby. You just stay here.'

She held her baby close, hidden safely inside Caleb's cloak and watched as he loaded up the cart once again.

The first people clambered down the beach bank and onto the land bridge.

'It's dry.'

'And firm!' they called through the gale.

Others began to join them, following where they had stepped.

Soon whole crowds of people were streaming down into the sea valley, family after family, flocks of sheep, carts laden with belongings.

Eliora couldn't wait to join them.

Caleb dragged the cart and lowered it carefully to men waiting below. Then he turned and supported Eliora down the bank.

The beach stood empty behind them.

Refreshed and well rested, the people moved fast. They walked briskly through the strangely beautiful landscape with the wind to carry them forward.

Eliora was stunned into silence by the scene. People rushed past her, eager to cross to the other side.

Down on the path everything was bathed in blue and green light. The gravel and sand were smooth beneath her feet with a few large rocks jutting out here and there.

The path was bounded by walls of water. Wind rushed at the walls in a constant blast, causing them to ripple, spray and foam.

No one wanted to talk and the animals travelled silently. The howling wind was the only sound that filled the watery valley.

Eliora was wide eyed, taking in as much of the scene as possible. There was nothing that could compare to this experience. As she walked, her freedom felt certain; she would never have to go back. Her God could be trusted no matter what impossibilities she faced. How amazing was her God that he would save someone like her and her people.

'Get in,' Caleb urged her. But before she could protest Caleb had lifted her into the cart. His cloak, draped over her shoulders, fell open, and there lay the tiny baby.

Eliora glanced up, her new felt love causing her to smile, but Caleb was frowning. She reached out and grabbed his hand. 'What is it?'

Caleb stood silently. The crowd bustled past set on their course.

'I'm not sure. It is difficult to explain.'

'I'm listening,' Eliora said gently.

'I can see you are happy, but I don't understand.'

'Understand what?'

'How you can be happy? Doesn't she just remind you?' Caleb asked.

'Yes and no,' Eliora admitted. 'But she isn't to blame.'

'I know.'

'Look at her. She is perfect.' Eliora offered Caleb the baby. He took her in his arms. 'She is a gift from God.'

'Gift? I thought ...'

'A curse?'

He nodded.

'I understand,' Eliora said carefully rearranging the shawl. The baby stirred as an arm was freed from the covers. 'She is a gift. Without her, I would have wanted to be Egyptian, without her I wouldn't know, really know about your love; how much you love me.'

Caleb glanced down at the little girl.

'You took me as I was,' Eliora whispered.

Caleb placed his hand over the baby and looked up at his wife. 'You know I love you.'

Eliora leaned close to him and kissed him. 'I know for certain that you love me,' she whispered. As she pulled away she heard Caleb gasp.

His face turned away from her and down to the baby. She had clasped his finger with her tiny hand. The hardness in Caleb's face, melted away. Suddenly he was beaming and tears glistened in his eyes.

'She is beautiful,' he said, 'Just like her mother. And I can't help it, I've fallen in love with her too. '

In a moment all has changed. A bond is formed in the love of a father for his child. Gold sparks shower the trio as a light floral scent of freesia permeates them.

The sun was beginning to lighten the strip of sky above and told her that they had been walking this path for some time. Eliora turned and all she could see was the path filled with her people and the beach was so far behind she could no longer see it. Ahead, the ground was beginning to rise.

The tribes were clambering up the steep banks to the shore beyond. Those that had already reached the other side offered hands to pull their companions from the path. Others carried heavy packs and small children to safety.

Caleb lifted Eliora and the baby over the edge then pushed the cart to waiting hands above.

The beach at this side of the sea was narrower but still large enough to hold all the people as they flowed slowly from the valley. The constant movement eventually stopped. The people had come through the sea. The passage did not close behind them.

In the distance the top of the cloud pillar shifted and rose high into the air flowing across the sky and re-joining the people.

'Ready yourselves!' Release commands.

The smooth sound of swords being unsheathed rings throughout the host, while others ready their bows.

We lie in wait, high above the sea bed behind the wall of water.

The cloud moves so fast and light is restored that the army on the other side are shaken by the sudden scene.

The frustrated bellow of the pharaoh raises a smile among my friends.

'Where are they?' he screams looking only at the beach where his prey had been trapped.

'They went through the sea!' A small creature announces darting back to its fiery master.

Pharaoh turns in the howling wind towards the land bridge.

'Get scouts to check the mountain pass and the shoreline,' Pharaoh spits out to one of his captains and a handful of men are sent out on foot to investigate. 'Could they have gone through there?' he asks.

'All the tracks lead that way, O great leader.'

'Then what are you waiting for?' Pharaoh shouts angrily over the wind. 'The mighty god Set has opened the water to trap them.'

'But this could be a trap for us,' a captain advises uneasily.

Pharaoh slashes his sword across the man's stomach and he falls to the floor.

'Who else defies the mighty Pharaoh?' He questions.

No one replies. Instead they urge all in their command to enter the sea valley.

The chariots are coming.

A few of the host dash from one horse to the next touching their eyes.

The ground is firm and the horses are blinkered to the dangerous place they are entering.

The seething mass of creatures is hungry for blood. They don't wait for Pharaoh's order to advance.

The battle cry of the Egyptians is lost in the wind and yelling of the horde. The collection of humans and demons funnel themselves into the sea entrance. The creatures mingle with focused warriors, laughing and shrieking, eager to capture the Remnant. Their desire is to annihilate the plan and destroy the promise.

We wait.

Gold encrusted chariots speed along the dry ground. The captains keep their battalions of men fixed on the mission as the sharp crack of the whip punctuates the battle cry.

We watch.

Line after line of the pharaoh's mighty army rush into the sea valley. Creatures sweep through the legs of the charging horses and weave through the soldiers.

We are ready.

The beach is empty.

The command is given.

The host flare into light. We dash into the organised lines, swords raised and arrows strung. The first attack is easy. Not one creature expected us. The air steams with sickly yellow vapour as hundreds of creatures are destroyed. I release an arrow that shoots through the ribcage of one creature before it catches the leathery wing of another, tearing a hole and making it useless.

We are gone before they have fully understood what has hit them.

But the army still travels deeper into the valley.

We swoop down quickly for a second attack. They have not recovered from the first but some were ready for us. Half a dozen of the host are caught in hand to hand combat, but we overwhelm the enemy with surprise, so even these skirmishes are dealt with fast. Many more are dispatched and the trace of vapour creeping over the sea bed is an encouraging sight.

'Ready your swords!' commands a rasping voice. 'Fight to the death!'

Our orders are to wait once again. The host use the walls of water as a shield.

The army moves on.

We follow, ready to burst in again.

The trumpet sounds. There is no need for stealth now.

I rocket over the wall, fire an arrow and discharge another in swift action. The first pierces the claw of a huge creature wielding a deadly mace. It screeches in pain and growls angrily. The second arrow finds its mark on the spindly creature that is throwing daggers with unearthly speed. Its eyes roll into the back of its head before it sizzles away.

I touch the eyes of the horses guiding the chariot near the front of the column. It whinnies as it sees the same scene that I see, kicks up onto its hind legs and panics.

All through the army, horses are crying out as their eyes are opened. Terrified, the horses run headlong into one another causing chariots to collide with ones that are being turned in circles. The men do their best to regain control but many are thrown to the ground. Hooves trample the overturned chariots and screaming soldiers. One squadron turns against another in confusion.

'Keep them moving!' the fiery leader commands. 'Get those slaves back!'

'Get those slaves back!' Pharaoh shouts over the commotion. He is so blinkered by his need to triumph that he fails to see the disaster around him.

The horde begins to regroup. They draw together into a closely knit pack. Obsidian swords, vicious spears and all manner of dangerous weapons circle the army.

But it is no use. The captains have no control, the soldiers are fighting among themselves and the horses are panicking.

The cloud stood at her back, but Eliora focused on her uncle.

Once again he stood at the edge of the beach. The wide opening was empty of her people.

Abruptly, the wind stopped.

Without the wind, the water could not be held back.

The howling wind stops.

The sudden silence only amplifies the sound of panic in the sea valley.

There is so little time to react.

The host are blasted into the air above as the water goes thrashing down into the gulf. The walls of water begin to fold in on themselves. The deafening roar of the collapsing and crashing walls mute the screams of death from the army below.

Beneath the waves the strongest struggle against the surge. The weak are already overcome. Soon, no one moves of their own accord and dead bodies swirl limply in the swell. Chariot debris either floats to the surface or lies embedded in the sea bed. Shards of wood and torn fabric are washed up along the shoreline.

I search for the horde.

They are not among the bodies.

'Look at the far side!' Release says as he approaches.

The bedraggled scaly creature is slowly creeping up the beach. A few others are climbing out of the water and following after it. It turns away from the water and flees to the mountain pass.

The scouts that were sent to look for the Remnant in the pass stand at the foot of the hills. The abrupt change in the wind and echoing crash of water called them back to the beach. They are left with the news to take back to Egypt, although there is no one to give them the command to return.

32

Song

The water lapped at the beach while the foam clung to the edge.

The roar of the crashing waters was replaced with the pounding silence of shock.

Eliora quickly passed the baby to Caleb and gingerly pushed her way through the crowd to get to the expanse of water. People tutted and huffed as she squeezed past them. She had to get there, to witness it, to know that she was free. She could hear Caleb following her but she did not turn. Tripping over a bundle left on the shore, she steadied herself before falling.

The scene could not have been more different. The vast walls of water had gone, the wind that had whipped at her hair and clothes had completely faded away. The water looked calm and harmless.

When she had stood on the far side, the sea had seemed an impossible barrier and a place of death. Now, the first light of dawn sparkled off the gentle waves.

Caleb wrapped his strong arm around her waist and rested his chin on her shoulder. His breathing was slightly laboured from the chase.

Eliora sighed as an unseen heaviness left her shoulders. For the first time she felt completely free. There was no one who could come after her now. She was free from slavery and free from the prince.

Floating towards the beach was the body of an Egyptian soldier. Eliora let out a squeal. He was face down, but all she was aware of was the untidy swirling hair that should have been tied and the once white tunic stained with grime. He had been stripped of his life and his Egyptian dignity.

Caleb made to turn her away.

'No. I'm fine,' she said calmly. 'I need to take this in.'

A shout further along told of other bodies reaching the shoreline, followed by the quiet buzz of whispering through a vast number of people.

Turning towards the sound, Eliora realised she had pushed her way through the Levite tribe, because her uncles stood shoulder to shoulder just a few paces away, her grandmother and mother not far behind them.

In the warming air Eliora heard a man hum the familiar notes of a song they had sung only a few days ago whilst working in the pits. The rhythm was one that would encourage a steady pace. She examined the men standing near to her trying to work out who it was, then the deep voice of her uncle Moses rang out. He had begun with just the tune, but now he was adding words to it.

'I will sing unto the Lord.'

A song of worship to the Creator begins. I see it stirring inside and long to hear it. I want it to bubble over. It is not for the Remnant, but they will hear it. They will witness this act of worship and it will inspire them. There is nothing as beautiful as worship from the heart. It has the purifying scent of eucalyptus that perfumes the morning air.

'The horse and the rider he has thrown into the sea. He is my strength and song. He has become my salvation.'

The Creator has truly done what no one and nothing else could have done. Moses has seen that when he relies on the Creator's strength, he will have victory. All he can do is sing! Salvation can only come from the Creator. They were caught in slavery, overcome by a powerful nation and then trapped between mountains and a sea. There was nothing that Moses could have done to earn the right to be saved, except trust in the one true God. It has been given freely to him.

'Your right hand has become glorious in power, Lord, you have dashed the enemy to pieces.'

The song rises above the heads of the Remnant. They hear the words and understand deeply. The Creator's right hand is both skilful and powerful. It is because of His greatness that the enemy is overthrown. The ones who were against the Remnant, were against the Creator. He has destroyed his enemies.

I laugh as Moses describes the events that he has just been a part of. He seems lost for words, as if his own language could not contain the marvellous things he has seen. His desire is to rejoice in the defeat of his God's enemies.

'Who is like you among the gods?'

Who is? There is no one like Him. He has defeated every false god that the Remnant have ever seen. They have seen so many, been subjected to the reign of gods over their lives for so many years, yet their God, the one and only Creator, came and redeemed them. He sought them out. He caused them, in Him amazing mercy, to turn to Him. They are dust, yet so precious. They are easily distracted and deceived, yet shown grace beyond measure.

They must remember this song. Remember that there is no one like Him.

He is their God and the Remnant are His people.

'The people will hear and be afraid.'

You have no idea how true that is Moses! These events will be reported throughout the world. Not only your close enemies will be shaken by the evidence of your deliverance, but others will be threatened by the fact that your God came to your rescue. Time will not be a barrier because this moment in history will send shock waves around the world that will rebound again and again.

'The Lord shall reign forever and ever.'

On the shore line the people believe this.

Eliora listened in silence to her uncle's song. The tune, once a song of slavery, had become a song of victory. Her eyes prickled as she took in the words. Echoes of harsh memories were fading in the light of his words. Tears ran down her cheeks. It really was over. At this sea the past was gone, now she could live.

As Moses came to an end, a familiar voice to Eliora took up the tune. The beautiful voice that had captivated the princess all those years ago began to repeat the words again and again. Eliora's grandmother sang with her arms held high.

'I will sing unto the Lord.

'The horse and the rider he has thrown into the sea.'

Suddenly her mother added a harmony to the tune and the two women smiled through the song. Miriam reached into the pack on the floor and pulled out a timbrel. She began a joyful beat. Jochebed could not help but clap along. She caught sight of Eliora and reached out her hand.

Eliora turned, kissed Caleb and then moved towards her mother.

Together they began to dance. Clapping their hands above their heads and twirling. The three generations sang in unison raising the song that rang over the people.

'I will sing unto the Lord!'

The timbrel and clapping, the dancing and unhindered joy began to spread. Soon Miriam, Jochebed and Eliora had linked hands with other women and were weaving gently through the people, collecting others as they went. Smaller groups caught the song and danced in circles with one another, joining hands and linking arms.

What had begun as a quiet song of worship had become a jubilant anthem of praise. The nation raised its voice.

Such a noise has never been heard before.

The Remnant are lost in the joy of praise, prayer and worship.

The aroma rises.

Energy spreads through the Remnant on ribbons of tangerine and nutmeg.

Frankincense weaves through the sweet spices of stacte, onycha and galbanum, a pure incense of worship. Cedar lifts it higher on a ripple of faith.

The rich and intoxicating scent of lotus floats down onto the people. The floral scent permeating the Remnant with rich blessing.

The smell of fresh rain speaks of their restoration as His people.

The final fragrance is hard to place. As the others disperse I can pick it up. Sweet and delicious, it sticks firmly on each person as they praise. Honey trickles from the Creator. The love and friendship of the Almighty blesses this people and sets them apart from any other.

'How will they react when trouble tests them once again?' I ask Release.

'We shall see, Faithful, we shall see,' Release replies.

'Surely with all they have seen and experienced they could not turn away.'

'But they are a prize to be captured. They had been held firmly by Egypt for all those years. I don't think the enemy will give up chasing after them for long.' Release looks to a spot in the reeds behind me,

I glance behind and see the once fiery creature crouched. The flames quenched by its defeat but its body still muscular and powerful looking.

It meets my gaze.

'If I have my way, he will never have a people to call his own,' it rasps. 'I want them all destroyed.'

I nock an arrow to my bow, but it is gone before I can attack. I knew I would not catch it.

'But will it ever have it that way? I don't think so! This people are marked for His glory.'

'This battle is won but the war still rages. We know that the enemy will continue to manipulate them, just as it did at the beginning.'

The Remnant are, as are the entire human race, plagued with a diseased heart, it has to be their decision to follow their God or not.

With thanks to ...

So many people helped me get this book into your hands.
Firstly, the inspiration to continue writing the Remnant series came from my love of the Bible. I thank my Creator for continuing to breathe life into his book. He has whispered, spoken and shouted so much through this whole process!
Without my husband to encourage me to keep writing while the housework tried to make me feel guilty and my parents continued support it would have taken so much longer.
Andy Back, you are a legend. I am so thankful for the time you put into reading my manuscript and pushing me to produce Eliora. I love the way you encourage the best out of me.
To those who read the draft and pointed out the typos, a very big thank you ... I hope they didn't miss any! Thank you Luella Bubloz, Pippa Pearson and Asher Hollway.
Many variations for the cover were mulled over and re-worked by Benjamin Hollway. Thank you for being patient.
For facebook friends who commented on book cover ideas and readers of my blog who enjoyed the first few chapters.
Lastly, to you, the reader of this book. Thank you for taking the time to enter my world. I really hope you loved the adventure.

Other books by the author in this series

Watch out for new titles by Katy Hollway